THE SHORT STORY

Previous work by the same author

The Romantic Survival (Constable, 1956)
The Characters of Love (Chatto, 1959)
Tolstoy and the Novel (Cambridge University Press, 1965)
Pushkin: A Comparative Commentary (Chatto, 1970)
The Uses of Division (Cambridge University Press, 1972)
An Essay on Hardy (Routledge & Kegan Paul, 1977)
Shakespeare and Tragedy (Routledge & Kegan Paul, 1980)
Selected Essays (Cambridge University Press, 1983)
The Line of Battle of Trafalgar and Other Essays (Collins, 1986)

In Another Country A Novel (Constable, 1954)

THE SHORT STORY

HENRY JAMES TO ELIZABETH BOWEN

JOHN BAYLEY

St. Martin's Press
New York

First published in the United States of America in 1988

Printed in Great Britain

ISBN 0-312-01669-7

Library of Congress Cataloging-in-Publication Data

Bayley, John, 1925–
    The short story.

    Bibliography: p.
    Includes index.
    1. Short story. 2. Short stories, English—
History and criticism. I. Title.
PN3373.B28   1988 809.3'1   87–36942
ISBN 0–312–01669–7

CONTENTS

Foreword   vii

Chapter 1. The theory of the short story. Poems as short stories. Larkin, Yeats and Wordsworth   1

Chapter 2. Conrad. Henry James. Todorov's theory of James's stories. 'The Turn of the Screw', 'A Landscape-Painter'   27

Chapter 3. Kipling's puzzles and paradoxes. Hemingway. 'Indian Camp'. The theory of the 'impossible event'. 'The wickedest story in the world'. 'Mrs Bathhurst'   64

Chapter 4. Chekhov. 'The Lady with the Dog'. Katherine Mansfield. D. H. Lawrence. Another kind of 'impossible event'. 'The Blind Man' and 'The Princess'. 'Love, he bawled'. Hardy's stories. 'On the Western Circuit'   109

Chapter 5. James Joyce: *Dubliners*. Epiphanies and 'studious meanness'. 'The Dead'. An Irish tradition. Elizabeth Bowen. 'Mysterious Kôr'   149

Chapter 6. Conclusion   179

Notes and Bibliography   190

Index   193

FOREWORD

Jorge Luis Borges, one of the most respected names in the business today, has said that, 'unlike the novel, the short story may be, for all purposes, essential'. It is a comment as delphic as one of his own stories, but it does indicate how conscious of his form the writer of short stories has become. No one now feels the need to say what a novel should be doing, for that comfortable article has always been, as D. H. Lawrence put it, 'incapable of the absolute'. But all its practitioners, as well as its critics, have an urge to define the task and status of the short story.

'At once a parable and a slice of life, at once symbolic and real, both a valid picture of some phase of experience, and a sudden illumination of one of the perennial moral and psychological paradoxes which lie at the heart of *la condition humaine*'. This definition by Kay Boyle may well leave us slightly dazed. The human condition has always sounded more impressive in French, and as 'essential' as Borges could wish, but she makes the perusal of the short story sound more of a duty than a pleasure. Is she protesting too much? Is there a hint of inferiority complex, making it necessary to emphasize that the short story is not just a brief tale, but something as special and as exclusive as a poem? The American novelist and storywriter William Gass uses that notion to exclude any others: 'It is not a character sketch, a mouse-trap, an epiphany, a slice of suburban life. It is the flowering of a symbol centre. It is a poem grafted on to sturdier stock.'

Yet the best short stories may have been written at odd moments by novelists or dramatists, or by a writer like D. H. Lawrence who was both novelist and poet. To specialize too exclusively in short stories may result in writing that is too 'essential', or too 'poetic', too purely literary. But that may be an asset in the critical climate of today, which lays such stress on 'literariness' as the goal and end of all fictions. Partly, at least, because of this critical attitude, the short story is said now to be in special favour. In his introduction to *The Art of the Tale*, an international anthology of stories written since the war, Daniel Halpern is enthusiastic: 'Regardless of whose pen fired the important moment, there seems to be general agreement that a serious revival of the short story is under way, as if at this particular juncture in the parlous history of our race we specially need its singular purity and magic'.

But to be pure and magical can also mean to be crude and heartless. Many contemporary stories seem cruel by nature, like fairy stories, yet far from naive: based instead on a formula which combines sophistication with sensationalism. Whatever their length they also seem to advertise their brevity, as much as their 'purity'. By contrast, the great masters of the form – Chekhov or Joyce or Henry James; Kafka or Kipling or Lawrence – seem to have all the time in the world for their stories, a leisureliness in which the reader can relax and look round.

None the less the short story today is still recognizably the same form and species that evolved towards the end of the nineteenth century. What special effects have been achieved by the best ones? And how do we know which are the best? If we enjoy short stories we probably enjoy discussing them, which is the justification for a study of those special effects.

THE SHORT STORY

CHAPTER ONE

We associate, quite rightly I think, the literature of the 1890s, and of the turn of the century, with two general ideas: 'art for art's sake' and 'the mysterious'. It was fashionable at the time, among its practitioners, to speak of the mystery of art. And yet on the face of it, the ideas associated with art and mystery are not really compatible: they even constitute a paradox. If all is 'art' in a work of art how can it also include a mystery, which by definition cannot be explained in art's own terms but must lurk somewhere outside of it? In practice, of course, nobody has much trouble in reconciling the two ideas. It is rather significant, none the less, that in the reading of a detective or murder mystery we often receive the impression – quite how or why is another matter – that the explanation is somehow outside mere words, as if it were not even under the control of the writer, but something which, like his reader, he has to accept.

The sense of mystery thus associates with the idea of an absolute, external reality, something that art cannot touch but only reveal. The relationship of the two ideas once caused little trouble or query, but it contained none the less the germ of a much greater controversy, and one that exercises critical theorists in our own time. Is everything in a work of literary art, including its 'truth', or the idea of the truth behind it, confined to its text, to its structure and the ways it can be deconstructed? Or does that text remain subject to facts, truths, circumstances outside itself, things with which we grapple in the course of living rather than in the process of reading? Put thus the problem seems quite unreal – a non-problem – and yet its formulation can be of use, and perhaps of particular use when we are discussing the effects peculiar to short stories. The reader may find it, or something like it, useful to bear in mind. By treating everything that is inside such stories as literature – that is to say, aspects of 'literariness' – some discussions seek to appreciate them solely in terms of function, to understand the plan on which they work. By applying the critical equivalent of Occam's Razor, truths or mysteries external to the workings of the story can be excluded, and with them all irrelevances of opinion.

Let us start the discussion of short stories with their possible relation to the poetic, and to poems; for this is where mystery in literature has by tradition most resided. In a famous passage in 'Tintern Abbey', Wordsworth writes of 'sensations sweet/ Felt in the blood, and felt along the heart'. The reader wonders, is there something wrong here? Shouldn't it be the other way round? – Felt in the heart, and felt along the blood. Doesn't sound so good? True. But more important that in taking a metaphor of feeling from physiology Wordsworth has got things mixed up, deliberately or inadvertently, and given a misleading picture of the circulation. It is at this moment that the critic steps in, telling us that any such consideration is irrelevant. We have to do here not only with transferred syntax but with 'literariness', a function of the body imagined inside art, not as and for itself. The rhetorical transposition of 'heart' and 'blood' within the poetic line is itself a normal function of 'literariness', part of the structure and convention of the poem which Wordsworth is writing.

That is both logical and helpful, as the guidelines of formalist criticism usually are. And yet it is also true that in 'Tintern Abbey' Wordsworth is seeking to communicate something in the nature of a mystery, one associated with the phenomena and experience of living, breathing, seeing. The emphasis that suggests this mystery comes in the phrase:

'Something far more deeply interfused'. Far more than poetry or than art extends? At any rate, the notion of something far more deeply located is potent in the words of the poem, seeming inevitably to lead us beyond and outside it. Just an aspect of the way it works, says the formalist, a sign in itself of its 'autonomy of discourse'. No doubt. And yet if the notion of a mystery seems to lead us beyond the poem we are already fixed in a paradox. It seems that the purpose of art is neither to declare nor to conceal but to transcend itself. At least, it appears that this might be so in certain cases.

It may be that the sensations 'felt in the blood and felt along the heart' themselves alert the reader – though probably not at a conscious level where either he or the poet is concerned – to the fact that in the world of the poem everything external, the natural world itself, is subtly changed, even inverted, so that as if in some kinds of science fiction we are living in a world through the looking-glass, or a world in which grass is blue, blood green, and so forth. It is, in fact, a wholly *poetic* world, a Wordsworthian poetic world, and once this has been accepted we can also accept the critical assumption that everything in it has become poeticity, has become literariness; an impression first conveyed, possibly, by the peculiarly serene transposition of heart and blood in the line we noticed; and confirmed, it may be, later in the poem, by hearing with the poet 'the still sad music of humanity', a line in which the unexpected word 'music' (try substituting 'murmur' or even 'mutter') transposes human association quite literally into a different key. The line suggests not human activity, but something more romantically lonely, the sound of wind in trees, or of a horn in the depths of the wood.

It seems we might agree, then, that everything in 'Tintern Abbey' has become its own sort of poetry, the sort of poem which confirms the contemporary critical view of formalist poetics that words in literature have no relation to things in life, so that 'heart', 'blood', 'music', have all acquired their special senses in relation to the poeticity of the poem. Things, however, are not as simple as that. The centrality of the poem is its mystery, and this evades any such impression, evades it all the more easily because of the serene otherness of the world in which the properties of the poem have their being.

The mystery's technical manifestation is, in fact, the paradox. By making everything in the poem so much a question of its art, Wordsworth suggests all the more powerfully the existence of the real world beyond it. Poetry here reveals and conjures up its opposite, the actuality which its verbal world has implicitly denied, of which it has substituted its own version. What is 'far more deeply interfused' than the champions of 'autonomy of discourse' can allow is that, in cases where such autonomy is most seemingly complete, the world from which it has been wrested is most subtly but intrusively present. Wordsworth's diction cannot but invite us to hear quite other sounds. The mystery itself may not be the one his own 'discourse' seems to invoke. The more native and autonomous the art the more effectively it may arouse foreign and external speculation.

Of course, formalist criticism can claim that no poem can crawl under the net of its language, and that the more paradoxical effects we see in it the more this confirms the nature of its purely linguistic and metaphorical life. That, in one sense, is self-evident. But the relation between what is in art, and what is outside it, still intrudes. Let us come to earth with a homely example very far from the world of 'Tintern Abbey'. A few years younger than Wordsworth, Charles Wolfe died many years before him, aged only thirty-two. They are poets of the same era and many of the same interests (Wordsworth also took a great interest in the Peninsula War) though Wolfe is remembered today only for one poem, 'The Burial of Sir John Moore after Corunna'. Wolfe was a Church of Ireland parson in County Down, and his poem, based on Southey's account in the *Annual Register*, first appeared in the *Newry Telegraph* in 1817. It was the golden age of epitaphs, funereal sculptures and plaques, and the public would have known exactly how to 'deal with' a poem of this kind; they would have identified its genre, that is to say, and brought to it the appropriate expectations. The hasty burial of Moore, killed in his successful holding action against the French before his army evacuated the port and temporarily left Spain, struck the imagination of visual artists too. Of the marble group in St Paul's, Barham was to write in *The Ingoldsby Legends*:

> The man and the angel have got Sir John Moore
> And are letting him down through a hole in the floor.

Painters seized the opportunity for chiaroscuro afforded by 'the lanthorn dimly burning', and the soldier holding it acquires a classical-type helmet – the sort that Byron ordered when he went to Greece.

The properties and type of the poem fitted in with what convention required, and the only reason for the poem's survival would seem to be the dramatic circumstances of Moore's death and burial, and the British fondness, where their armies are concerned, for heroic failure as a context for lasting memorial. But there is more to it than that. The hypnotic life of the poem, conveyed through its soldier-narrator who speaks as and for the anonymous 'us' of his mates, depends on details chosen from the stock account of what happened. Moore was buried like all soldiers after a battle (except that most would have been pilfered and stripped first by their comrades or by the enemy) without time for the ritual of shroud or coffin, so that 'he lay like a warrior taking his rest/ With his martial cloak around him'. The circumstances of the campaign that led to the evacuation may be criticized at home ('Lightly they'll talk of the spirit that's gone,/ And o'er his cold ashes upbraid him'), but Moore in his anonymous grave ('We carved not a line, and we raised not a stone') will be quite indifferent. There is a strong popular element in the poem's convention, not at all unusual at the time, and one which will be fully exploited by Kipling at the end of the century, together with the always welcome sentiment that the 'high-ups' may disapprove, but that 'we' know what it's all about.

From the point of view of 'autonomy of discourse', however, there are two details which are disproportionately compelling because of the effect they exert on the poem's structure, opening it up and exposing it to the standards and reactions of a non-literary world.

> But half of our heavy task was done
>   When the clock struck the hour for retiring;
> And we heard the distant and random gun
>   That the foe was sullenly firing.

The narrator's awkwardness, as if he were using the convention in a heartfelt but clumsy way, can be heard in the opening lines of this penultimate stanza. The narrator accidentally gives the rather quaint impression that the clock strikes the hour for bed, in a scene of tranquillity; through it the lines convey the terse message that the hurried business of getting away by sea at night gave them no time even to finish digging the grave. The two lines following impart a military technicality which would be lost on almost all readers, unless there were a few old soldiers perusing the *Newry Telegraph* and the subsequent volume in which the poem appeared. Artillerymen had a term for a gun set up in daylight to fire on a fixed line at a point by which enemy activity had been observed. This would be fired at irregular intervals during the night in the hope of killing or dispersing working parties, etc. In practice, the recoil of such a 'random' gun meant that it usually lost its carefully laid point of aim during the darkness, thus making things not too unsafe for the soldiers on night work who were its target. In any case the enemy gunners have laid their piece at a discreet distance from the troops who have recently repelled their much larger army, and are firing it more out of boredom and disgruntled routine than for any better reason.

These facts are in the poem but not of it. In sharp contrast is a detail in the second stanza, also available to Moore through Southey's account.

> We buried him darkly at dead of night,
>   The sods with our bayonets turning ...

This is a perfect example of bogus authenticity, of the falsely effective detail, dished up by Southey, or his informant, as a civilian for civilians. Anyone who had carried a musket and bayonet would see the absurdity of trying to dig a hole with a weapon shaped like a large needle, useful only at its point. It could pierce a sod but not turn it, and Moore would never have been got underground had it been the only implement available. In practice, foot soldiers carried picks and shovels as a matter of course, and the effort vividly to suggest a hasty improvisation, bright idea of a literary man who has never been involved, recoils upon itself.

But these two moments in the poem reinforce one another, rather than cancel each other out. The soldier-narrator accepts the literary man's idea about the bayonet and uses it faithfully, as if aware that this is how things are done in poems, while at the same time reserving, as if unconsciously, his own sense of what really happened, like the firing of the 'random' gun. These confusions blend into the hypnotic nature of the poem, the reader being dimly but satisfyingly aware that he is being given both the soldier's view of the episode and the equally memorable and proper official version. There is a contrast between the two but no hostility, for everyone recognizes that art must do its work in a different style from that in which the facts do theirs. The poem makes no attempt to be an 'autonomous discourse', and its success is due to its simplicity and its modesty, its combination of elements incompatible in art, but not in terms of the kind of emotions which receive it, the emotions which grasp that soldiers digging a grave do not speak 'a word of sorrow', and probably feel none either, but know, none the less, that art and feeling must later have their turn together.

The formalist critic of course has a simple answer to all this. These things are indeed in the poem, if they can be deduced from it, and in so far as they are relevant to the structures and conventions on which it is based. These exist *a priori* in terms of the complete poem, and the poem cannot reach out into the reality of the situation it describes. But it must do, since it gives the impression of so doing, and in ways in which 'Tintern Abbey' so emphatically does not? Wolfe's poem has muddled its own conventions so thoroughly that it has ceased, or failed, to be a work of art, a 'text', in the sense that 'Tintern Abbey' is one. Our sense of oddity in 'Tintern Abbey' ('Felt in the blood and felt along the heart') turns out only to confirm the poem's distance from life, as from physiology. The mistake about bayonets and the accidental authenticity about guns, together with numerous other unrelated, heterogeneous touches (there is a suggestion of an Irish lament, found also, in a more transmogrified form, in the poems of Wolfe's contemporary, Darley) help to rush 'The Burial of Sir John Moore after Corunna' into the confused centre of things, where feeling and apprehension are as

muddled as if in experience; make it too, though undoubtedly
a masterpiece, very much an accidental and unrepeatable one.

I have said that the atmosphere of 'Tintern Abbey' is one of
inversion 'almost suspended', as if 'laid asleep', and that
everything in the poem subtly reinforces the totality of this.
Living cannot be felt along the blood because its motion *is*
suspended: the reader has become a 'living soul'; the phrase is
a careful contradiction or oxymoron which itself suggests the
paradox between art and the mystery which is outside art.
(Souls by implication do not normally 'live': only when the
functions of the body they inhabit have become 'suspended'.)
The poem, then, is an early example of a kind of art which
came into its own at the end of the nineteenth century and has
continued to flourish into the twentieth – the art of the short
story. 'Tintern Abbey' is a short story as 'The Burial of Sir
John Moore after Corunna' is not. In creating a world so
entirely and homogeneously involved in art Wordsworth also
insists on a mystery which has nothing to do with it, which is
'far more deeply interfused'. Art can only work with total
success by conjuring a world which is its opposite, which is
dedicated wholly to moments in life, when the soul itself is not
the disembodied thing the word normally defines, but is
actually 'living'. It is the same contradiction that is involved
in the 'music' of humanity. Art, of which music is a portion,
can summon up what is opposite to it – 'the dreary intercourse
of daily life' – and appear to hold each suspended and separate
in the same mystery.

At about the turn of the century the sort of paradox which is
unconsciously present in Wordsworth's poem begins to be
more consciously developed as a formula, and it is then that
we begin to have the concept of the modern short story. James
Joyce would speak of its process as an 'epiphany', a term
which carries overtones of Pater's view of art and Pater's own
stories, with which Joyce was familiar; but also goes further
back to Wordsworth's statement in his *Prelude*, that 'There
are in our existence spots of time' – moments which are
essential to moral meaning and the moral well-being of the
individual, but which can be exploited in a different spirit by
the artist. The significant moment is at once art's
demonstration of its own completeness, and of the mystery of

being which lies outside art. For this reason the more complete the art the more capable it is of arousing speculation, speculation to which art has already ensured that there can never be an answer. To suggest that there is one, 'far more deeply' embedded than art can reach, is itself art's most vital achievement.

The short story effect, if we can agree to call it that, the epiphany, or 'spot of time', may be met with everywhere, and in almost any genre – poems, novels, *nouvelles* – though the short story itself, of course, affords it complete and conscious existence. But it may even be present in a play, as it is in *Hamlet*, while in Shakespeare's little poem, 'The Phoenix and the Turtle', it achieves its neatest and most concentrated appearance of enigma. Its evidence of solutionlessness, and of totality as an aspect of that state, may be very declared, or it may be so implicit as hardly to be recognized. What we can be quite sure of is that such a recorded moment as 'The Burial of Sir John Moore after Corunna' belongs to quite a different species of art; and that is at least partly due to the interweaving in it of factual truth and falsity, and conventions confused and brought off with unexpected success, revealing human elements in their artless and natural state. Such elements, in this type of art, can themselves be carefully counterfeited, expertly presented and devised, exploited to give an effect of naturalness, or as a mask for real confusion and insufficiency of grip.

To make my point, and before going on to other examples, it would be worth exploring further the questions raised by the example of the Sir John Moore poem, in order to demonstrate more fully how different the art of it is from that which produces the short story effect. Wolfe's poem is a simple example of what might be termed the investigative anecdote, an event used as the occasion for opinion and enquiry. The soldier-narrator is explaining how something came about which impressed itself on him then, and still moves him now, because it took the opposite form from the way things should be done. What struck him, and what strikes the reader who reflects on the poem, is the way in which the burial took place, in fact was not a burial in the proper sense at all. The corpse was hurried along, laid in the ground as if in a camp bed; while the narrator perhaps has even convinced himself, after this lapse of time, or at least has made it a graphic touch in his narration, that the grave had to be dug with bayonets. There was no funeral music except the occasional report of an enemy gun, and no grave watch. It impresses the speaker that Moore was left *alone*, and this reversal of rites which are intended to suggest the opposite, to make the one buried not only seem particularly part of the human family but accompanied by appropriate memorials, makes the reader exceptionally aware of the solitude of death. Moore was left 'alone in his glory' – a contradiction of a very moving kind, because glory, a social affair, was no possible good to him. His conduct of the retreat will be criticized, questions asked in Parliament, votes of censure taken; and the reader is even half-aware, though the speaker may not be, that Moore will *not* be allowed to 'sleep on/ In the grave where a Briton has laid him'. Human compulsion will reassert itself and compel Moore, as it were, to join the family of death and be conventionally honoured among them.

A great part of the success of Wolfe's poem comes from the obvious emotion with which he wrote it, presumably having been greatly moved by Southey's account. Our sense of the author's feeling, which he projects in an amateurish manner on to his imaginary soldier-speaker, fuses with our own complex sense of how the poem works, and how its main impression – of a funeral in reverse – defines and signifies itself. Unlike Wordsworth in 'Tintern Abbey', Wolfe does not withhold a mystery, which in being withheld reveals how completely the promise of it has been achieved as art. Like a novel, 'The Burial of Sir John Moore' embarks on a joint enterprise as between writer and reader, collaborating in their investigation through the persona of the soldier-narrator, a figure who is himself not properly realized, so that he embodies both the fervent but unmilitary emotions of the author himself (as in the gaffe about the bayonets) together with the reader's own growing awareness of the exceptional nature of the event, in relation to most funerary commemorations; the emphasis laid upon Moore's solitariness, and separation from the mechanisms of official praise or blame, mechanisms which the poem implies are still operating. This suggestion of the provisional is one of the most effective things about the poem. 'If they let him sleep on' is the proviso which contrasts with the isolation of Moore, and it also operates a new line of reflection. Why this hurried burial in any case? The answer is clear: that by burying Moore, however unpermanently, his army confirmed the positiveness of his last victory over the French, whereas if his soldiers had left the French themselves to do the job (no doubt with full military honours) they would have conceded retreat as defeat, and Moore himself would have become a sort of posthumous prisoner.

No considerations of this sort could be imagined as possible in a poem like Wordsworth's. They belong to the world of the novel, not to that of the short story. The nature of the poem helps to define the two quite separate genres, and the difference between them can best be shown through the medium of a third genre – the poem – which can demonstrate the characteristics of either. In the world of the novel, as in the world of a poem like 'The Burial of Sir John Moore', there is no mystery, and there *is* an answer. The reason for the burial, the subject of the poem, is not inside the poem, nor explained by it, but none the less can be correctly inferred, for the world of actual events is also the world of the poem. The converse is true not only of 'Tintern Abbey', in which a mystery is suggested which the art of the poem is too necessarily absolute to explain, but in other short story poems of Wordsworth such as the 'Lucy' sequence. In 'Strange Fits of Passion I have known', the significance of the moon, which accompanies the traveller, and at the end drops out of sight below the roof of the cottage, is never explained, nor could it be. It is part of the mystery of the poem, conveyed by its arts but not carried by it back into the world of exterior query and response. The poem even imagines an impossible condition for its own 'understanding': that it should only be told by the poet 'in the Lover's ear'. On the other hand, certain short poems of Wordsworth, such as 'Advice to Fathers' and 'We are Seven', are simply investigative and anecdotal; while others again, like 'Resolution and Independence' – the Leech-Gatherer poem – are both investigative anecdotes and true short stories.

The same could hardly be said of Philip Larkin's poems 'The Whitsun Weddings' and 'Dockery and Son'. The latter requires for its understanding a good deal of external information, much of which can be deduced by a reader who has had the same sort of educational background as Larkin and has shared at least some of his experiences. As with 'The Burial of Sir John Moore' we can be carried along by the poem and by its subdued mastery of feeling, but in both cases there is much we must pick up from outside if we are to understand the whole context and continuity, both poems having a rhetorically conclusive ending which has already been pre-empted by further query. 'Dockery and Son' is founded on uncertainties not fully covered by its presentation, and is also provisional, in this case by reason of its unrelenting autobiographical accuracy. Starting with a flourish, Larkin seems to be creating a suitable persona for the poem, only to make it unmistakably clear that that persona is himself, as he thinks of himself. So complete is the poet's seeming preoccupation with the occasion he describes, and what he deduced from it, that he makes no attempt to explain matters. Such an admission to his confidence means expecting us to know, without being told, why in the poem's third line he describes himself as 'death-suited'. Whatever funeral he may have been attending does not enter the poem, but the poets rumination, begun by the news that Dockery's son is now a student at the college, sees the invisible death ceremony as the background 'of finding out how much had gone of life'.

The poet is 'death-suited, visitant' ... the rarefied second epithet conveying a modestly ironic view of his status; also suggesting the more normal word, and condition, of being hesitant. From other poems we know that their author is obsessed both with death and with the choice of not becoming involved in life, of 'ignoring' it as he himself feels 'ignored' as he leaves Oxford after the visit, to take the train back north. Each regular eight-line stanza ends in mid-sentence, a hesitation turned into hiatus, indicating the dislocations in a thought process already sufficiently familiar and boring to the thinker. Such thoughts about life and death are a normal and wearisome routine, like falling asleep on a railway journey.

> Well, it just shows
> How much ... How little ... Yawning, I suppose
> I fell asleep, waking at the fumes
> And furnace-glares of Sheffield, where I changed,
> And ate an awful pie, and walked along
> The platform to its end to see the ranged
> Joining and parting lines reflect a strong
> Unhindered moon.

That pie, now one of the most celebrated exhibits in the museum of contemporary poetry, is also a characteristic property of the short story. Together with the moon it promises to set the tone for the short story's effects, of epiphanic mystery, of an experience and moment set in art, 'recalled' by the writer, and fixing itself as permanently memorable in the file of literary experiences kept by the reader.

But these promises are not fulfilled. The awful pie and the unhindered moon are not true short story effects, like the cold and the love-feast and the empty dress dwelt upon by Keats on St Agnes Eve, or the snow, the singing and the refreshments in Joyce's story, 'The Dead'. Rather, they exist as part of a deception, almost a parody of the short story's completed art and withheld mystery. Epiphany is in its nature a moment that is unique, a drawing together of event and experience into a singular impression which art can render whole. 'Dockery and Son' seems to be going to do that, but in fact falls asleep, as it were, out of boredom with the familiarity of the reflections that come to mind. So good is the poet, and the poem, that the reader prizes this familiarity as if it were something wholly new; and by accomplishing this the poet has things both ways: tacitly showing how artificial is the short story in its need to make itself uniquely memorable, and at the same time managing to make his title and poem uniquely memorable anyway.

At the same time there is an answer, of a simple and prosaic kind, to everything in 'Dockery and Son'. Like 'The Burial of Sir John Moore' it has a large number of facts both in it, and pertaining to it. Also a large number of hypotheses which offer themselves as part of the pleasure and interest of the poem, but which are not necessarily in themselves a part of its

specification or autonomous structure. They bring us close to
the poet, and in tune with his preoccupations, instead of
exerting the short story's emphasis on the unknowable event
which art alone had made to stand out clear. The poem tells us
in passing a good deal about the way colleges work, or used to
work. The Dean as informant and acquaintance is also the
college's disciplinary official, who used to summon the young
Larkin and his friends – correctly clad in their gowns for the
interview – to give him 'our version' of 'those incidents last
night'. This is undoubtedly the poet as he really was –
reminiscence turned into creation. And both Dean and poet
take it for granted that Dockery's son will follow his father to
the college.

One of the many fascinations of the poem is the way in
which the reader can separate in it the short story element and
the novel element. All this material has the workmanlike
accuracy of the novel. Dockery himself appears documented
as if in one.

> Anyone up today must have been born
> In '43, when I was twenty-one.
> If he was younger, did he get this son
> At nineteen, twenty? Was he that withdrawn
>
> High-collared public-schoolboy, sharing rooms
> With Cartwright who was killed?

In this moment of reflection on his exact chronology the poet
compresses with impish blandness the spacious materials of a
novel (materials about to be dissipated in a yawn and train
doze: 'How much ... How little ...') and adds the ghostly
suggestion of another kind of art. The impishness extends to
Dockery himself, remembered doubtfully, if the poet has got
him right, as 'that withdrawn/ High-collared public-
schoolboy'. The collar detail, not easy to imagine and explain
accurately after this lapse of time, goes with a general class
impression quietly given its importance in the background of
novel/poem. Again, enquiry can get the answer right,
although the reticent essentiality of the class set-up might
permanently confuse an American reader, for whom 'public
school' would signify the oppisite of its English meaning. In

this, as elsewhere in Larkin, the background of novel in poem can only read fully by a reader accustomed to the ways of Larkin's Englishness.

The short story, though, does not demand this knowledge, and reveals Dockery in a different light. That withdrawn figure, associated with' 'Cartwright who was killed', himself takes on the truly enigmatic and unknowable short story persona, in this case that of the sacrificial victim associated with the wars of this century, whose country house and upper-class background make it all the more inevitable that he will disappear into the limbo of the lost: missing in action, went down over France, leaving behind him the young heir who will continue the tradition, maintain the estate, receive the Oxford heritage...Seen in this light and according to the short story's process, Dockery becomes a figure almost like that of Michael Furey in 'The Dead', a faceless figure standing forever in half-darkness, under a dripping tree. But the poem as novel knows quite well that the real Dockery is no doubt still prosaically alive, living out his days somewhere in his own snug or depressing routines, only marginally aware that the possession of a son at his own old Oxford college is a matter for self-congratulation. This real Dockery was not especially convinced 'he should be added to'; and he and his fiancée, under war-time conditions, probably found her pregnancy, if no worse, just one more of the many difficulties and trials of the period. But for poet and story-poem Dockery cannot but be in some sense an heroic figure, who sternly took 'stock/ Of what he wanted', and in so doing paradoxically joined the legendary givers – 'Their sons they gave, their immortality', as Rupert Brooke phrased it in a famous sonnet – in the sacrifice suggested in the background of the poem, the college war-memorial, the death-suited visitor, the black-gowned merry undergraduates of yesteryear ('Unconscious of their doom'), the locked door of what might almost be 'Jacob's Room' ('I try the door of where I used to live').

The short story element in the poem can thus be seen to be determined by an unexpressed paradox, a very common story formula, for not only is there nothing to be said or invesigated about such a paradox, but the story's effect would in any case depend upon not overtly expressing it. The poet himself did

not, does not, in any sense wish to give, to be a sacrifice, either
to life or for death. But he equates Dockery's act in having a
son as at one with those who give their lives, who in fact gave
up their sons. A true short story would emphasize this
paradox discreetly but with much greater pointedness,
making it the *trouvaille* or realization, the situation not to be
got behind, on which the form usually depends. But as novel
the poem is not a bit like that, which makes the whole
consideration of poem as either story or novel so revealing.
The poem is full of latent humour, embodied in pauses and
syntactic movement:

> I try the door of where I used to live:
> Locked.

– a movement ponderously and deceptively innocent, like that
in 'Church Going'; ('Yet stop I did; in fact I often do'.) A
'significance' – the past, like the Garden of Eden is
irrecoverable? – is kept firmly out: what matters is that the
room he used to live in is locked.

The poet knows well how to relax as himself, privately
(which in terms of the poetry means accessibly) entertained
by the undoubted shock the Dean's information has given
him. 'But Dockery, good Lord ...' has become a way of
seeing, and saying, how natural to oneself one's own life is. In
fact, after the shock, it still seems 'quite natural', a matter for
the novel's space and absorptive rumination – 'Well, it just
shows/ How much ... How little ...' – a cue to fall asleep on.
Although Dockery is identified both with a legend in history
and as a portent in the poet's own life, he belongs, as so much
in one's actual purview must do, to literature rather than to
life. Even the notion of him and son – Dombey and Son –
echoes literature. Awful pies and vague meanderings along
railway platforms are more in one's own line. As in the novel
the reader is fully involved in a joint exploration, in which the
neat droll 'story' subject of Dockery, as dead hero and living
father – each somehow equalling the other – is itself a subject
for amusement within the leisurely, friendly sphere of the
novel poem. Since we don't – very sensibly – want to be dead
heroes, we don't want to be living fathers either; and the poet

takes us with him as he rises, without haste or embarrassment, to a comforting commentary on the futility of life. Yes, we all know that it makes no difference whether you use it by sacrificing yourself and getting sons, or spend it in just hanging about. It's all the same in the end, thank goodness: we can't control our hidden choice; and thank goodness, too, that the only end of age is – well, you know ...

Larkin's version of time-honoured poetic pessimism is very much his own, although it is clear that as the main cause of his poetry's great popularity it has much in common with the tone of such equally popular works as *The Rubaiyat of Omar Khayyam* and *The Shropshire Lad*, as also to such a famous bravura passage as the one from Dryden's play, *Aurungzebe* – 'When I consider life, 'tis all a cheat,/ But, fool'd with hope, men favour the deceit' – a speech which we know Larkin admired, and which gave a title, *Sprightly Running*, to the first selection of his friend John Wain's autobiography. The vigour of such pessimism is its own reward, poetically speaking, and a job in that line well done invariably gives satisfaction. Larkin's handling of the theme is both expert and recognizable enough to satisfy its time-honoured place in poetry, and at the same time purely original. Having children would be 'dilution' to him; his lifestyle with its 'innate assumptions' seems natural, and his own, until it suddenly hardens 'into all we've got/ And how we got it'. A strange and frightening image ('looked back on they rear/ Like sand-clouds, thick and close') turns these natural assumptions into predetermined nightmare in which 'we' are all in the same boat, whether or not we share the poet's obsession with not raising a family. With remarkable ingenuity the poet persuades us that his own personal lifestyle – all he's got – is also all there is, so that the sudden transition in the last four lines to the old-fashioned poetic authority of gloom seems both inevitable and true. The personal element in life becomes universalized, as if the poem were relating a novel, something like Arnold Bennett's *The Old Wives' Tale*.

More important for our theory, however, is the part played in the perspective of the poem by the short story element. The young live in, or are remembered in, a short story situation, which the old can look back on but not regain – their lives

have hardened 'into all we've got'. And yet the poet himself
has, ironically, given up all for art – the poem itself is a living
proof of that – as if he were a character in a Henry James story.
The poem uses the promising density of short story situations
– notably that of the humdrum living Dockery both as dead
hero and figure from legend, a Siegfried whose son Sigurd is
ready to carry on his role. That role, implicit in the social
background of the poem, shows the poet's idiosyncratic
attitude towards facts and ideas about class. His class position
enables Dockery to become a father, to 'carry on the line'; and
the poet's own position, outside such class considerations, is
shown by the fact that it is 'quite natural' for him not to do so.
Class is a form of literature, a style of looking at the world, and
can be taken no more seriously than the time-honoured
situations of literature. But without literature, or class, what
do we have? – Nothing. That is where the seriousness comes
in. Human activities and displays, like Dockery's or Dickens',
exist from Larkin's point of view in order to show the simple
unillusioned honesty of his own art.

It is a device, and like all good devices comes with complete
naturalness to the poet. His position of total deprivation *vis-
à-vis* others puts him unexpectedly in the position of a Henry
James story hero or heroine. Not ripeness but realization is
all. He has 'no son, no wife, no house or land', and life itself is
a rapidly diminishing possession. The experience of this, in
art, is what remains and what can be registered. As Larkin
puts it in another poem, 'Symphony in White Major', 'Where
other people wore like clothes/ The human beings in their
days,/ I set myself to bring to those/ Who thought I could, the
lost displays'. This artist can have nothing in life except his
art, regarding other people as 'lost displays', like Dockery;
unable to use them with the casual and unconscious egotism
of love or possession.

Yet this fact at once confronts the reader with a disarming
paradox. For the poet is really not a bit like this, in his art or in
anything else, nor does he really think he is. The point is that
'To have no son, no wife, no house or land still seemed *quite
natural*', and no doubt for him will always seem so. The
naturalness is that of Larkinian communication and
forthcomingness, of the sort the novel form also uses by

custom and by nature. The poet and short story writer are 'death-suited', confined to the momentary vision and portent of Dockery, and his creation of a story, but the novelist in the man who wrote the poem wanders freely around within it, exchanging confidences, as it seems, with the reader about how he *feels*, about the fact that his instinct is to preserve himself from life (as a story is preserved from it) not to be diluted and distracted among events and contingencies (as a novel can be). In the process he gives himself away, as inevitably as everyone does in shared speech: most obviously so in his own half-hidden, wholly muffled suggestion of a sexual comparison between Dockery and himself.

> Dockery, now:
> Only nineteen, he must have taken stock
> Of what he wanted, and been capable
> Of ... No, that's not the difference: rather, how
> Convinced he was he should be added to!

For a moment the poet seems ready to concede that Dockery has superior virility, in addition to all the other kinds of status, in terms of art and society, in which he himself is lacking. But he balks at that, turning the implied imputation back on Dockery as a figure of almost conditioned stupidity, so blinkered that he must needs be fissiparous, like an amoeba. Dockery is momentarily worsted; the poet's superiority (and virility too) confirmed; but the gambit has not been lost on the reader, who is taking a dialogue-like part in the rumination. Of course, it is a trick in which the poet deliberately lets himself be seen through as part of the process of writing the poem, but it confers, and far more effectively than any mere autobiographical confidence, a remarkable impression of intimacy and truth. The poem lets itself be seen to be kidding on the level, perturbed by some implications of the story it is contriving. One knows a short story not to be 'true': it cannot be in terms of epiphany and its artfully contrived moment of vision; but Larkin is adding something unexpected to this foregone conclusion; adding the certainty that what he is telling actually happened to him, in exactly this form.

That impression, so overwhelmimg in Larkin's best poems, makes them contrast markedly with less good ones, such as 'An Arundel Tomb', which are crafted on a predeterminal basis. Conversely, contemporary poems which seem plainly and honestly confiding, like those of Seamus Heaney, are apt also to be curiously dull. The marvellously discreet element of showmanship in Larkin's best poems depends on the combination of a set-up story with the poet's own attitudes and tone of voice, the two engaging in a subtle rivalry with each other. Their funniest and most obvious clash occurs in 'I Remember I Remember', where the poem and the poet dourly nudge off the story which the context of a lost childhood (' "Why, Coventry!" I exclaimed. "I was born here" ') tries to horn in with. For the childhood was not even lost; it is recollected only as 'unspent', a non-event from which people like Dockery and his son have been exempted. They escaped from the 'real' life the poet has to lead, the 'nothing' which, 'like something, happens anywhere', into the world of story. For Larkin, naturally enough, there is no such luck. His poem sends up every literary version of the past, from fond memoirs to the story situations of D. H. Lawrence, but, more important, he is again recounting things exactly as they happened, and as he feels them to be. The poem shows how essential stories are, and how much the poet relies upon them, even as he sets up that cunning opposition between what literature can make of experience, and the un-thing we actually find it to be (it is part of the poem's forthcomingness that we know, and Larkin knows we know, that those childhood holidays were quite fun at the time, really).

   In 'The Whitsun Weddings' the contrast is at its most subtle and most rewarding, for the 'story' and 'natural life' (the poet's life) keep changing places. The brides and grooms of the Whitsun weddings have all the glamour of otherness, and are disappearing into a mysterious world, the more mysterious because its beginnings are described by the poet in a fashion at once so deadpan and so humdrum ('A dozen marriages got under way'). Seen thus the transaction – weddings at Whitsuntime for down-to-earth tax reasons – acquires all the fascination of a mystery, the railway journey itself the entrance to a land of strangeness and power. The just-marrieds are seen with relentless romanticism, in all the exotic trappings of their class background ('The nylon gloves and jewellery-substitutes/ The lemons, mauves and olive-ochres ...') which seems for Larkin to have just the same attraction as the background of Dockery, his son, their college and social status: two 'other' worlds – one high class, one low – which show how completely Larkin himself is outside both their respective spheres of influence and expectation. The appeal to the poet, in fact, is that of the story; a moment in time, which those who made it will never be aware of.

> – and none
> Thought of the others they would never meet
> Or how their lives would all contain this hour.

Only the poet thought of them, and created their story; and his solitariness in the experience is an unspoken comment both on the pretensions of the short story (we are sharing its big experience) and also on the mystery which those who are making it for the spectator – whether as human beings or aspects of nature – are themselves unconscious of. As in 'Dockery and Son' the poet is being totally honest, or his art is, about his own real place in life, and his relation to the romance of what he sees. His honesty as an artist is of the same order as that of Wordsworth in 'Tintern Abbey' or 'Resolution and Independence', confiding in the reader without seeming to do so, and suggesting the presence of a mystery which is beyond art, and which the poet can only partially explain.

It is resolved only by cessation, as the train with the wedded couples and the poet arrives at its terminus in London.

> We slowed again,
> And as the tightened brakes took hold, there swelled
> A sense of falling, like an arrow-shower
> Sent out of sight, somewhere becoming rain.

This presents an image of otherness as complete as

Wordsworth's 'still sad music of humanity', or 'felt in the blood and felt along the heart'. But its mystery is a great deal more complex, and, as a climax of showmanship, more satisfying. It is easy to dismantle the unparalleled metaphor, more or less, and see that the bridal train trip has resolved itself into an image of erection, penetration, fertility. But in terms of the short story that is unnecessary, even irrelevant. As with Wordsworth, the language has dropped absolutely the simplicities of its meaning, has become the mystery that the story seeks for. Indeed, it would be true to say that the impression of the last few lines is in a sense oppositional to what their image conveys: the poem ends in a conception which has nothing to do with the normal goals and privacies of marriage. It is the mystery of its own being and arrival that is celebrated, 'the sense of falling', the poem's declension into its own static story world, while the unknowing and uncaring lives of those who inspired it continue their own inevitable human parabola towards fulfilment and death. This is why story and contingency change places in the poem; and the deep humour of the poem lies in the way the unknown lives of its anonymous *dramatis personae* are placed in opposition and in parallel with the known lives and reactions of poet and poem.

Unlike the situation in 'Dockery and Son', where the poet is left master of the field, the story worsted, 'The Whitsun Weddings' contrives to attach itself so closely to the persons whom the poet has observed that it is he, and not they, who are left in abeyance. In completing itself the poem has pushed the poet and his personality – usually so gloriously if unobtrusively assertive – into temporary limbo. By invisibly celebrating its own self at the end, rather than the poet's views on life, and his well-known attitudes, the poem has also kept in foreground the potent magic and mystery of its weddings. Dockery receded and vanished, but the relations the wedding ceremonies have inaugurated – relations from which the poet, but not the fancy of his readers, is excluded – seem to swell into independent substance, and live on.

The 'frail Travelling coincidence', in 'The Whitsun Weddings', has obvious affinities with some of the poems of Hardy, although Hardy's poems are anecdotes rather than short stories. They do not have the tension between the conditions of story and the processes of reflection which Larkin in various ways exploits, nor the fulfilment in inconclusiveness which is a speciality of the short story method. Perhaps not suprisingly, in view of Larkin's early passion for Yeats, it is Yeats and not Hardy whose poems exhibit many of Larkin's characteristic kinds of showmanship and craftsmanship; though what is subdued and ironically intimate in the younger poet – perhaps by deliberate contrast with the elder – is, in Yeats, always a matter of energetic *tour de force*. None the less both poets can tell us a lot about the internal workings of the short story form, for both use its *topoi* with the strong element of parody which their own share in the poem requires, and thus reveal the way such a story functions from an unexpected angle. In the first poem of *The Winding Stair* the idea of the short story's 'moment' is subjected to the panache of Yeats' rhetorical process; knocked about, as it were, by his poetic will, and by his determination to resolve the story situation he has evoked in the way most suited to his style.

As with many short stories of the type, 'the moment' is set by means of incantation, but made laconic to the point of parody:

> The light of evening, Lissadell,
> Great windows open to the south,
> Two girls in silk kimonos, both
> Beautiful, one a gazelle.

The moment is magic and a mystery, but Yeats establishes that in the tersest and simplest terms, a parody in miniature of the short story's *topos*. Every reader is gripped by it, and by the magic name, even if he does not know it refers to a house, or to which house and where. Yeats, like Larkin, is playing the totality of the story against the total incompleteness of the personal and reflective genre. The magic moment is cut off by futurity and by what happened to happen: the story tone is equally disrupted by the poet's change of manner:

> But a raving autumn shears
> Blossom from a summer's wreath,
> The elder is condemned to death

> Pardoned, drags out lonely years.
> I know not what the other dreams
> Some vague utopia ...

Although the reader knows that the poem is in a sense a familial one, and that he is overhearing Yeats talking about his friends, it does not greatly help him to know from the memorial dedication that these are Constance Markiewicz and Eva Gore-Booth. Yet the poet's spell is effective; so much so that it does not greatly surprise the reader that one of these beautiful creatures should have been 'condemned to death': it is the kind of thing that might happen in such magic circles. But the precision has given way to a tone of throwaway impatience – 'some vague utopia' – as if such things were not worth the specificity of poetry. Yeats is getting away with his usual lordly line: if you don't know my friends you don't know anyone. The two rebellious Gore-Booth sisters were in fact deeply involved in Irish militant nationalism, and the one who became Countess Markiewicz had been condemned for her part in the Easter Rising and was subsequently reprieved. After relaxing into the personal criticism expressed by those two tellingly twinned epithets, 'raving', and 'vague', the one as biting as the other is patronizing and dismissive, Yeats rounds off his first long stanza with symmetric perfection, turning back to the storied moment of memory, and the two beautiful girls.

In their moment they live in the same world as Dockery and the couples of the Whitsun weddings. Yeats could have ended the poem there. But the picture as painted would have been too unexceptional – the moment of art outside time, and the poet's comment on the diminution into vulgarity and pathos which time has brought. The naive (which does not mean simple) art of Hardy allows his most touching poems to remain sentimentally anecdotal, his spots of time fixed by physical means, as in 'Green Slates', the sight of which reminds the poet of the girl he once glimpsed 'standing in the quarry'. Hardy has no further implications to disturb his scene, or his poem. But Yeats has deliberately invoked these by the way he has talked about the girls at Lissadell. He must produce a moral, an opposition, a commentary that will satisfy queries without answering them. His 'dear shadows', who have degenerated into fatuous and fallible females, must be exonerated and sanctified by other means than presenting them as once gracious and beautiful (and one like a gazelle). So one of the most venerable of literary conventions is employed. They know better now. They know 'all the folly of a fight/ With a common wrong or right.' And now Yeats' dependence on cliché becomes overwhelming, almost insolent, and his style flexes itself to bemuse the reader with its sheer virtuosity. Larkin, at the end of 'Dockery and Son', pulls off a brilliant effect by absolute baldness, his audience not even being expected to agree but only to acquiesce in glum and admiring satisfaction:

> Life is first boredom, then fear
> Whether or not we use it, it goes
> And leaves what something hidden from us chose
> And age, and then the only end of age.

Yeats is much more obviously full of tricks, but his point is as simple as Larkin's and less straightforward. 'The innocent and the beautiful/ Have no enemy but time'; and then a highly virtuoso metaphor is mounted whose function is to distract the reader from the shortcut in ordinary poetic intelligence that Yeats is taking. 'Bid me rise and strike a match/ And strike another till time catch/ Should the conflagration climb/ Run till all the sages know.' The rhetorical self-command masks the absurdity of the gesture, absurdity compounded by the repetition and break in the last line – 'Bid me strike a match and blow!' Yeats intends to blow upon his fire of stupid and forgettable past events in order to fan the flames that consume them, but the last line could also be said to blow out the metaphor, as it seems to blow out the match. The match-lighting business is not serious, no more serious than Yeats considers the political activities of the two girls to be. In the weakness of the metaphor he seems to join their own weaknesses, an act of friendship in terms of style which is touching, and gives warmth and complex fellow-feeling to the poem's second part. (That 'Bid me' – is the kind of glib speechifying gambit that the girls must have heard at political rallies, and perhaps uttered themselves.) In cancelling the story, and the timeless, legendary figures created for it, the poet and the two girls come closer to us in the ordinary muddle of being human beings. The metaphor of time as the only 'enemy' of aesthetic perfection has done its job and can be forgotten. The poet's fallibility, and too great facility as a stylist, blends with the very absurdity from which he had disassociated himself, and the two women whom he is celebrating.

The result is a masterpiece which, as in the Larkin poems, combines our short story element with other unstable and almost accidental effects which the compass and genre of a poem can bring together and hold in solution. Though unstable they may not be uncalculated; it is part of Larkin's strategy, as we have seen, to seem to reveal himself as if by mistake, or through the inadvertence of concentration on his own ruminations. With Yeats, of course, rhetoric is its own reward: he is not playing to be seen through as part of its effect. Nor has he Larkin's scrupulousness – that of a poet in a deeply conservative tradition of discourse – in taking pains to make quite sure the reader is with him. It is part of Yeats' romantic attitude to mystify and overawe the reader through his social and personal utterance, and to let his commentary be its own version of 'Now you see me: now you don't'.

And yet if we examine Yeats' text closely, as in the case of the poem discussed, both his art and his mystery give way to something more humanly accessible, in a saving sense more commonplace. Poetry and the short story are always close together. But poetry, as in these examples, can allow itself to be reduced to complex human considerations, by means of which it affords its own commentary upon itself. The short story must supply that commentary without giving it; while suggesting that its mystery cannot be yielded up; is far more deeply interfused; not to be understood.

CHAPTER TWO

Persons in stories are of two kinds: contextual and anecdotal. In most cases there are permutations and combinations of the two, as in 'Dockery and Son', where Dockery is presented with the status of an anecdote, while the poet as character lives in the world of context, the world where it seems 'quite natural' to behave in certain ways and to have acquired unconsciously certain lifestyles. The same is true of 'The Whitsun Weddings'. Poems which tell stories usually make, as part of the genre, a sharp distinction between the two kinds; and in Larkin's case this is particularly insistent, though unobtrusive. The world beyond him, the world that might have happened, acquires the status of anecdote, and by the same logic, that of mystery. Wordsworth's 'light that never was on sea or land' dwindles into the discovery that other people are fascinating, in terms of art and as art objects, because they lead lives that are not one's own.

Wordsworth's anecdotes are themselves illustrative of the difference, and of its significance. In 'Resolution and Independence' the Leech-gatherer is a figure of mystery, impenetrable, and for that reason, wholly satisfactory to the eye of art:

> In my mind's eye I seemed to see him pace
> About the weary moors continually,
> Wandering about alone and silently.

Yet Wordsworth is also, and without seeming to find
anything incongruous in it, feeding into his story at least two
other ways of seeing the Leech-gatherer. He is a strong-
minded old fellow, deeply religious, like most simple folk in
lonely situations, and inclined to garrulity when he gets a
chance to talk to a sympathetic stranger. Wordsworth is quite
conscious of the difference between the old man as he is, and
as he appears to the poet's eye.

> The Old-man still stood talking at my side;
> But now his voice to me was like a stream
> Scarce heard; nor word from word could I divide;
> And the whole Body of the Man did seem
> Like one whom I had met with in a dream ...

The point is emphasized again and again ('While I these
thoughts within myself pursued/ He, having made a pause,
the same discourse renewed') as if the writer were determined
not to blink the fact that what the old man means to him has
no relation to what he is in and as himself.

The poem is based on the contrast between the contextual
being of Wordsworth, and what the old man means in the
poem as a happening, both anecdote and apparition. The two
are naturally confused, even though the poet and his readers
are aware of them separately, for the old man as he appears in
Wordsworth's imagination, 'wandering about alone and
silently' ... 'not all alive or dead,/ Nor all asleep –' is not the
old man who still doggedly pursues his occupation, 'Housing,
with God's good help, by choice or chance'. The poem, with
its own kind of inspired awkwardness, shows us both, in a
setting whose parts are quite open, and make no more
pretence than does Sir John Moore's burial to blend together
in the secret harmony which would constitute a short story.
Both form and speech in the poem are incongruous, like the
old-fashioned Spenserian stanza, the diction often
conscientiously archaic ('a flash of mild surprise/ Broke from
the sable orbs of his yet vivid eyes') as if the poet felt that the
impression the Leech-gatherer made required a traditional
poetic utterance. On the other hand, that impression, as
recorded factually by Wordsworth and his sister Dorothy,

was of an immensely decrepit old person in a lonely moorland; and what originally struck the poet so strongly was a combination of the misery and helplessness of age with the desolate spot in which the encounter took place. All this is brought into the poem, but accumulated haphazardly, so that the immediate impression, and what was subsequently built on it, merges into a confusion that threatens to be self-cancelling. That it is not so is the result of the poem's egocentric inward concentration, which holds the materials together in its own spell of absorption. Something has happened, a 'dire constraint of pain, or rage/ Of sickness felt by him in times long past' (The rhyme word 'rage' becomes startingly effective in terms of the old man's present tranquillity) to give the old man's frame its air of extreme decreptitude; and the poet's inner world has been equally darkened by that morning's reflections on his own life and possible fate.

Wordsworth's inner faith in the poem's experience is the correlative of the old man's necessary and unquestioning resolution. Each endorses the other, and Wordsworth does not hesitate to conclude that God is the mainstay of both. And yet the *incompleteness* of the poem can be felt almost as a solid presence, a palpable entity in the way it has been structured into being. Though there is a short story in it, this has not any real atmosphere and status of its own, as the short story element has in 'Dockery and Son'; and though the conclusion is equally and firmly logical in both poems, it is a logic that remains outside the bounds of secrecy in a story's completeness. Dockery, as we have seen, is fully accounted for: the poem suggests both his legendary status as a possibly dead hero, and his actual humdrum contextual existence as a, presumably, living father. Both anecdotal and contextual, Dockery completes the poem; though the fact that he is not fully one or the other means that it does not have a short story's completeness.

But the contextual aspect of 'Resolution and Independence' involves an omission which the reader is naggingly aware of, and which yet has neither the mystery proffered and withheld in the form of the Tintern Abbey poem, nor the kind of mystery which the short story achieves through its own totality of aesthetic effect. Wordsworth's omission throws a good deal of light on the nature of that effect, for it is not one that an artist would consider and weigh in the balance, but a problem involving the poet's sense of 'real life'. Incidents and episodes from this always ambiguous category of being are what Wordsworth claimed to give, and, as we shall see later, the short story has a special technique for revealing a reality about life over and above the one which it purports to show. In the case of 'Resolution and Independence' this occurs as part of the contrast effect between Wordsworth's own being and the one imputed to the Leech-gatherer. The most deeply felt realization in the poem, it might be said, is Wordsworth's about his own feelings, situation, impulse of resolve.

And yet this itself depends upon the success – the undoubted success – with which Wordsworth has also realized in the poem the figure of the Leech-gatherer, which is where the omission comes in. To be seemingly complete, a legendary or mythological figure, a figure of story, the Leech-gatherer must forfeit the truth of his actual trade. He must be a Leech-gatherer in name and in idea only – a sufficiently striking name and idea upon which Wordsworth is leaning heavily; putting forward, indeed, as an earnest of 'real life', the variety and the pathos in humanity's still, sad music. Leech-gathering is both a touching and a picturesque exemplar of how the poor live, the strange necessities which find them a humble employment. But having emphasized this point, and brought the old man to the verge of the pool in which he operated, Wordsworth flinches from revealing how this was done. It is possible he did not know himself, for the leech-gatherer he met, and who was the occasion for the poem, was not actually engaged in the business; but it seems more likely that he knew very well, and was silently contrasting his own happy *physical* existence, rambling across the natural beauties of mountain and moor, with the gruesome department of physical nature in which the old man was compelled to live and have his being.

Mystery has the old sense of craft or profession – the executioner in *Measure for Measure* fears that a mere amateur will 'discredit' his 'mystery' – and the unrevealed and incongruous mystery in 'Resolution and Independence' is how leeches were actually caught. They attached themselves to the feet and ankles of the hunter, who indeed stood 'motionless', but not 'upon the margin' of the 'moorish flood'. Wordsworth transposes his vision of the old man, seeing him as a boulder upon the moor, or as 'a Sea-beast crawled forth, that on a shelf/ Of rock or sand reposeth, there to sun itself'. Behind this vision it is possible to see another – that of the crippled ancient bent double as he stood as unmoving as a heron in the shallow water.

Wordsworth's silent comparison of himself with this uncomplaining figure is very touching, but it means that the old man who is the occasion of the tale is both contextually and anecdotally incomplete. Good short stories have the air of telling themselves, but this story will not let itself be told. Were the poem to be explicit about the wretched discomfort of the trade, as Hood or Mayhew would have been, the status of the leech-gatherer would be a quite different one: he would cease to be an anecdotal portent and become a fact about how the poor live. Yet, in withholding the fact, Wordsworth surprisingly achieves one of the most vital effects of the short story – the impression that there is something more to come – even though the artefact of the poem reposes in a state of arbitrary finality, as a short story would not and could not allow. Wordsworth's poetry usually has a provisional quality; and with good reason, for he often went back to modify or to enlarge, but 'Resolution and Independence' has the right air of there being nothing more to say, and a significance, which could be spoiling, withheld.

The curious thing is that the poet was persistently blamed for making a ridiculous fuss about the Leech-gatherer and their conversation; and he himself replied to this mockery with energy, referring, as any Romantic poet would, to the visionary strangeness of such an old man in such a place. And it is true that the poem avoids the bathos imputed to it by keeping its myth figure always just ahead, as it were, of the mockery which seeks to patronize the poet's account of their meeting. Formally speaking, the poem trembles on the verge of the absurdity the unsympathetic reader finds in it, but consistently avoids it by a withholding and withdrawing

tactic, related to the 'something far more deeply interfused'
tactic of 'Tintern Abbey'. The persistence that Lewis Carroll
found ludicrous in fact serves to emphasize the way in which
both Leech-gatherer and poem retains what appears to be
their secret and their 'mystery'. Like a character in a fairy
story Wordsworth is convinced there is a solution to the
riddle, which will solve his own problems.

> Perplexed, and longing to be comforted,
> My question eagerly did I renew,
> 'How is it that you live, and what is it you do?'
>
> He with a smile did then his words repeat;
> And said that, gathering Leeches, far and wide
> He travelled; stirring thus about his feet
> The waters of the Pools where they abide.
> 'Once I could meet with them on every side;
> But they have dwindled long by slow decay;
> Yet still I persevere, and find them where I may'.

The smile is typical of a situation in which the hero is trying to
tease out something which his interlocutor does not seem to
recognize the existence of. Also the stanza treads the edge of
another sort of revelation: the method by which leeches are
caught. The smile goes with the rhyme on 'repeat' and 'feet',
bringing us as close as possible to a problem which has now
incongruously doubled itself: what is the 'secret' of the leech-
gatherer has now both expanded, and substituted itself, for
the more homely secret of catching leeches. Both these are
turned aside by the simple naturalism caught in the old man's
reported speech, telling the poet merely what we all know:
that old men repeat themselves, and always know that things
were once much better than they now are; that birds used to
be found on every bush and flocks of leeches in every pond.
This well-worn truth is the first that substitutes for the
Leech-gatherer's hypothetical secret, the next being the
poem's emphatic but still elusive conclusion – 'God', said I,
'be my help and stay secure;/ I'll think of the Leech-gatherer
on the lonely moor!' This utterance parallels as a cliché the
old man's reported remark on the former abundance of

leeches and their present scarcity; but it also has the true
Delphic doubleness. Although the first sentiment seems to
follow from the second, the second is all we can be sure of. All
the poem can do is to ensure that we shall continue to think of
the Leech-gatherer.

The poet's response is to that aspect of the Leech-gatherer
which is like the gatekeeper in Kafka's story, before whose
gate a man stands until he dies, waiting to find out the secret
of life. In this it is as much of a true short story as its form
permits, for Wordsworth's stanza and poetic style allow for
lapses, incongruities, and alternations of tone and style which
a conscious prose can also contrive for itself. It would be
wrong to say that the comedy of the poem is wholly
unintentional, for the tone he adopts cannot but seem aware –
as in a comic anecdote – of the poet's preoccupation with his
own state of mind, first in relation to anxieties that develop as
a result of his first morning joy upon the moor, then as a result
of his encounter with the Leech-gatherer, and the enigma of
his being. Such a close history of self-preoccupation is sure to
produce comic effects, as it does in 'Dockery and Son', and
both poets seem to exploit this, like raconteurs. (Compare the
absorbed preliminary 'Now', opening Wordsworth's eighth
stanza, with Larkin's 'But Dockery, good Lord ...') Larkin,
the showman, is more delicately aware of the comic elements
in his narrative, but both poets seem to expect an audience at
once sympathetic and amused, as if by a good 'story'; nor
should we discount Wordsworth's disappointment at the
reaction of his first audience, whom he had evidently failed to
carry along.

This latent element of comedy is essential to the short story
form, and these poems show with some precision how it can
operate, with no apparent intention or effort on the part of the
writer. Wordsworth, indeed, usually misjudges the art, in his
too great concern to let the reader smile, so that he is also
moved.

> O Reader! Had you in your mind
> Such stores as silent thought can bring,
> O gentle Reader! you would find
> A tale in everything.

In his zeal to domesticate in rural England the highly popular Romantic fables of the time, full of high-minded orphans, chaste affections, young women abandoned but *toujours sensible*, Wordsworth was anxious to let his readers be touched by the incongruities involved. But he can seldom let these appear naturally: more often he contradicts his own advice to the reader. 'Should you *think*, Perhaps a tale you'll make it'. Too often the poet misunderstands the direction his reader's thought may take. Metre does not help, and only in poems like 'Resolution and Independence' does there seem a true subterranean contact between the way Wordsworth's mind is working, and the way in which his reader follows. In the worst cases the writer himself seems to have missed the point of his own tale, as in the beautifully told 'Fidelity', which relates how a shepherd on the mountains finds a dog; the dog has stayed for three months by the skeleton of its master, a traveller killed in a cliff fall.

> How nourished here through such long time
> He knows, who gave that love sublime;
> And gave that strength of feeling, great
> Above all human estimate.

God knows, but the poet does not seem to. The dog must have eaten its master, and stayed by the body as the only point of reality to which it was accustomed. Does Wordsworth know this? It is the idea of *feeling* he wishes to bring home to us, and his account of the dog unused to mountain country, with its 'timid cry', is very moving. It is even possible, in the last verse, to imagine the poet's gaze fixed deadpan on the reader, as if daring him to interrupt the rush of *feeling* with the knowledge of brute reality; and to remember Hazlitt's observation of the 'convulsive inclination to laughter' around Wordsworth's mouth; to wonder if 'a heart more wakeful' has not already anticipated our awareness of the true story in the poem.

But which is the true story? The form is not, in fact, susceptible to the query, however much it may use the tactic of withholding a solution, or evidence, or the enigma of what it is really about. A story may intrigue us, as hypothetically in the case of 'Fidelity', by seeming unaware of what it is itself recording; or the narrator's absorption in his own condition may mislead him, as in the case of 'Resolution and Independence', or some of Kafka's stories, about the nature of things as it appears to the reader. Kipling's later stories are full of blind alleys and irrelevant clues, whose purposes may be other than those which the reader guesses them to be. Thus in 'A Madonna of the Trenches' one of the characters tries to deceive the others about the causes of his breakdown at the end of the war; and this deception becomes the stalking-horse for the much greater one about Kipling's intentions and beliefs in presenting the story – is its real focus, for instance, on the inexplicable motivations of suicide? In an early story, 'At the End of the Passage' (whose title itself has a formula significance in this context), a much more straightforward contrast emerges, between the story's mumbo-jumbo horror out of Poe, and the stark fact of a man so overstrained into insomnia, by the heat and loneliness of his job in India, that he becomes terrified by the idea of sleep itself. An even more remarkable story, 'The Strange Ride of Morrowbie Jukes', offers a graphic scenario, of the adventure-story type, as both image and substitute for the nightmare that would follow a breakdown in the conditioning of one of the English ruling class in India. Each 'story in it' needs the other: without the other each would function at an inferior level of art.

The ideal short story has controlled all the possibilities in it, but continues to live in terms of their own actual and lively existence. An impression of deadness in the story may arise from too meticulous a control on the part of the writer, and too methodical an awareness of the effects to be achieved. The writer's mastery can make its own dead end. Numerous excellent story writers – two examples that come to mind would be Karen Blixen and Flannery O'Connor – create an extremely powerful effect, whose only drawback is the lack of doubt in the reader's mind that this particular powerful effect has been sought after and created. Such stories depend upon their own absoluteness, and that absoluteness, which can seem the goal of the short story writer in terms of the form's success, may also be its nemesis. The 'short story', a genre as self-conscious as the literary context in which the term itself was invented, carries a kind of excuse in its very description, and also a promise. It will give us concentration instead of length. Other forms, like the poems I have been discussing, can do the same thing. But fully to succeed the short story must forgo its self-conscious emphasis on concentration, and appear both leisurely and enmeshed in the speculative, as any other genre may be. It must seem both formally to preclude, and secretly to accept, speculation on matters exlcuded by itself; speculation about the author and his being, his relation to the matter in the work, and to matters outside it. The incompatibility between its art and its mystery must become its own justification.

This can be seen triumphantly to occur in Conrad's *Lord Jim*, which began as a story, almost as much a 'short story' as Conrad's 'Amy Foster', but which grew (as the conventional distinction between italics and inverted commas shows) into a *nouvelle* or short novel. Henry James was familiar with the same kind of growth, and with finding that what he had taken to be a story was expanding into a larger form. The point would be not so much that any story can become a novel – or James's 'blessed *nouvelle*' – as that in doing so it retains many of the qualities the story form emphasizes. Jim in a novel, even in a *nouvelle*, could not be the enigmatic figure that he remains in Conrad's presentation. The 'subtle unsoundness' that Marlow finds in him would be verified and exemplified as comprehensively as is the unsoundness in George Eliot's character of Lydgate, in her novel *Middlemarch*. Although *Lord Jim* became almost as long as a novel, Jim remains a character in a story. He is a character, that is to say, in the same sense in which the Leech-gatherer is one, or Akaky Akakyevich, the hero of Gogol's story, 'The Overcoat'.

Like them, Jim is primarily an anecdotal person, although as the story turns itself into a short novel he acquired a contextual existence, first as a 'water-clerk' in an eastern seaport, then as adventurer and trusted adviser to a native ruler. In both these roles he seems curiously unreal, and this is part of the effect of the story, for Jim is a man continually seeking the role that will give him what he feels to be his ideal reality, and hence never finding it: he is real only at the moment when he jumps, and that jump is for the story its end in itself. Its anecdote is both begun and completed by the history of the moment of Jim's jump from the Patna's deck. Thus Jim remains a mystery, however much the *nouvelle* may go on to exemplify and complete the analysis of him, inventing a sequel suitably heroic and colourful, and contriving a suitably ironic ending. In terms of the short story the special interest of *Lord Jim* is that Conrad goes on to supply in it, and at length, the kind of material that the story would only *imply*, holding it in a deliberately concentrated area of query, of a future cut off and impalpable.

Gogol, in 'The Overcoat', pursues a different technique, reducing the contextual side of his hero to grotesque parody. Akaky's daily routines are entered into in detail, the kind of detail over which the novel would linger, but consist only of the endless copying which absorbs his whole capacity for pleasure and comfort, and which engrosses him so completely that he does not even bother about the cockroaches in the perpetual beef and onion stew dished out by his landlady. In spite of this background there is something withheld and mysterious about Akaky, of which we get a glimpse when his new overcoat is finally finished, and he goes off in it to his colleagues' party. Wearing his overcoat he notices for the first time a prostitute, and gives a little skip at the sight, as if the overcoat were a magic garment which has changed his whole life and let him see and feel things never experienced before.

This is indeed true for the reader who experiences the story, the overcoat being its own anecdote, and an enigmatic one. The theft of it is the end of its owner, who catches a fatal chill from misery and agitation in his attempts to get it back. The overcoat is heaven for Akaky – heaven always being a suitably equivocal concept – and heaven has been lost after a single moment for vouchsafement. What this means for Gogol is equally mysterious, but the reader can feel the deep involvement of his own secret life, all the more because the tale itself is so breezily and triumphantly complete. This paradoxical contrast between surface and depths is of course familiar enough in all sorts of fiction. Gogol's 'secret', associated with his own clandestine homosexuality, is pored over by the most learned Russian critics; and, in a quite

different context, one of the oddest cults in the novel of our
time has been that of Barbara Pym, whose 'secret' appears to
be that she was exactly like one of her own 'excellent women',
and yet one endowed with the power to observe and to write
like the recording angel. All her devotees seem to feel, in some
sense, the seduction of this contrast.

Our sense of the writer himself, in the short story, is one of
a rather specialized kind, as we might imagine; and Henry
James is a good instance of it. As a critic and commentator on
his own art, James himself of course knew exactly what was
involved. He knew that the writer as novelist was in fact
present 'on every page' from which his own art had tried so
hard to remove him. But the case of the story was rather
different. In it, any sense of authorial presence might actually
be turned technically to account, might be built into the tale
as one of its specific and individual effects. This has occurred,
whether or not of set purpose, in Conrad's *Lord Jim*, and in
'The Secret Sharer'. In both cases the anecdotal hero remains
incomplete, seen in terms of hints and suggestions. In both
the narrator – Marlow in the one case, the young captain in
the other – is used as a stalking-horse, to increase both the
reader's interest in the anecdotal hero, and a sense of the
latter's continuing mysteriousness. Conrad himself thought
'The Secret Sharer' the best thing he had done in the story
line, and as a story it stands out not only from the humour and
unusualness of the anecdotal situation, but because of the way
in which the notion of a secret is explicitly made the guiding
principle of the tale – the tale considered as a yarn which
Conrad had picked up about an incident that took place on the
windjammer *Cutty Sark*. The title itself can be taken two
ways, according to whether the word secret is noun or
adjective: the man who shares the captain's cabin, in secret, is
also in collusion with the author and narrator as a sharer of
secrets. And a secret remains one by definition. even if it is
shared; and shared, in whatever fashion, with the reader.

In fact the unspoken collusion of the two young men of the
story – former 'Conway boys' – carries no sexual overtones, as
the critics have sometimes suggested, but is an image of the
inevitably and flatteringly secret relation between the writer
of the tale and his reader. It is more important that he should

be telling us – sharing with us – something of significance, than that we should grasp – that there should be any possibility of us grasping – exactly what this is. The writer's secret – what it may mean to him – has itself become the justification of the tale, its subject the reader's sense of fascination and curiosity. This is formally emphasized, and the reader's curiosity whetted – by the offhand reference in the opening paragraph – offhand, one should add, only in the tone and not in the careful and beautiful nature of the writing – to the mysterious structures which stick out of the shallow water of the gulf of Siam; seemingly pointless, unless they are perhaps fish-traps, but in any case something the western mind brushes away from its purview. The low-keyed way the story slides into being contrasts with the dramatic climax of its ending, with the secret sharer of the cabin striking out for the unknown shore, 'a free swimmer confronting his destiny', and the young captain risking his first command close under the cliffs of the island archipelago. The beginning of the story seems implicitly to criticize the way it ends, as if the real mystery, like the objects in the water, remained too ordinarily incomprehensible for there to be any validity in a resounding conclusion to the anecdote. The narrator, and thus the author, willed it so; and, as in *Lord Jim*, the author was determined to make *something* of the story by giving it an appropriately big-scale ending. It is important to the story, however, that the quietness of its opening sequences make more impression on us than the loudness of the closing ones. The author seems to admit as much, and in the admission there is also secret information passed – about himself, and about his sense of art and the story. Where the latter is concerned, the free swimmer seeking his destiny is less important than our glimpse of the motionless dark head in the water under the ship's side – the glimpse that really matters about this particular anecdotal man – and though the story knows that it has to end as it does, it stresses the fact in such a way as to add to its undermeanings, in the same way that the impressions and speculations that accumulate around Jim and his jump mean more than Jim's subsequent history and the contrivance of his death. The short story always tries either to avoid an ending, or to suggest there is none, and one way of doing this is to draw attention to the way it has been arranged, a way that does not seem of a piece with the story itself. The story can disassociate itself by arranging an ending suited to a novel or *nouvelle*, which clears up the event without dispelling the mystery.

Conrad could be said to avoid the implications of some of his best stories, and this itself tells us much about him. He avoids them, so to speak, as a man and not as an artist. D. H. Lawrence tells us that we should trust the tale and not the teller, but this advice is particularly unhelpful where the short story is concerned, since many of its best effects come from the covert interrelation between the artist – the 'teller' – and the man inside the artist. It is here that the secrets begin on which the form flourishes. In the depths of 'The Secret Sharer' there stirs Conrad's own irresponsibility, the vulnerable and invisible part of us that is not on public display; just as *Lord Jim* provides the area of mystification in which can circle Conrad's own personal sense of having abandoned his post – his country and people. Conrad's reticence as a man seems fascinated by the challenge to it that the story provides, and returns to it as the moth to the flame.

Even when young, Henry James seems to have contemplated this area of secrets in the short story with remarkable self-possession. One of his earliest, 'A Landscape-Painter', shows him sharing the secret with the reader on his own terms and in his own way. It is a remarkable performance, so remarkable that one may wonder whether James, even in his years of sophistication, ever produced a better, or a more characteristic one. His description of the anecdote was 'something that had oddly happened to someone'. What oddly happens to the Landscape-Painter is that he dies, still young. That we discover on the second page of the story. The anecdote is thus framed as a history, because we know – or we infer, rather – that his wife too has died, later on. The 'I' of the story, who makes an appearance only in the first two pages, has a jaunty manner traditional to his office and derived mostly from Poe, though James has cunningly infused this with the rather self-conscious worldliness of a young New Yorker. The story opens with a smoking-room question: 'Do you remember how, a dozen years ago, a number of our friends were startled by the report of the rupture of young Locksley's engagement with Miss Leary?' This is just the tone, and convention, which the young Kipling will take up twenty years later; and something similar will be used by another young friend of James, Robert Louis Stevenson. It is James's equivalent of Plain Tales from New England.

Locksley is short and dark and not particularly good-looking, whereas Miss Leary has the 'heroic proportions' of the Venus de Milo. But Locksley is rich; his prospects of wealth 'believed to be enormous', a phrase which looks forward to the hush and the excitement that attends on Milly Theale's status in *The Wings of the Dove*. Already the story is bifurcating: on the one hand, mystery – the mystery of wealth and the fates which attend it – on the other hand, the atmosphere of farce. Mrs Leary, a widow with four daughters, is known to be 'an inveterate old screw'. Miss Leary is compensated by 'marriage with a gentleman of expectations very nearly as brilliant as those of her old suitor'. And what about Locksley? 'What was *his* compensation? That is precisely my story.'

It is not quite the end of the official story-teller, who survives for another page to disappear in a sentence whose cumbrousness seems deliberately to court the reader's notice. 'The recent passing away of the one person who had a voice paramount to mine in the disposal of Locksley's effects enables me to act without reserve.' Who is this person? Locksley's wife presumably, although she seems to be of no interest to the story-teller. But although the opening indicates obscurity, as well as the mystery of money, and although 'Locksley disappeared, as you will remember, from public view', some matters of chronology receive a very marked emphasis. The narrator lost sight of Locksley. 'He died seven years ago, at the age of thirty-five. For five years, accordingly, he managed to shield his life from the eyes of men'. His diary came into the narrator's hands 'through circumstances I need not go into', and 'extends from his twenty-fifth to his thirtieth year, at which period it breaks off suddenly'. The narrator suggests that 'if you come to my house', he will show you some of Locksley's pictures; and that 'meanwhile' he will place before us the last hundred pages of the diary.

These exact figures suggest an unspoken problem and a possibility of solution, which a reading of the diary will now no doubt confirm. It is always a disappointment to find that people haven't gone to the dogs, and the narrator anticipates our satisfaction in finding that Locksley has done the next best thing. He is no longer around, and his history, his doing and being, can now be patronized, can appear wholly in an anecdotal light. That, at least, is the suggestion in the narrator's tone. But the diary itself now abruptly begins, and the whole atmosphere of the story at once changes. *Chowderville, June 9th*. The facetious tone, the story as farce, appears for the last time in the place name, that of an archetypal New England fishing village. The diary's first sentence introduces something quite different. 'I have been sitting some minutes, pen in hand, wondering whether on this new earth, beneath this new sky, I had better resume this occasional history of nothing at all.' He goes on: 'I think I will at all events make the experiment. If we fail, as Lady Macbeth remarks, we fail. I find my entries have been longest when I had least to say.' The short story has declared its hand. It has nothing to say, and its art consists in not failing in the way it does this. James as author has also shown his hand, taking over from the gossipy cub narrator of the opening sequence. He has become the diarist, the *alter ego* of the artist, the young man who is about to produce 'a number of remarkable paintings'.

The extraordinary richness and charm of 'A Landscape-Painter' is the more remarkable when compared with the very elementary tales, often heavily influenced by the allegories of Hawthorne, which James produced about the same time. He had himself made the attempt at Newport to become an artist, and he had a great feeling for the New England coast, its scenery and atmosphere. As painter he had attempted in the spirit of Lady Macbeth, and he had failed; but the attempt was not fruitless, for as a short story 'A Landscape-Painter' is founded on the pictorial eye, the vision of rock and water; the 'blue darkness' of the night outside, in which nothing stirs except the rising tide; the figure of the young woman,

daughter of a retired sea-captain, in whose house the painter
takes up his lodgings.

> I remember, when Miss Quarterman stepped ashore and stood
> upon the beach, relieved against the cool darkness of a recess in
> the cliff, while her father and I busied ourselves with gathering
> up our baskets and fastening the anchor – I remember, I say,
> what a picture she made. There is a certain purity in the air of this
> place which I have never seen surpassed – a lightness, a
> brilliancy, a crudity, which allows perfect liberty of self-
> assertion to each individual object in the landscape. The
> prospect is ever more or less like a picture which lacks its final
> process, its reduction to unity.

'Its final process, its reduction to unity.' James was already
expert enough to intuit that, whatever might be the case with
a painting, the short story could derive its particular effects
precisely from absence of such a reduction: its composition
might depend on the artful exhibition of elements that
remained uncomposed, so as to leave a query, an air of
interrogation, about the whole. Miss Quarterman herself is
vividly suggested by the landscape-painter's prose, which yet
– as in a picture – leaves her an enigmatic life of her own.

As it composes a pictorial self the story doubles back to play
in literary terms. 'How can a man', the painter's diary gravely
enquires, 'be simple and natural who is known to have a large
income? ... It's bad enough to have it; to be known to have it,
to be known only because you have it, is most damnable.'
This, as we already know from the facetious opening, is the
first line of the tale, from which it will successively operate a
planned withdrawal. Locksley's sententiousness on the
subject gives us a hint, and leads us to suppose that some
irony will follow. In the meantime an idyll develops, as if in a
picture, centred on the sleepy routine of the town and
Locksley's delight in it, in walking, painting, and fishing with
the delightful old sea-captain. The chief figure in the idyll is
Miss Quarterman, seen in her brightness and freshness like
the sky and the sea, as if in 'a clever English water-colour'.
She goes out to teach the music lessons from which most of
the family income derives, and 'when she comes home, with
the raindrops glistening on her rich cheeks and her dark
lashes, her cloak bespattered with mud and her hands red

with the cool damp, she is a very honourable figure.' She is attended, in the eyes of Locksley, with traditional romantic simplicities.

At the same time 'she is rather a puzzle'. Her comments on his paintings – she 'called everything beautiful and delightful' – disappoint. 'Is she, indeed, a very commonplace person, and the fault in me, who am for ever taking women to mean a great deal more than their maker intended?' These uncertainties go with precisions, and a significant renewal of chronology. Locksley's first idea of Miss Quarterman was of a teacher in a young ladies' school ('I suppose she's over thirty. I think I know the species') but when he meets her, in her 'fresh white dress, with a blue ribbon on her neck, and a rosebud in her button-hole – or whatever corresponds to the button-hole on the feminine bosom' – she seems 'about twenty-four'. Later he has 'collected a few facts. She is not twenty-four but twenty-seven years old'. She reads only novels, but 'likes only the good ones. I do so like *The Missing Bride*, which I have just finished.' Locksley decides to 'set her to work at some of the masters'.

It is 'a very happy little household', and the innocent patronage of his diary – James clearly took an artful pleasure in its sententiousness – none the less reveals to the reader, as it were beside and apart from Locksley himself, that it really *is* one. The reader apprehends, in fact, that he is not to be given the simple irony of sophisticated town-dweller who is really a pawn in the hands of scheming country-folk, the nature and quality of whose Eden he has naively mistaken. Then what is he to be given? The idyll, over which the diarist dilates so happily and so meticulously, must be leading somewhere. Or is its still-life an image of the story, the anecdote as it ought to be; indeed the anecdote perfectly coincident with context? That has a truth about it, for the point about Eden is its reality, not that it is like a dream which has to give place to the cold light of continuing experience. The reality of absurdly named Chowderville penetrates the reader with calm delight, the tranquil daily aesthetic pleasure taken in it by Locksley himself, and with that goes the same sense of the Quartermans, father and daughter.

The strangeness, the charm, of the place is the strangeness

and charm of art, but it also has that of 'The Great Good Place', the story – so much less natural and convincing than 'A Landscape-Painter' – which James was to write many years later. All art is the recapture of innocence, and that of the short story particularly so, because it deals with a charmed moment, whatever its duration. Nor is there any serpent in Eden except the chronological nature of life itself. The reader continues to expect that the knowing tone of the first few sentences will in some way be cleverly repeated (it is typical of James to use the word in a wholly innocent sense, as when he speaks of 'a clever English water-colour'). A clever short story is a banality, and James reserves the adjective for something to be admired not only for its art but for its real simplicity, as in the setting and description of his own story.

But the reader's expectations are not to be disappointed. Money brings deceit, as Locksley fears, and as he had plenty of opportunity to observe in Newport or in New York society, as had his creator. But exactly what is 'deceit' in this situation? Miriam Quarterman is indeed, in the old phrase, as honest as the day. The reader will be disappointed of any hope of finding her as venal as Miss Leary in New York, neat as that discovery might be, and suited to the kind of little stage comedies, based on his stories, with which James hoped to keep the pot boiling in his later years. And how venal, in any case, was Miss Leary herself? Miss Quarterman, were she so disposed, could probably give as good an answer to that as anyone else. What happens, of course, is that Locksley falls ill – the good old Victorian literary standby of a slight fever – and that while looking after him she reads his diary. Naturally enough the diary, as it continues, remains ignorant of this, and Miss Quarterman herself gives no sign, other than by refusing her other suitor, a young lawyer of the town. Locksley proposes, is accepted; the pair have a quiet wedding and go for their honeymoon to another small place down the coast. Here Locksley fatuously proposes to himself, in his diary, a great aesthetic pleasure. He will 'give her the book to read, and sit by her, watching her face – watching the great secret dawn upon her.'

Naturally enough he is cheated of this wish. The story ends with the last entry, which begins: 'Somehow or other I can write this quietly enough; but I hardly think I shall ever write any more'. He goes on to record how his wife tells him she had read the diary. 'I read it because I suspected. Otherwise I wouldn't have done so'. She always thought there was something wrong in his story of being a poor art student. 'You cheated me and I mystified you'. Now they can be honest with each other. 'If you really love me – and I think you do – you will not let this make any difference.'

Again there is the suggestion of stage comedy – Shavian comedy – in the *dénouement*. Miss Quarterman talks – when she talks –. like a good actress with a good part, and she has already administered a fine lecture to the hero on his characteristically masculine vanities and vices. Women are honest about their wishes, their envies, their desire to compete with each other: men deceive themselves, prevaricate, like to feel their fine feelings. 'All women are like me in this respect, and all men more or less like you.' Masculine complacency, even considerateness, is a form of patronage. 'You are considerate of me, because you know that I know that you are so. There's the rub, you see: I know that you know that I know it!' They have been playing a game with each other, but, as the girl tells him at the end, she is 'incapable of more than one deception' ... 'Didn't you see it? didn't you know it? see that I saw it? know that I knew it?' But Locksley has singularly failed to understand. Not only the cunning of his own vanity but his essential innocence, his romanticism, his artist's vision itself, have prevented him from doing so.

As the reader apprehends, Miss Quarterman's comedy persona and speeches, both in the middle of the story and at its end, are more or less water under the bridge. The young James knew enough about comedy conventions and smart endings to execute that side of the business. Much more significant is the way he understands and sympathizes with the heroine, indeed identifies with her. His feminine sensibility, at one with hers, pervades the tale, lending it – and to other early stories as well – a complete understanding of the female situation, and a remarkably unsentimental delicacy about it. More than that: he was highly responsive at this stage of his artistic life, and in a way that he was not to be later on, to the physical presence and charm of women; and it is this which he so powerfully conveys in 'A Landscape-Painter'. His hero is as responsive as he, but James has a far greater understanding of Miss Quarterman than Locksley does. An important side-effect of the story is the contrast between diarist and author, in their relation to the heroine, which the reader apprehends in the same way that he feels, as a part of the story's perspective, the difference between the 'real' Miss Quarterman and the girl seen and fallen in love with by the landscape-painter in the New England coast setting about which he is so lyrical.

The riddle or mystery which James has managed to get into his story is associated with this double vision. 'I hardly think I shall ever write any more' is the formula by which a short story expends itself, in becoming its own self of which no repetition is possible. But the significance of the story being thus so definitively over is that it reveals another unwritten story behind it, whose outlines we glimpse in the fact given by the narrator 'I' at the beginning. This story cannot be written because the diarist who might have done so is silent, and will shortly be dead. And the narrator who gives us these posthumous facts about him clearly has no interest in writing a story at all.

What then is the significance, the unknown quantity, which lurks outside the diary, and is suggested only in the facts related of the diarist's life, and in his final entry? 'He died seven years ago, at the age of thirty-five. For five years, accordingly, he managed to shield his life from the eyes of men.' His private diary 'extends from his twenty-fifth to his thirtieth year, at which period it breaks off suddenly.' The last five years of the diarist's life, the years of his marriage, were silent. And since the diarist was also a painter we infer that no pictures were painted during that time, either. The strong assumption is that there is something silent, sad, and, final, that surrounds the idyll in the New England fishing village, and puts a necessary end to it, also putting an end to the artist's vision that made it possible. That something is of course death, but death may also be the arbitrary cipher for something else, for an aspect of life to which the vision of art has no admission.

The art of 'A Landscape-Painter' gives rise to such speculation, and indeed seems intended to persuade the reader to speculate in some such way. It supplies a great deal of invisible commentary which in no way disturbs the authentic simplicity of its art. Each enhances the other as in the best short stories, without giving rise to the *relativity* which is specified by the novel's form, and which is a feature of a *nouvelle* like *Lord Jim*. Although there is a kind of mystery or query in the background of 'A Landscape-Painter' it is there not only to be examined but to supply answers to such an examination, answers which are a part of the general atmosphere of thought and meditation surrounding the tale.

In relation to James's art of the story this is important, because several of his critics have emphasized that their specification depends upon a riddle which is itself the object and point of the story. To put it in terms of the opening of our first chapter, art solves the problem of the mystery outside itself – the 'something far more deeply interfused' – by making that something the condition of art. As Todorov, the clearest and most forceful of the French structuralist critics, puts it: 'The Jamesian narrative is always based on *the quest for an absolute and absent cause*' (his italics). The appearance of a revelation keeps the narrative going, and revelation is itself automatically effected by cessation of the narrative. Thus, for instance, in 'The Turn of the Screw', which in spite of its length has all the characteristics and purposes of a short story, the quest is ended by the death of the boy, Miles. Once 'his little heart has stopped' there is nothing left but 'the quiet day', in which the reader, like the governess, is 'alone'. All query about what has actually happened – for example, whether the governess has herself supplied the hallucinations, as Edmund Wilson believed, or whether the children were themselves consciously haunted – is not just irrelevant, but actually incompatible with the tale's specification.

If my analysis of the technical frame of the story is plausible – the engine of the narrative being the continued beating of the boy's heart, and its stopping the logical end to it – then we may feel that the story has cheated us in some way, and no really good story can afford to do that. Todorov's incisive formula has a brilliant French logic about it, but it ignores the actual untidiness, the effect of sheer accumulation, which even the most calculated verbal art cannot but produce in the course of the way it works on us. The mysteries and queries of art are in their nature no different from those we encounter in living with and experiencing other persons. The governess of 'The Turn of the Screw', for instance, if we met with her in life, would probably present to our imagination some of the same data for reflection and enquiry with which we consider her in terms of her own story. Of course, in the background of Todorov's formulation about James's narrative technique in his stories is the more general structuralist premise that, as Todorov puts it, 'words imply the absence of things', and that in all narrative art 'the presence of the truth' is 'incompatible with the narrative'. Again, there is more of logic in this than there is of human experience. The desire to reduce literature to its own laws is a natural one, and makes everything tidy, but it runs counter to the appetite and experience of any but the most preconditioned and brainwashed reader. Todorov's observations, like those of any good critic, increase our interest in James's, or any other, narrative, in so far as they widen the field of speculation and response, but no one would wish to read James's, or any other stories, if each were intended to put a full stop to curiosity in the manner that Todorov describes.

As his art became more set in its ways, and he himself more observant of these, James himself might be said to have become to some extent his own critic *à la* Todorov, and to encourage in his readers a sense of process rather than of possibilities and effects. His story, 'The Figure in the Carpet', is a kind of parody of his own processes, playing with the reader, or the critic, in the rather elephantine manner which the play of art had come to assume for James in late middle age. Todorov is no doubt right in asserting that the figure in James's narrative carpet is indeed 'the quest for an absolute and absent cause', and that 'the cause is what, by its absence, brings the text into being'. James would himself have had the fondest of reactions to a formulation of his process as intrinsically elegant as 'the essential is absent, the absent is essential'. James might well have recognized *that* to be the figure in the carpet, what the author Hugh Vereker calls in the story 'this little trick of mine'. The strength of art, its alcoholic strength as it were, is increased by the factor of uncertainty. The point is made openly – too openly – in the late story 'In the Cage', in which the mechanism of the plot is left in a state of deliberate obscurity, so that the most ingenious reader could not deduce anything positive from it. 'If nothing was more impossible than the fact, nothing, on the other hand, was more intense than the vision', as the story blandly informs us. Maybe so, for the artist himself, and perhaps for his heroine, the telegraph girl 'in the cage' who becomes absorbed in a vision of the love-life of a society couple whose telegrams go through her office. But for the reader the story is apt to be a disappointment, if only because the author and heroine are so much more fascinated by its possibilities than he can be. The story has the odd air – in this very much the opposite of 'A Landscape-Painter' – of being completely unconcerned with its reader, who tries in vain to make out what the excitement is all about.

As we shall see, 'In the Cage' has a significant point of resemblance to 'A Landscape-Painter', and so has 'The Turn of the Screw', but it is more important that the two later stories have an air of total structuring, as stories, which deprives both of them of the special features of interest which protrude, as it were, from the achievement of the early one. Such a protrusion is, I believe, an essential part of the really good short story, because such a story contrives to be both complete in itself, as art, and also significantly incomplete. Todorov, like most structuralists, is keen on the story form as an exemplar, because in length and technique they offer good illustrations of the theory that words in literature obey their own logic and are incompatible with things. As Todorov rather engagingly puts it, the public in general prefer novels to stories, 'long books to short texts, not because length is taken as a criterion of value, but because there is no time, in reading a short work, to forget it is only "literature" and not "life".' Looked at from another point of view, it may be that the best accomplishment of a story is to give us the feeling that it is life and not literature, despite the fact that it has not much space in which to deploy this illusion.

Where 'The Turn of the Screw' is concerned, the illusion is present only in a rather unexpected form. James himself considered the tale as a mere pot-boiler, and expressed surprise at its comparative popularity. In crafting the story and introducing it, he went to some lengths to emphasize the nature of its artificiality, its status as a tale told – or rather read aloud – at a country house party, and the ingenious idea that animated it. What, in the artificial world of ghostly horror, gives more of a *frisson* than the haunting of a child? Why of course, the haunting of *two* children! Thus launched, the tale bids fair to be an ingenious specimen of its highly formalized genre, and it superbly succeeds in its aim. But if we read it more than once we may find our attention being distracted more and more away from the haunting, and its handling, to a consideration of the children themselves, or rather to the phenomenon of childishness in relation to the adult world. Again and again in the course of the tale, and all the time-honoured elaboration of its stages (time-honoured because necessary to postpone the climax and increase the expectations of the audience) James draws attention to the impossibility of knowing what, if anything, is going on in children's minds. To adults their world is opaque, obscure without even being mysterious. The governess necessarily adopts the convention of all adults, at that time, that the children are not only little dears, but little dears whose thought processes and consciousness are particularly pure and transparent, touchingly accessible. While engaged on his business with the ghosts James continually, and with seeming inadvertence, contradicts this convention, while appearing, both for himself as author and on behalf of his heroine-narrator the governess, to endorse it. The innocent children have been corrupted by the unspeakable evil of the ghostly contact. But the real impression the story begins to leave is just that children are like that. Between them and their secret affairs, and the governess, there is a natural if unbridgeable gulf.

It is here that the story begins to resemble 'life' rather than 'literature', the more so as literature seems hardly to be aware how much and what kind of life it is letting in. In the context of the old house, Bly, and under the conditions of her employment, the governess might indeed find the natural secretiveness of children to constitute a questionable mystery, one for which she casts about for an explanation; and what explanation more disturbing than that her predecessors, a *pair* of them, *were* in the children's confidence, a part of their secret life. James's formal specification for the ghosts, as he himself observed, is almost demure. They are evil, 'bad', with an evilness never enlarged upon. To a friend who came up with the all too naive question of why he always managed to impute unnaturalness and perversion to such characters, James replied in his most feline way that the friend had been allowing himself to get ideas about the nature of evil, and 'I never do that'. In fact, and in terms of the 'life' that penetrates the elegant shell of the ghost story's conventions, the suggestion comes over that Peter Quint and Miss Jessel, the sinister ex-valet and ex-governess, were really *like children too*, a depraved pair, the dark twins, as it were, of the angelic pair which the governess finds little Miles and little Flora to be.

There is humour, as well as a disquieting situation from life, in the idea of the governess in confrontation with not two but four children, two present in the flesh and the other two present in them, lurking in the very secretiveness of their good manners. No wonder she is disturbed and jealous, although there is no need to claim, as Edmund Wilson did, that it is the governess's own neurosis and hysteria which brings on the delusions and the crisis, of which the children remain uncomprehending. It is not that there is a true explanation of the story lying behind the apparent one, as Wilson argued, but that the story is divided in two: being on the one hand a conventional if ingenious tale of haunting, and on the other a highly Jamesian probing into the subject, the *donnée*, of a governess taking over two children in rather unusual circumstances. The second could be the subject of a nouvelle. In fact such a *donnée* would have been too slight and too homely to have responded to James's narrative elaboration as a tale in itself. He could only have made such a theme wholly artificial, as he did in 'What Maisie Knew', or make it, as 'The Turn of the Screw', follow the time-honoured conventions of the ghost story.

None the less, James's sense of children, of what it means to be a child, comes over more vividly in 'The Turn of the Screw' than anywhere else in his work. It is clear that he regarded them with a kind of knowing suspicion, and also with that species of enquiry he brought to all aspects of life which constituted a mystery; something superior in its exclusiveness, withdrawn, withheld; the thing that started off his literary process and eventually became its technique and justification. But though a very good story can have, as I put it, protrusions or extrusions from it, a sense of the relative and incomplete, it cannot remain wholly alive if it is divided in two in such a way that the literary convention side of it keeps the 'life' side of it so firmly under control. 'The Turn of the Screw' remains a *tour de force*, but one that is cold, calculated, literary, and seems more so with each re-reading; whereas 'A Landscape-Painter' moves in the opposite direction, revealing more interest and more of the pathos and feeling of life the more we go into it.

The death of little Miles is the climax of 'The Turn of the Screw', whereas the death of the landscape-painter, noted only in the worldly social tones of the voice that introduces the tale, might seem outside and barely connected with it. But who cares about the death of little Miles? The stopping of his heart is so obviously a piece of plot mechanism, designed to bring the story to a correct and logical finish. Even the fact that he has been 'dispossessed', driven by the governess's remorselessly well-meaning inquisition out of whatever shared and childish world of secrecy he had lived in, does not touch the reader or truly interest him. It is quite clear that James himself is not deeply involved. But his involvement in 'A Landscape-Painter' is very deep indeed, and the manner in which he has managed to write and present that story puts it in a living and harmonious relation with something genuinely mysterious. Very moving too. It is a simple trick, but the reader is aware all the time he is reading that the diarist is dead, the idyll over, and also the marriage to which it was a prelude. We are in touch with a man, now dead, whose vision of art, of happiness, of a possible life, is remarkably real to us. What happened to them? That is the hidden theme of the story, and our growing realization of it makes the diarist's life and death seem a real thing, and not like the contrivance of a story at all. *Pace* Todorov the diarist's death seems indeed a thing, a true sad fact, whereas that of little Miles is a piece of literary ritual.

Art, happiness, a possible life? The answer seems to be that in 'A Landscape-Painter' James was exploring, perhaps unconsciously, the way in which his own life was shaping, or might shape. His early story is a masterpiece of the same kind as 'The Secret Sharer', or Joyce's 'The Dead', or Chekhov's 'The Lady with the Little Dog': with the difference that whereas all these have the quality of retrospection, 'A Landscape-Painter' is a prospective picture where its author is concerned, the more so because the painter himself is framed at the outset, as in a picture, by the news of his death. The art of the story arranges this, as if emphasizing by means of it the story's hermetic completeness, and thus paradoxically releasing the elements of query and possibility in it. At the end the situation, for James and for the reader, is still very much alive, whereas the end of 'The Turn of the Screw' is definitively the end both of the story and of its meaning.

The literary style of the painter-diarist, mildly and pleasurably parodying that of James himself (as Gabriel Conroy's reflections parody those of Joyce in 'The Dead') tells us what he is like and makes us at home with him. His impressions at Chowderville are recorded with an exact vividness, but soberly, as talented painters have sometimes done in prose; and his early adventures there have a deliberately mythic quality. Hiring a small boat, he manages to get himself across to an island that lies opposite the little town. 'I sailed for half an hour directly before the wind, and at last found myself aground on the shelving beach of a quiet little cove.' In this uninhabited place he can scramble about and feast his eyes. 'The only particular sensation I remember was that of being ten years old again, together with a general impression of Saturday afternoon ...' But his boat has been left high and dry by the tide, and he is 'rescued' by the old sea-captain, who offers his accommodation with himself and his daughter. The childhood paradise of the island is now happily joined to a perfect mother–father situation, in which the mother, moreover, is available to be fallen in love with.

If this is a dream of James it is a singularly compelling one. Miriam, the captain's daughter, is more vividly and agreeably present to the reader than any other of James's heroines, early or late, and is very possibly modelled on one of his young acquaintances at Newport or elsewhere. But the progress of the myth is inexorable. Two days after his marriage the diarist records his arrival at the honeymoon hotel.

> It was a raw, black day. We have a couple of good rooms, close to the savage sea. I am nevertheless afraid I have made a mistake. It would perhaps have been wiser to go to New York. These things are not immaterial; we make our own heaven, but we scarcely make our own earth. I am writing at a little table by the window, looking out on the rocks, the gathering dusk, the rising fog. My wife has wandered down to the rocky platform in front of the house. I can see her from here, bareheaded, in that old crimson shawl, talking to one of the landlord's little boys. She has just given the infant a kiss, bless her tender heart!

The passage is shot through with signs and equivocations. Although the diarist is still looking forward to the revelation to his wife of his riches, he is already feeling he has made a mistake, although a mistake only in not going to New York. Climatically the idyll is over. His wife has wandered off and is talking tenderly to little boys. The diarist is no longer the ten year old of the island. Miss Quarterman had proposed a picnic there, gauging her moment exactly, and the day the three of them had spent in the sun on the island gave the diarist painter one of his most lyrically beautiful and humorous entries. Shortly after it he had himself proposed, and been accepted.

The myth, almost invisible in the texture of the table, is inexorable, like life itself. Miriam has not deceived the painter; she has acted intelligently and with the best intentions, both for himself and for her. But already Locksley perceives with growing horror that they are diverging – she into marriage, the absorptions of home and children: he into the superfluous role of money-provider, cut off from his art and from what fed it, the youthful life of the island, and of love with the not so young Nausicaa – he quickly found she was twenty-seven and it worried him not at all – whom he had found beside the sea. The humour of the situation is deep, and remarkably understanding in so young an author. Locksley's wife has a tender heart, as he rather desperately exclaims, but it was not and will not be tender exclusively to him. The deception, neatly echoing that of Miss Leary, is part of the purely 'literary' aspect of the tale, its conventional structure: the true deception is that practised by life itself, for reasons which are at once the best and the worst.

Which are they for James? That is possibly the most absorbing, as it is the most imponderable, achievement of the story, the something deeply interfused in it. That he is, so to speak, deeply attracted to Miss Quarterman, now Mrs Locksley, there is no doubt whatever. To that extent the story, to use the terms dismissively employed to Todorov, is as much concerned with 'life' as with 'literature'. James is at once fascinated by Miss Quarterman and deeply apprehensive of her. The story is an exorcism, but it is also a tribute, even a declaration. In these ways it is certainly unique among James's tales. But James is also in the odd situation of identifying with Miss Quarterman. He understands her intuitively; he is in a sense on her side, as he is on the side of the young heroine of another very early story, 'The Story of a Year', which comes second in the first volume of James's collected tales, as 'A Landscape-Painter' comes third. The story concerns a year in the civil war, not long over. A young man off to the war becomes engaged to a young woman. They write each other love-letters, and James is sympathetically aware of the difficulty, for the girl, of keeping up the *idea* of their love. Furtively encouraged by her fiancé's mother, who is possessive for her son, the girl goes into society and meets a rich man, who falls for her. Her fiancé is severely wounded and brought home. She is terribly moved by the sight of his white wan form, and the way in which his eyes 'wandered over her with a kind of peaceful glee'. She vows 'to love you and nurse you forever'.

But the fiancé is aware of the situation, and also knows he is going to die. He tells her to accept the man who wants to marry her, because 'Life *is* as good as death'. 'My great pain is in leaving you. But you, too, will die one of these days;

remember that. In all pain and sorrow, remember that.' He asks her to be kind to his mother – 'She will have great grief but she will not die of it. She'll live to great age' – and they hold hands till he dies. Such scenes were very common indeed in the fiction of the time, and although James uses its rhetoric with a good deal of devotion ('O imposing spectacle of death! O blessed soul, marked for promotion! What earthly favor is like thine?') the story is remarkable for its honesty and its penetrating understanding of what is really going on in the young woman's mind. She resents extremely her fiancé's mother ('Before the scorn of her own conscience (which never came) ... she was ready to bow down – but not before that long-faced Nemesis in black silk') and she feels an hysterical desire to do 'justice' to her 'old love' and renounce her own suitor. But the story, and its author, knows she will not, just as it picks its way with the most tacit nicety between true emotions – like Lizzie's grief for her fiancé – which none the less require her to 'act the part', and the unemotional necessities – marriage, a home – which inevitably urge her on to fill a part in life.

The young James understands all these matters and in a manner that suggests very forcibly, where some of the early stories are concerned, that he and his future are deeply involved in them. The ideal short story, in addition to all its other apparently incompatible tasks, should be an exploratory form. Chekhov's 'The Steppe' is such a story, one of the finest of all, and it ends with the young hero Yegor's arrival – after his adventures on the steppe – at the place where his new life is going to begin. Chekhov toyed with the idea of continuing Yegor's further adventures in another story about him, but he wisely concluded that such a continuation would spoil the effect of the original story, which the critics had hailed as a masterpiece when it appeared in the *Northern Herald*, comparing the writer to Gogol and to Tolstoy. 'Threshold' stories, as one might call them, require to have a particular finality, which is paradoxically immanent in their form. 'A Landscape-Painter' gives a special twist to the genre by making the beginning in life a false one, a debut of whose ritual ending after five years we have already been informed.

Those five years are enigmatic. What took place in them? They are of the story and yet not in it. Locksley, and his bride, exist only in his diary – in art, that is – and the frankness with which the story admits this makes it peculiarly effective. Those five years after marriage cannot come into the story because James has no idea what they were like, or would be like, either for Locksley or for himself. On the face of it, this might seem a perfect example of Todorov's thesis that the Jamesian story is always based on the quest for 'an absolute and absent cause', and that in a story 'words imply the absence of things'. But in fact, exactly the opposite is true. Words here imply the *presence* of things, and imply them with a forcefulness which makes the story what it is. Over the diary, and the whole idyll it describes, broods the knowledge for the reader that the diarist has taken, in some sense, a fatally wrong turning in the course of his progress through life. If dying young can be said to be taking a wrong turn this adds to the invisible irony, for both in marrying and in dying Locksley could be said to have behaved involuntarily: he had no choice in the matter. The story implies things – that is, achieves its reality – all the more successfully because the reader grasps on the very first page, when the chronology is carefully revealed to him, that this has all the arbitrariness of art, words, inventions ... Locksley is going to be killed off, and yet the story triumphantly persuades us that he lives and breathes in it, that he is a true pilgrim through life, like the author himself: that both are setting out on it, and the story itself is a vehicle for them to do so.

If Locksley's highly fictional 'death' is a factor that makes him and his diary so particularly alive in the story, this may be partly because the story itself ends so simply and so abruptly, with the last recorded words of the two days-married Mrs Locksley, telling him that he may abuse her in his diary if he likes, as she will never peep into it again. We believe her. Everything the diary contains and represents is over, and a new life has begun, a new life about which the diarist has already made the oblique comment: 'I hardly think I shall ever write any more.' The words are both moving and ominous. The reader hears them with a surprising kind of dread, because they signal the end of his intercourse with the young man whose company has grown so familiar; and the reader (like a real friend) is selfish enough to feel that Locksley could not be happy and successful in any kind of life from which that company is excluded. The emphasis of the thing is born by the reader's sense of James himself, and James's own feelings about young men who get married – himself too, perhaps. Whatever else may happen to them they can no longer be articulate, no longer be 'friends'. From one point of view Locksley's demise is immaterial to the story: he might still be living his new unknown life to which James and his reader have no access. Many threshold stories end in this way, but its own sort of finality is important to 'A Landscape-Painter'. Its almost supererogatory clean sweep (Locksley's wife is dead too – did they have any children?) makes it unnervingly full of queries.

And these are, so to speak, real queries; not the theoretical sort which can be formulated *ex post facto* after little Miles's heart has stopped at the end of 'The Turn of the Screw'. 'In the Cage' has an ending which is formally definitive in the same way: it ends with the heroine getting married, to her worthy shopkeeper suitor, and putting aside the romantic, upper-class puzzle which she, and the reader, have been poring over. The ironies of this story are both heavy and flat. The girl in the telegraphist's cage has engaged, like an artist, in free speculation, and in the challenge of style and mystery. Though confined in the flesh she was free in the spirit. All this will disappear into silence and vacancy when she gets married, and the story of her experiences comes to an end.

The ending is very similar to that of 'A Landscape-Painter', yet it could not be more different. Formula has displaced the odd kind of luck which makes the early story so alive and so moving, as well as complex. That it was luck is shown by the inferiority of the other early stories, in the same volume, which have a rather similar theme. 'My Friend Bingham' is most engagingly bad, though it has interesting points of similarity to 'A Landscape-Painter'. Bingham's friend, the 'I' of the story, acts as a benevolent intermediary for his shy friend with an impoverished widow, whose child Bingham had the misfortune to cause the death of in a shooting accident. (This odd episode is related with

wonderful ineptitude.) Once again, James's sympathy with
the interesting widow amounts almost to an identification,
and yet she remains for him a mysterious figure, with
unknown powers and motives. James fails to convey the
innerness of what remains only an interesting *donnée*: that the
accident which killed Mrs Hicks's little boy has given her a
special relation to the man who was its inadvertent cause, as if
he could be a substitute for the lost child. In striving to
imitate the manner of a young man who would be a bosom
friend of the worthy Bingham, James becomes both laborious
and arch, particularly in the emphasis he lays on an odd
feature of his friend's happy marriage.

> She has made a devoted wife; but – and in occasional moments of
> insight it has seemed to me that this portion of her fate is a
> delicate tribute to a fantastic principle of equity – she has never
> again become a mother.

In his conclusion James underlines heavily the kind of points
implicit in the delicate atmosphere of 'A Landscape-Painter'.

> In saying that she has made a devoted wife, it may seem that I
> have written Bingham's own later history. Yet as the friend of his
> younger days, the comrade of his belle jeunesse, the partaker of
> his dreams, I would fain give him a sentence apart. What shall it
> be? He is a truly incorruptible soul; he is a confirmed
> philosopher; he has grown quite stout.

This, one feels, will never do. And yet there is both a charm
about it and a significance of meaning hovering in James's
way, the kind of significance which will later on become more
stylized and polished. He is experimenting with varieties of
tone and ending, and the dismissal of Bingham in the
concluding sentence of the story, as having 'grown quite
stout', shows just how James has deliberately taken his
character into the hand of total, if invisible, patronage. The
same patronage extends, on different scales and in a variety of
different ways, to Miles and his governess in 'The Turn of the
Screw', to the heroine of 'In the Cage'. The true story
contrives to let the author remain puzzled by what he has
created, fascinated by it, not altogether sure of it; while at the

same time the art of the author has fully completed the story's circle.

His characters were no longer a puzzle to the mature James; and he was no longer feeling his way into life by exploring his impressions of them in a tale. Of course, even in his late maturity, James could be shaken internally by strong emotions and sorrows, and the realizations these brought with them; and such realizations find their way into stories like 'The Bench of Desolation', and his last New York stories; but the habit of manipulation and of 'process' means that the persons in his tales no longer have the freshness that comes from being seen rather than used. The early ones tell us a great deal more about the way really good stories are written, and there is something endearing about the way James shows his hand. 'The Story of a Masterpiece' is an early instance of a theme which James was to embroider on all his working life. A rich widower falls in love with a charming young woman, and feels the same anxieties that so many of James's men entertain in these tales. Is he loved for himself, or does the needy Miss Everett merely view him as a catch? Again, the point of the story is that the author is well aware of the many modes of feeling and behaving that lie between these two extremes – much more aware, of course, than his hero is. Author, and reader, are more into the situation than hero, but this does not mean that they feel the kind of superiority often proffered by a narrative of this kind. James, at this period, had a curious, almost boyish, knack of arranging the participation of all three parties together, through the medium of what his friend William Dean Howells called our 'perpetual delight in his way of saying things'. An early tale of his is often 'like a nice informal little social gathering' in which the persons of the narrative are partaking along with himself and his reader.

Lennox, the would-be husband in 'The Story of A Masterpiece', engages for his fiancée's portrait a young painter who was formerly in love with her, but who became disenchanted with what he came to consider her flirtatiousness and cold heart. When he paints the portrait, which is considered a masterly work, he represents these qualities in the sitter, in such a way that they can only impress themselves on someone intimately involved with her. Lennox is so disturbed by the way the portrait seems to look at him that he destroys it, as if by doing so he could exorcise those traits of which it seems to accuse its original. Lennox behaves as if art were so much outside life that the removal of what was uncomfortable in it could make life comfortable again; but it is more significant that, like the Landscape-Painter, he comes to disbelieve in his own love for the girl when he begins to think of her as incapable of love for him. Being a man of honour he decides to go through with the marriage, because 'if he had mistaken and overrated her, the fault was his own, and it was a hard thing that she should pay the penalty. Whatever were her failings, they were profoundly involuntary, and it was plain that with regard to himself her intentions were good.'

In the unfathomable world of emotion which these stories explore, and which in one case succeed in making into an admirable world of art, the feminine emotions are felt to be 'profoundly involuntary' on the one hand, and to have on the other the 'sweet infallibility' which Bingham's friend the narrator finds in Mrs Hicks. There is no overt irony at all in this combination. Irony only appears in James's too explicit dismissive tricks, such as the endings of 'My Friend Bingham', and the even more visible flourish with which he concludes 'The Story of A Masterpiece', dismissing in the same sentence our interest in Lennox. 'How he has fared – how he is destined to fare – in matrimony, it is rather too early to determine. He has been married scarcely three months.' It is the same ending with which he will dismiss Verena Terrant of *The Bostonians*, when she finally allows herself to be carried off in marriage by Basil Ransom, and is discovered to be in tears, which would seem, in the far from brilliant union she has entered into – 'not the last she was destined to shed'. Such conclusions emphasize by contrast the very different relation which the young James appears to have with the personnel of his best stories, with whom he communes as with his own wonderings and reflections. This is the reverse of knowing, or of any need to let the reader know how knowing it is. All the more surprising because the thematic material *is* there – the use of puzzles and the threshold of abstentions – underlying the life in the stories but never channeling it into a formula or authorial world. What is there can surface later on as a conscious influence, and a vulgarizing one, expressed for instance in the jingle that 'a good man married is a good man marred'. And those are his own words for a theme picked up and exploited by the young Kipling.

CHAPTER THREE

With Kipling the short story could be said to enter a new phase. On the one hand it becomes all art: on the other, all exhortation. These two have mingled in the form before, as they have in other kinds of literature, but the short story gives them a special kind of concentration, suited to its nature, so that both appear in strong relief. Their relationship can be very moving, or it can be bizarre, but in Kipling's work it is almost always compulsive. Compulsive, that is, in the sense that we cannot stop reading, and that when we have finished a very strong impression remains, so strong as to put aside for the moment any question about how it was done, or even what it is supposed to be telling us.

The showman in Kipling is also what he called his daemon; the subterranean power, that is, which dictated what he wrote, and on account of which he refused to accept ranks or honours which he felt were not due to him personally. Obviously, there is something defensive about this attitude, and it is paradoxical as well, for the writer might seem to be refusing responsibility for the nature of the power that worked through him. In a famous phrase, which he gave to his cousin Stanley Baldwin to use in a speech, he referred to certain public figures and bodies, such as the press, as exercising 'power without responsibility – the perquisite of the harlot throughout the ages'. Where his conception of his own art is concerned the charge might rebound upon himself. In fact in his public pronouncements and views, as well as in the open or disguised messages in his work, Kipling was highly responsible – no writer more so. Whether we agree with him or not is another matter. But Kipling seems to have seen his daemon as responsible for his art, and his own view of life as something quite different; and in practice, as usually happens, he saw no special problem in reconciling the mystery with the message.

All this goes to make an altogether unusual impression of Kipling in his stories as writer and man. Nothing could be less like the continuum of James's ruminative apprehension of things, as revealed in his earlier stories. In some of Kipling's we have the impression of a deep and humane intelligence functioning purposefully and unflamboyantly beneath all the hypnotic brilliance and the cocky assertiveness: other stories seem to indicate a man helpless in the grip of violent emotions and prejudices. Giving vent to these in all the freedom and virtuosity of his art seems to afford him a necessary but almost repulsive satisfaction. It may be that both these impressions of Kipling in his stories are true and correct ones, and that only in his art – the art of the 'daemon', if we choose to accept Kipling's view of it – can they be reconciled.

Such a reconciliation, if it exists, takes place out of sight, in the reader's unconscious as much as in Kipling's. His own observations about art, and in particular his own art, are few but far from reassuring; as if anything in that mysterious area which is consciously examined is bound to sound not quite real. All his stories have the intention of instructing us, even lecturing us, but the early ones do this with such bravura and immediacy that the intention disappears. The young Kipling, like the young James, seems more to want to share his traffics and discoveries with us, however insistently he points out what is to be learnt from them; for instance from the tales about India and east of Suez, where deeds and responsibilities are rather different from what they are at home. A feature of many of the best of these tales is the way in which 'truth' and 'literature' are virtually separated in them, although in a manner so subtle and so natural that the reader hardly notices

what is happening. The cruder example would be the story I
mentioned earlier, 'The End of the Passage', in which a
horror device from Poe is used to give punch and climax to a
grim little tale of insomnia, exhaustion and overwork on an
outstation in India during the hot season. The reality of the
story, and the meaning it points at us, is that this is what the
servants of the Raj have to put up with in doing their duty,
duty which not infrequently leads to breakdown and death.

But the reality in the story, created with all Kipling's
hypnotic sense of detail and atmosphere, is exaggerated by
the unknown terror which is added on, and so placed in the
comfortable department of the macabre. In apparently
turning the screw, and heightening the horror, the story in
fact softens and relaxes it. It is as if the young Kipling had
enough instinctive wisdom to let his reader off the hook.
Having shown him what things can really be like on an Indian
outstation he soothes him with a tall tale, full of virtuoso
literariness. The district doctor who views the body of his
civil service colleague, dead through unknown causes, is
haunted by the dead man's story of seeing terrible things in
dreams, and so photographs his eyes which are open and
staring wide. Having developed the pictures in a dark room
he comes out white and trembling, and tells the other
colleagues who have gathered that he has destroyed the
negatives and that nothing came out on them. The dead man's
bearer, suddenly become wise and inscrutable in the literary
style suited to the situation, opines that his master had gone
very far away in his dreams, and had not been able to get back.
The dead man had dreaded sleep and striven to stay awake,
because of a recurrent dream – 'a blind face that cries and
can't wipe its eyes'. He knows that if it catches up with him he
will die.

The true horror of the story – a man on the verge of
madness from heat, insomnia and loneliness, and the
responsibilities of his job – is overlaid by the false nightmare
of the dead man's eyes, and the quasi-scientific verification of
its mystery. Delusions, as Kipling himself knew well, have
their own kind of reality, but his art has a tendency to go in for
overkill at this stage, and to call in literature to complete its
truest effects. 'The Strange Ride of Morrowbie Jukes' is a

more remarkable and more interesting example of the same tendency. It is indeed one of Kipling's best stories. Its generic structure of falsity is so graphically convincing that the reader only begins to query it when he has developed a theoretical interest in the way Kipling's narratives work. Then he can detect what the limits of 'truth' in this one are, and how some scrap of anecdote concerning a 'village of the dead' has been turned by the writer into a powerful and accomplished tale of adventure, in the tradition which Stevenson and Ambrose Bierce had also excelled. Out of this very accomplishment, however, emerges the outline of the real story, which is Kipling's sufficiently nightmare sense of the utter strangeness and foreignness of India, things in it which makes sense to its inhabitants, but which to the outsider are enclaves of desolation and meaninglessness. There is fascination for him, though, in the very thought of such things, and their seduction could cause him to fall into chaos as Morrowbie Jukes fell into the village of the dead. E. M. Forster undoubtedly borrowed the outlines of this real story for his account in *A Passage to India* of the Marabar caves and the effect they have on certain westerners.

'The Strange Ride of Morrowbie Jukes' is a title which seems to try to emphasize, in a jaunty manner, how much of a 'story' it is. This in itself gives a clue to the tale's effectiveness, for it is as if the author were trying to exorcise the true significance of his own story by taking it more lightly, and in more literary fashion, than is proper to its perturbing nature. Whereas 'At the End of the Passage' superimposes a mechanism out of Poe on to a story situation which might have been handled by Chekhov, the two narrative modes in 'The Strange Ride' need one another and act powerfully in combination. As so often with good short stories an invisible synergism is taking place below the surface, the traditional art of the form compounding in this case with a meaning the author seems reluctant to give, because it hardly coincides with his ideas about the duties and obligations of empire.

'The Strange Ride', and 'The Man Who would be King', in which two adventurers attempt to found an empire of their own in a remote corner of Afghanistan, are two of Kipling's best; and the reason is certainly the harmonious though secret combination in them of adventure story with something very like a search for a secret cause, a deep and disconcerting mystery. It is in these stories, as with the best of the 'Soldiers Three' ones, that we have the clearest sense of intercourse with what I called 'deep and humane intelligence'. But the impression does not last. His stories about the Boer War show us the other Kipling, in the grip of strong emotions, determined to proselytize the reader and inculcate in him his own strongly-held beliefs. These stories are extremely vivid and memorable, with a vividness which is beginning to have a sort of Madame Tussaud effect, with every moustache hair meticulously in place. 'The Comprehension of Private Copper' and 'A Sahib's War' give us a good deal of insight into feelings and events of their time and place: they also show the way in which the intensification of 'art' in a Kipling story means a corresponding increase in the mechanism of persuasion and exhortation. Kipling's art grows artier as his view of history and Empire and England becomes more possessive, more insistent, more pretentious. *Puck of Pook's Hill* (1906) and *Rewards and Fairies* (1910) claim a great deal of authority, the more so since Kipling adopts the convention that they are addressed to young people. As with all really good stories of this type they can and do appeal to all ages; and in *Something of Myself*, his single autobiographical study, posthumously published, Kipling refers specifically to the care he had taken with the 'overlaid tints and textures' which would make their separate appeals to readers of different ages, and impart their separate salutary truths.

This is not reassuring. What reader wants to feel, like a diner in a restaurant where kiddies are catered for, that a special literary meal has been laid on, and accommodated to his powers of perception and mental digestion? But in practice the concoction works brilliantly. It also discloses a great deal about Kipling's techniques, so much so indeed that it is hard for the experienced and mature reader not to feel at times that he has been invited to participate in a kind of elaborate joke; that the storywriter, poker-faced, is shutting one eye at him above the heads of a spellbound youthful audience. This impression must be false, but it is no more false than many of Kipling's own brilliant structures and compulsively gripping moments of detail. Does he actually rejoice in their implausibility, or is their implausibility itself one of the glories of his art, a sign of how wholly manufactured it is, according to its own original specification?

The Kipling daemon designs no answer to this, and Kipling certainly would not reply on his familiar's behalf. Yet it is perhaps true that as his stories become more and more dazzlingly artificial, so they also become more memorable, more moving even. It may be no coincidence that the Roman soldier sequences in *Puck of Pook's Hill* are by common consent the ones that readers are most struck by and most vividly remember, and yet it is these stories which contain both the most bogus magic and the most insistent exhortation. Kipling strains so far the parallel between the Roman and the British Empires, Hadrian's Wall and the Indian north-west frontier, that even the most bemused and unsuspecting reader may find some of the things Parnesius tells him decidedly odd. What is he to make, for instance, of the centurion's astonishing observation that Scotland is bitter cold in winter but burning hot in the summer, a fact that is no doubt true of the Khyber pass? Or that Parnesius's men of the detachment he took to the wall were 'Roman-born Romans', as if to be born in Britain was the only alternative, in the Roman army, to being born in Rome? Once again the fact suits the difference in Kipling's time between being British-born and raised in the colonies, but it makes no sense in terms of the Roman empire and army. Odder things still are negligently conveyed through the expertise of the young/old soldier, as that the best way of catapulting enemy ships is to heave bags of stone at them which lodge in their sails ('Bolts only cut the cloth') and thus neatly capsize them. The reader might well rub his eyes but in fact he does not, though this is the side of Kipling which was to bombard his youthful son at the front in France with exhortations to stretch tennis-netting across his trench as an ingenious device to keep out hand-grenades.

No, Kipling gets away with it, at least in the stories – John Kipling had no time left to take the advice about tennis-netting. As a poem puts it: 'The cool and perspicuous eyes overbore unbelieving.' And to overbear unbelieving is the function of detail in Kipling's stories. In some of the least successful it takes the whole story over, but that certainly does not occur in the historical sketches of *Puck of Pook's Hill* and *Rewards and Fairies*, where the construction of history is effectively contrasted with moments of timeless truth, like the feeling of utter loneliness and desolation which overcomes the young officer when he reaches the wall and sees the word 'Finis' scratched on the bricked-up archway. That, we know, could happen anywhere, any time; and the young centurion has remained a potent symbol of military romance and duty, as we can see from Anthony Powell's curiously moving account, in *A Dance to the Music of Time*, of the rather pathetic officer who in 1941 tries to model his military attitudes on a hazy recollection of the Roman scenes in *Puck of Pook's Hill*. He was probably one of many, and his incompetence is an indication of the way in which the appeal of the Kipling ethos is to the weak rather than to the strong.

The fact is, however, that the art of Kipling's stories often seems to tremble on the verge of absurdity, and seems strangely divorced from their capacity to move us. A late and very notorious tale, 'Dayspring Mishandled', is from one point of view a parody of Kipling's love and attention to expert detail. Its hero is a Chaucer forger, who produces a fragment so convincing in terms of technical provenance that it fools all the scholars, particularly the one whose reputation the discovery of it makes, the one on whom the hero wishes to revenge himself. But although the details about the language and the manuscript are done with great gusto and flourish they would not deceive a comparatively casual reader, let alone a bench of experts. And this is in one sense the point of the joke. For the real 'mystery' of the story has nothing to do with revenge and the relish of experts, but is about the obscure and terrible sadness of lost opportunities, vanished chances of happiness, irreversible errors of feeling and judgement. All these are summed up in the inspired phrase which gives a title to the story, a phrase which has nothing to do with Chaucer or Chaucer's poetry, but everything to do with Kipling's own powers of suggesting loss, and emotional impoverishment and destruction, and suggesting them in an oblique but extremely moving way.

In the *Puck* series Kipling seems to take over history as an expert technician and forger could be said to take over an author's work, and he produces the same air of brilliant falsity or hypnotized reality. He does the same thing when imitating the speech and manners of a narrator, like Parnesius, or a subaltern just back from Burma, or one of the Soldiers Three. The deep-down truth in Kipling, or his power to move us as well as hypnotize us, seems to depend on a unique relation between itself and the expert falsity of his art. When we recover and say, 'I don't believe a word of this', there is something left none the less in which he makes us believe very deeply. The relation between the two is very odd, and can produce the feelings of embarrassment and exasperation which is the response of many readers – particularly intellectual ones – to Kipling's showmanship. Dickens is an obvious parallel, but Dickens gives no illustration of Kipling's narrative and short story flair, which uses the false mastery of art to bring out the discoveries made by something much more deep, because uncertain and vulnerable.

The combination can work in peculiar ways. In the last story of *Rewards and Fairies*, 'The Tree of Justice', the broken old beggar who turns out to be King Harold of England sits by the fire with elbows on knees and his face in both hands. Such a way of sitting, we are casually informed, is 'Saxon-fashion', for a Norman always sits with one hand on his chin. This is to create one's own truth as well as one's own history. It seems to work for the reason that art always works if it can create a completely confident or convincing surface or story pattern. Authenticity is in the look of the thing. Kipling's stories might seem to be good examples of Professor Gombrich's thesis, in *Art and Illusion*, that nothing on the surface of a painting is itself either true or false. If the thing comes off, if the paint creates a composition totally actual on its own terms, it is irrelevant to ask – as a critic is said to have once asked Delacroix – whether an object in one of his pictures was the back or the front of a man. 'Neither', replied Delacroix, 'it's painting.'

The analogy is tempting when it comes to describing how

Kipling works, but it won't quite do. For it is also very much a part of his effect that such things do *not* work, that they are too obvious to do so. Their falsity none the less puts us in a frame of mind for the truth, which has nothing to do with how Normans and Saxons sit round a fire. It is the vision of the old man himself, left out of history and behind it, that moves us; and this old man is necessarily left out of the expertise of the story too. He fits in neither to history nor to Kipling's insistent art, and that is why he is strange and memorable. Another way of putting it is that Kipling's 'world' requires the presence behind it of another world, which he does not seem so much in control of. The all too articulate and inventive expert seems to need the presence of a quiet man who thinks little of art, who has feelings about which he is silent, or which he cannot express.

It is this man, the deep and human Kipling, the lurking Kipling, who seems to have a considerable part in the earlier story in *Rewards and Fairies* about Bishop Wilfrid and the conversion of the South Saxons. The public Kipling disliked missionary activities, experience having shown him that communities were best off with their own traditions and beliefs. Meon, the heathen Saxon king, is a noble figure, and Eddi the missionary priest a slightly ridiculous one. As in 'The Knife and the Naked Chalk', in which a neolithic hero acquires the new technology of iron for his tribe, and pays the penalty of a personal alienation from them, an educational moral is equally pat in 'The Conversion of St Wilfrid' (a suitably ambiguous title, which gives the reader a knowing nudge). A more light-hearted tale than the neolithic one, it depends on the joke of a miracle. The two Christian priests go out fishing with Meon, and are wrecked on a small island where they are likely to starve. They are saved by Meon's tame seal who brings them fish, and whose appearance is hailed as a miracle by the priest Eddi. The miracle might in fact just as well be credited to the heathen's god Wotan, on whose help Meon had called, since he had refused to abandon the old gods in the last extremity. But when safe back in his hall Meon allows himself to be baptized, with all his people. The working out of things at different levels of understanding, the didactic message, is as tiresome as it is at any point in the two collections; and shows, incidentally, why Kipling was so much admired and imitated by the official writers of Soviet Russia. The historical dialectic works out its purposes, having things both ways: progress must come, though there is always a price to be paid for progress. The ideals of a heroic society were fine in themselves and suited to the men who practised them, but they must yield to the new belief, just as communities will lose their sense of purpose, and die, if they do not yield to new technologies.

All this is sufficiently discouraging, and as unreal in its way as the methods by which Kipling's art seeks to establish an absolute historical authenticity. Authentic art should produce authentic social diagnosis, but false authenticity works both ways, making Kipling's message as fundamentally unreal as his details. This indeed might seem the case, and yet it is not quite like that, and we can see why from the way Kipling's good stories work. The mystery behind them, the mystery of the man himself, saves the day. In spite of its pat moral and its all too obvious joke, 'The Conversion of St Wilfrid' can still bring tears unexpectedly to the eyes. Kipling himself seems genuinely moved by something in his story, which lies outside the lesson he is giving us with the aid of the Daemon Puck's offhand omniscience about how history happened.

Nearly dead from exposure on the island, Wilfrid wakes from a doze to hear Meon calling on the old gods 'in that high shaking heathen yell which I detest so'. He explains that he is giving Wotan his chance. And the miracle occurs. It is not the miracle that is moving but the courteous humour of Meon, trying out something in which he no longer believes, and in the primitive idiom which he knows to be repulsive to his new friend, on what seems the non-existent chance of saving them all. That is an aspect of faith or courage which has nothing to do with miracles. It goes with Wilfrid's knowledge of a Meon as a wonderful man who 'never looked back – never looked back' – praise which has the true ecclesiastic flavour. It is Wilfrid's words, combined with the sound of that 'Heathen yell', which give the episode such an extraordinary and involuntary pressure of reality, acting on the reader almost physically. Kipling is full of such moments, but they occur unexpectedly and without flourish or prelude. They are in fact the *opposite* of Kipling's parade of authenticity, and seem to suggest the man behind the artist; while at the same time it is the mesmeric falseness of the artist which gives them by contrast their own kind of simple truth.

Kipling's authenticity is always disingenuous, and the ally of the message he is getting across. It would be fair to say that his conception of the daemon is disingenuous too, since that entity is so evidently in league with Kipling's own views. It is difficult to say how far he had his tongue in his cheek when he wrote 'The Finest Story in the World', which, as the title suggests, affects to give the recipe for the best possible story. Did the still youthful Kipling, at the time he put together the collection *Many Inventions*, in which the story appeared, really think this? From the tone of the story the likeliest thing is that he was kidding, and yet kidding, as they say, on the level. The young man in the finest story is a genuine case of daemonic possession, for at moments, and unaware that he does so, he can recall episodes from past lives. He has been a Greek galley-slave and a Viking explorer. (It is a curious thing, as J. B. Priestley once dryly observed, that people who can recall their past incarnations always turn out to have been something suitably exotic, never some mindless member of the faceless masses.) Since he has actually seen things which no one else today can even imagine he has the total authority to write the finest story in the world. The joke is, of course, that in his normal self as a bank clerk with literary aspirations he can only produce derivative trash.

There seems no doubt that *Puck of Pook's Hill* and *Rewards and Fairies* are based on the same idea: that a person summoned up from the past is the perfect literary raconteur, because everything he says and does must be overwhelmingly authentic. The finest fiction is the most offhand truth. Parnesius the Roman centurion gives the children a demonstration of the Roman salute, 'which ends with a hollow clang of the shield coming into place between the shoulder-blades'. A detail one could remember forever, without ever pausing to reflect that the physical movements involved are an utter absurdity, as much so as Parnesius's ship-sinking catapults. Kipling is giving an ingenious variation on the perennial notion of the tall story, with the difference that the authentic is established by means of falsity, rather than falsity being used as a mode of narrative entertainment. 'I beg your pardon', says the subaltern 'slowly and stiffly' to the enthralled novelist in 'A Conference of the Powers', 'but I am telling this thing as it happened.' A further variation on this insistent point in Kipling's view of art occurs in the story 'A Matter of Fact', in which two journalists on a tramp steamer see a sea-monster, blown to the surface from great depths by an underwater eruption. One tries to write the story as the greatest scoop of all time: the other decides to do it as fiction, realizing that no reader of the papers is going to believe an absolutely true account.

The idea that the 'finest' story is also the 'truest' is so manifestly absurd that it is clear Kipling himself could not have taken it seriously. Yet it remained a potent idea which was to have great influence. What it means is that the story-teller creates his own truth by means of an absolute and offhand authority, such as the eyewitnesses of history possess in the *Puck* stories. The trick is to give the reader the impression that 'at last' the truth is being told, to make the initial impact compulsive. After that, if he reads the story again, the reader can only admire the way it was done, yet his fascination with this remains just as great. In terms of narrative method there is a straight line from these stories of Kipling to those of Hemingway. Indeed Kipling's first readers felt, as Hemingway's were to do, that here was the truth at last, that this was completely authentic, up to the moment, and 'In our Time'. The title of Hemingway's first collection is an indication of what it will do and how it will do it, and the stories are in their own way as didactic as Kipling's. Authenticity shows us exactly what to think and how to respond, and we read on in a trance of obedience, Hemingway's facts having the same status and authority as Kipling's pseudo-facts. The news shots of made-up war between the stories of *In Our Time* have something of the same vulgarizing overemphasis as Kipling's verses between his tales. And we are always conscious in Hemingway that it was Kipling who began the idea of the truest story as coming from the man who saw it happen, and stylizing this until 'seeing it happen' becomes total invention.

The trouble with 'seeing it happen' is that the happening itself loses interest, depth, the goal of the mysterious. Kipling avoids this by the exotic nature of the happening – India, the jungle, sea-monsters, galley-slaves, Roman centurions – and, more importantly, by the sense the reader gets – as in 'The Conversion of St Wilfrid' – of a more involuntary and subdued Kipling, a quieter, unliterary personality, who is in the background. This sense of multiple consciousness can also be present in reading a Hemingway story, particularly a very early one, but it quickly disappears as the Hemingway style takes over and acquires a unitary purpose and authority. For example, though the atmosphere in such small masterpieces as 'Cat in the Rain', and 'Out of Season', is subtly and indirectly indicated, there is not the smallest doubt in the reader's mind about what the composer of those tales is intent on, and the way he is working towards it. The former story is a particular favourite with critics, who have pointed out the ambiguities in its structure. Was the cat the American wife sees in the rain outside the hotel the same cat which is brought up to her room at the end of the story by the maid? If the Italian hotel-keeper ('She liked his dignity. She liked the way he wanted to serve her. She liked the way he felt about being a hotel-keeper. She liked his old, heavy face and big hands') a symbolic figure, a father figure? Does he send the maid up with a cat in order to show that he understands her situation – dissatisfied with her present role as a wife, wanting to have children, to be more feminine, to be looked after?

Conveyed, as they are, with all Hemingway's complete sureness and confidences these things have only the air of being enigmatic. Like the details offhandedly told by Kipling's narrators, their function is to suggest a complete absence of falsity, to freeze the reader into an awed concentration on what the writer is showing him. There is no suggestion of another, a more uncertain or more deeply involved writer, behind the one who is telling the story. In both 'Cat in the Rain' and 'Out of Season' the atmosphere of dissatisfaction is perfectly caught, so perfectly that no alternative or dissociated atmosphere is possible; and none of that sudden shift in perspective which – to go back to our previous examples – made Meon appear in a different light as a pagan, and Wilfrid exhibit for a moment those comic traits that inevitably attend on the ecclesiastical persona.

No doubt Hemingway caught the personae of his two stories straight from his sense of himself and his wife on an Italian expedition. His first wife Hadley wanted a child, Hemingway did not: and he registers with an incomparable economy the range and nature of the tensions involved. It is a chilling economy, suggesting by its very success that the shortest narrative can none the less have corners and pockets where it idles in a genuine perplexity or irrelevance, and that a sense of inevitability in a story's atmosphere may have drawbacks as well as advantages. The deadpan humour in the two stories does not lighten them but confirms their compacted weight, solid as the 'piombo' which is missing from the fishing equipment in 'Out of Season'. Moreover, Hemingway's own personality, so rigorously kept out of the story's frame, is startlingly present as a purely external phenomenon. It is his will which is in question, and which broods over the atmosphere of both stories, determining what they are like and what will happen in them, just as the real Hemingway imposed his will – to fish, to write, to make or not to make love – on the people in his life.

We have to know about Hemingway before we can, in this full sense, *read* the stories, and especially before the real significance of their humour can penetrate us. For its point is that the author is fully aware of how he is behaving, and yet insulates the tale wholly from that awareness. Hemingway is himself the source of the dissatisfaction whose weight he catches so perfectly in the prose, for it is his own behaviour which has produced it. His self-knowledge is perfect, as perfect as one of the fishing casts his heroes can throw, and is devastatingly immanent in the story's style. Hemingway has nothing more to discover about himself: there is no element of exploration, only a clinical certainty. In 'Out of Season' the will expresses itself positively – the young wife drags along behind her husband on their way to try to fish. In 'Cat in the Rain' the will takes an equally overpowering negative form. The husband lies on the bed reading while his wife wanders about and sees the cat in the rain outside, crouching under one of the dripping green tables. The husband is amiable enough, in an absent way, while his wife does the equivalent of miaowing and prowling restlessly to and fro in the bedroom. But his amiability ends with the suddenness of a whiplash. ' "Oh shut up and get something to read," George said. He was reading again.' The humour of the separated Hemingway, and his will to make us read what he has written, seems also able – within the cell of the writing – to compel even the wife in the story herself to read this story about the cat in the rain.

'Indian Camp', the first story, and notable for the absolute perfection of its confidence, also has a surprising amount of 'give' in the style, capacity for variation and for the suggestion of different feelings and personalities in the writing which is found in very good stories but which the Hemingway manner soon blots out. He has already acquired the trick of repetition which can make spoken speech sound like a foreign language, but which is so convincing because it embodies not so much what the character would have heard as 'what the Narrator heard'. The phrase is that of Anthony Powell, discussing in his memoirs the principles of naturalistic speech in a story; and it indicates exactly why speech of that sort sometimes sounds totally unconvincing, and sometimes is instantly accepted by the reader. The reader believes it if he knows the writer heard it, and is not just reproducing something which he believes to be authentic. And what the writer heard is, of course, up to him. There can be no possibility that the narrator's father, in 'Indian Camp', could really have said about the Indian squaw who is having a baby: 'But her screams are not important. I don't hear them because they are not important'. But this is exactly what the narrator *feels* his father to be saying, and his relation with his father dominates the tale at a deep level, exercising a shadowy displacement of the surface material. The least attentive reader feels that something is wrong with the father; and that his son, the narrator Nick, is close to his father in terms of this knowledge. The levels of the story interlock in a surprisingly complex way, giving it a freedom and flexibility of structure quite absent in 'Cat in the Rain' and 'Out of Season', and much more like the early stories of Henry James. In the later stories and novels what Hemingway 'hears' has become predictable and mechanical (though his method of hearing how, say, Spaniards talk to each other is by no means unconvincing) but in 'Indian Camp' and other very early stories he hears his characters in different ways and at different levels.

A section of characters in 'Indian Camp' – the squaw who is trying to have the baby, 'Uncle George', even the squaw's husband, the Indian who cuts his throat – are display personnel, who are only on the outside of the action and whose role is virtually a comic one. That does not make them any less effective. The caesarean operation which Nick's father performs on the Indian woman is imitated by the Indian husband in the throes of the *couvade* who cuts his own throat. The squaw bites the arm of Uncle George, who with the other Indians is trying to hold her down. After the delivery Uncle George has leisure to look at his arm, and the young Indian who had laughed at him 'smiled reminiscently'. The phrase shows how closely Hemingway's style was to be imitated by the humorous writers of the New Yorker school, and how natural in his early work is the relation between event and comedy. 'I'll put some peroxide on that, George', says Nick's father; and because this is part of comic event it is what the doctor would actually say, and not what the narrator 'hears'. After the operation the doctor is 'feeling as exalted and talkative as football players are in the dressing-room after a game'. The end of display comedy is signalled by the disappearance of Uncle George, who had remarked: 'Oh, you're a great man, all right,' when the doctor talked of having done 'one for the medical journal'. 'Doing a Caesarean with a jack-knife, and sewing it up with nine-foot, tapered gut leaders'.

Nick, the notional narrator, turns away from the world of action summed up in that sentence. 'His curiosity had been gone for a long time.' All the things that Hemingway will go for in his art and his life are repudiated in the tale, or rather they are situated in the terrible and meaningless, the frenetic and comic area of living. As daylight comes, and Nick and his father walk back to the lake, his father with 'all post-operative exhilaration gone', the story settles into its deeper and final phase. What has happened to Uncle George? His vanishing seems of deep but unexplained significance. For now the tale is a matter between Nick and his father, and the idea of death that holds them together as they row across the lake, whose water 'felt warm in the sharp chill of the morning'. Rowed by his father, as if by Charon, across the still lake in the early morning, Nick 'felt quite sure he would never die'.

The irony is so complete and so successful that it has sunk without trace. Under the story is the same free depth as there is when Bill and Nick discuss their fathers in 'The Three-Day Blow'. And that free depth, in which is suspended the unexpressed relation, anxiety and affection between the sons and their fathers, acts to guarantee the truth of the whole tale, its depth of uncertainty and its surface of deadpan comedy. It is this truth which Hemingway loses so quickly, supplying instead of it the offhand authenticity which is so false and yet so effective in Kipling. Hemingway's version of it takes the form of the narrator holding us by the eye and going over the details at the same steady pace. Like Nick in 'Big Two-Hearted River' he does not want 'to rush his sensations any'. And it is the unitary nature of these which produces an effect of almost inevitable falsification, even in the trout stream, still more on the battlefield, in later narratives.

There are plenty of signs that Kipling became aware, as his art matured and grew more conscious of itself, that though false authenticity might make a story compulsively readable, it had other drawbacks. It could be seen through, and although this might not affect the impact of the tale itself, it diminished the importance of the message. Kipling's techniques started to go underground, in order that the curious and persistent reader might find things out for himself, and in so doing attach all the more weight and significance to them. He was well aware of the danger that arose, for himself and for his art, from his own popularity, and from the syndrome which Auden was to put into a verse epigram.

> With what conviction the young man spoke
> When he thought his nonsense rather a joke;
> Now that he doesn't doubt any more
> No one believes the booming old bore.

Conviction in the early Kipling goes with a light-heartedness which can indeed have the air of 'rather a joke', as well as adding – as all humour does – further dimensions and possibilities to the tale.

'At the End of the Passage' is a case in point. The mesmeric force of the story consists in its presentation of the four men who come together for an occasional evening, travelling long distances to do so from their isolated work in the baking Indian plains. They don't like each other a bit, but their need for each other's company is of course compulsive; and just as automatic is their instinct to look after the one among them who is most obviously sickening and falling out of the iron routine that keeps them going. This situation has something in common with that in Melville's story 'Bartleby the Scrivener', in which Bartleby gradually drops out of the routines of life, and in so doing out of the grip of the story itself. Kipling's instinct as a narrator is not to be portentous about things, and above all not to make a direct appeal for 'pity' for his four Indian civil servants trapped in their hellish hot weather routines. The real impact will be greater if the tale can be turned into 'rather a joke', with all the business of the occult horrors that lurk in India, the dead man's eye, the nameless things and fears which went with the sensational literature of the period.

The true sense of desolation can be enhanced, not diminished, by delicious terrors incongruously added on, to give the tale another dimension. Kipling does the same thing in another early story 'The Phantom Rickshaw', a thoroughly uncomfortable and disquieting tale disguised as a conventional ghost story. Kipling himself gave a clue to its effect when he commented in 'Something of Myself' that 'Some of it was weak, much was bad and out of key'. This was no doubt in part natural modesty, but the phrase 'out of key' in fact suggests one of the best aspects of early and middle period Kipling stories, though presumably one that had no appeal for him as a judge of his own work. No serious artist is likely to want to hear that the most effective aspect of his tale is overlaid and yet enhanced by its most trivial and conventional aspect.

This none the less is what happens. The title of 'The

Phantom Rickshaw' sufficiently indicates the conventional side of it. A British member of the Indian service, one of Kipling's usual characters, has a love affair with a young widow, Mrs Keith-Wessington. He soon tires of it, but she does not, and is constantly seeking him out and repeating, with an exasperating pathos, that there must be some sort of 'mistake' somewhere. The action takes place in Simla, the hill and leave station, and Mrs Keith-Wessington goes about in her rickshaw, drawn by coolies in a black and white livery. The official, Pansay, falls in love with a young girl, Kitty Mannering, and is determined for this reason to break off once and for all with his former lover. He does so, as uncompromisingly as possible, and soon after hears that Mrs Keith-Wessington has died. He sets himself seriously to court his new sweetheart, and on a ride with her sees the rickshaw with the black and white attendants, and thinks it must have been taken over by somebody else, until he sees Mrs Keith-Wessington leaning out of it and repeating that it must be all a mistake.

The rest of the tale is predictable, following the time-honoured pattern of every ghost story of the kind. Kipling must have read many of them, and he uses the medieval motif of the demon lover in another Simla story. Pansay's doctor says there is nothing wrong with him; his new girl casts him off; he becomes a pariah figure suspected of drunkenness, and observed in earnest conversation on Simla Mall with an invisible woman in an invisible rickshaw. This end is obvious and 'cannot be far off': as in most such stories the victim himself is writing his account of what has gone wrong.

What has gone wrong, though, is something quite different from the seeing of a ghost, a multiple ghost with a bit of mechanism thrown in, such as would appeal to Kipling, a sort of variant of the ghost train idea. The centre of the story is what Pansay, an unreflective character, himself considers to be the sheer unfairness of things. Mrs Keith-Wessington's eternal cry that it is all a mistake, and that 'we shall be as good friends as ever we were', does indeed seem offkey, in terms of the conventional part of the story. As with 'Bartleby the Scrivener' there does seem to be something wrong which nothing can put right, and which pursues its own logic irrespective of the melodrama of the ghost story. What is wrong is connected both with the conditions of life in India, where emotional attachments are subject to so many artificial strains, and where service breeds its own kind of mental habits and attitudes; but also something deeper than that, some primal mistake in the nature of love and emotion itself. The power of the story is not in its ghost motif, nor that the first person narrator is 'a doomed man', but in the sense of hopelessness which Kipling conveys and seems evidently to feel himself, in his usual obscure and elliptical fashion. The commonplace moral associated with the ghost convention – a moral of revenge, retribution, suffering exacted for a wrong done – is undermined by the tone of the story with its emphasis on a 'mistake' – 'it's all a mistake'. The impression the story leaves, and it is a disturbing one, as in the case of many of Kipling's best, is that the author himself is struggling against something his art cannot help revealing. He is struggling to identify with what might be called the 'clean-limbed' interpretation of the story: that Pansay did 'honestly, heartily' care for his new love in a way that he never did for Mrs Keith-Wessington, and that though he and the ghost are to be deeply pitied, the author and his reader must none the less cling to the fact that there is a difference between a 'sickly' and a 'healthy' love. A mother figure must be exorcised.

The form of the short story can contain and exhibit the drama of this in its own special way. 'The Phantom Rickshaw' disquiets the reader all the more because the author seems to strive to avoid giving the impression of any such disquiet, emphasizing instead the strange pathos of Pansay's delusion. But as in the case of 'The End of the Passage' and 'The Strange Ride of Morrowbie Jukes', the real feel of the story is of the blank terror of an existence in which love and duty mean so little, and drop so quickly out of sight. Such an existence is indeed 'all a mistake', breeding delusions and neuroses which have the grim utility of concealing the primal fault, and of concealing too, incidentally, the kind of reality that shows itself in the depth of Kipling's artifices.

These grew more elaborate as time went on, as if they were a kind of defence against the involuntary effect, and a way of keeping the story well in hand. Indeed, the striking thing about the famously complex late stories is how diminished in them the area meaning has become. Kipling controls each effect by means of its own obscurity, and oversees all by means of what has aptly been called his 'loud reticence'. The meticulous art intensifies and makes more raw and more visible his own griefs and preoccupations in these years, so that some of the stories exhibit to an astonishing degree a combination of artistic stoicism with sick misery or hopeless resentment. Not only are they intensely gripping to read, any number of times, but they can also send a frisson down the back on each occasion, as if we were in almost physical contact with the author. Much has been written about these stories, many of which – 'Dayspring Mishandled' is a prime example – have the air of conundrums that have to be unriddled. Some of them, like the notorious 'Mary Postgate', are explained in order to show that Kipling was quite in control of himself and his material, and was methodically exploring, with a sort of haunted clairvoyance, the interaction between a personality and a society involved in the traumatic shock of the first war.

This is plausible enough, although many among the late stories turn out, under their mask of obscurity, to be very simple, narrowed to a single focus as if by the microscope lens in 'The Eye of Allah'. In the two stories about war hysteria, 'Swept and Garnished' and 'Mary Postgate', both of which are dated to 1914 and 1915 and appear at the end of *A Diversity of Creatures*, the collection published before the war ended, it is absolutely clear that Kipling's hatred of the Germans has sought and found the perfect correlative in seemingly objective studies of the delusions of two women – one German, one English – in relation to the unprecedented monstrosity of the times. The remarkable impact of the two tales is due to the reader's sense of Kipling's own violence controlled and yet also exaggerated by his sense of the shock that women at the time were experiencing, and the emotions that were coming out under the then unfamiliar impact of horror propaganda. If the stories were really clinical studies of delusion, done with the most cunning and detailed art, as Kipling's closest critics and most intelligent apologists have suggested (though there seems no reason why he should have to be excused for feeling such violent emotion at that time and in those circumstances) they would certainly not have the extremely powerful and disturbing effect they do.

Kipling in fact gets it both ways. His visible hatred exercises its own catharsis on the reader, who at the same time is able to 'understand' why in such circumstances people – women more particularly – feel and act as they do. It was, of course, a collective hysteria which was over even before the Great War itself had ended, so that both stories are in some degree historical curiosities, fixing the mood of a period in the most vivid imaginative terms. In spite of that neither story has dated in the slightest. 'Swept and Garnished' has something prophetic in its theme of a bourgeois German woman's fixation with order and tidiness, and her delusion that the apartment is invaded and dirtied by a group of Belgian children, who have been told to come and 'wait' there. 'Mary Postgate', which follows it, is in every way more remarkable, chiefly because Kipling seems so completely at home with the heroine. Her hatred for the Germans is his hatred, even though he is meticulous in showing how irrational and propaganda-fed her emotions are. When the young man whom she has helped to bring up, and to whom she has become entirely devoted, is killed on a training flight, she and her employer regret that he did not first manage to kill any Germans; and although he has showed her the arrangements for dropping bombs from his plane she still takes for granted, after getting it into her head that a little girl in the village has been killed by a bomb from a German aeroplane, that her own boy could not possibly do anything like that. 'Wynn was a gentleman who for no consideration on earth would have torn little Edna into those vividly coloured strips and strings.'

The reader can feel Kipling letting himself go in such utterances: there is nothing distancing or calculated about them. For him, as for Mary Postgate and young Wynn, the Germans are 'bloody pagans', who have been tossing Belgian babies on to bayonets. In 'Swept and Garnished' a particularly horrible and gratuitous propaganda story of the time – that the Germans were systematically cutting off the right arms of little Belgian boys that they should never grow up to fight against them – is obliquely referred to as if it were certainly true. In her delirium the German woman who imagines that the Belgian children have come into her flat has this final horror pointed out to her by one of them. She 'looked, and saw', and it causes her final breakdown, when she is found by the maid trying to scrub the blood off the immaculately ordered appointments of her flat. But the reader has to infer just what it is she sees, and this makes its seeming *authenticity* all the more certain.

The particular technical interest of 'Mary Postgate' is that Kipling uses the same device on a much bolder scale, and with so cunning an appearance of authenticity that it could be said to backfire on him. Probably he would not have minded about this, intuiting that if he had persuaded the reader to *share* Mary's delusion – that is to say, to suppose that she really has refused to help a German airman, and has enjoyed every second of his long drawn-out death throes – he has not only increased the horror of the tale but has enabled the reader to share in Mary's hate feelings, as he himself has done. No wonder his cousin Oliver, Stanley Baldwin's son, called it 'the wickedest story ever written'. The wickedness, in a sense, consists in the fact that it is a *story*, that there is no time for the nightmare it produces to be explained, and that this is Kipling's intention. Every time we read it, it reasserts its power wholly to fascinate, as if the reader were a rabbit before a snake, and breaks off leaving him in the same state of daze. It is a hallmark of Kipling's stories that they do not 'grow' in the mind; indeed they seem smaller and clearer in the mind, as part of their specification, leaving only a static imprint of extreme vividness, like a waxwork or a tableau. This procedure is the keynote of his originality as a short story writer, and the reason for the story being, as it were, the predestined form of his particular genius. The vivid images they leave behind may not be the ones most emphasized in the story.

Yet there is no doubt that this story has been planned to deceive us, and to achieve its peculiar effectiveness by doing so. The critics have always disagreed about it, and in various ways sought to show its impartial intelligence and perspicacity. This can indeed be done, but not in terms of the story's actual effect: we are back once again with the ideal of the narrator who holds his audience spellbound by his negligent authenticity, his taken-for-granted knowledge of what took place. (This, of course, is the opposite of the much more common device of the unreliable or partial narrator, which Kipling sometimes uses by bringing two or three of his wholly reliable narrators together so that they cancel each other out, so to speak, and leave everything ambiguous.) But the narrator in 'Mary Postgate' is above suspicion, and he relates Mary's experiences as if they were historic events, like those of the centurion on the wall.

Kipling is at home in falsity, and he now makes his most cunning use of it to give what seems the authentic experience of the reader. In his two essays 'What Happens in "Mary Postgate"', and 'The Nationality of the Airman in "Mary Postgate"', Professor Norman Page pays Kipling the craftsman the compliment of weighing up the evidence with the most scrupulous care. His essays are the most enlightening written about the story, and they quite obviously come to the right conclusion. Page points out that there are two interlocking delusions: first, Mary's conviction that a German bomb has killed little Edna, whereas it seems likely that this has occurred through the collapse of a decayed outhouse. Second, Mary's discovery of a wounded German airman when she is lighting, in the shrubbery at home, the bonfire that will destroy Wynn's heterogeneous possessions, and, incidentally, 'burn her heart to ashes'. Mary has actually *seen* little Edna's body, torn into 'vividly coloured strips and strings'. And she is burning in the destructor, and turning over and over with the kitchen poker, a heterogeneous mass of real objects from the past, Wynn's past. The list of them given by Kipling is quite extraordinary in its detailed pathos, based no doubt on the destruction of his own son's belongings after he was killed in France: the longest, most absolute, most authentic swarm of detailed information to be found in any of the stories.

These two bunches of fact, it seems to me – the 'strips and strings' of Edna's body, and the coagulated mass of Wynn's burning possessions – support the delusion and turn it into a third fact. Mary, and the reader, are quite convinced that the apparition in the shrubbery behind the incinerator is a real

German airman. Not the faintest hint escapes the narrator
that Mary might be 'imagining things'. And where I would
part company with Professor Page is on the question of the
story as such: it is no use asking 'what happens *in* Mary
Postgate?' when 'Mary Postgate' itself is so complete and
appallingly authentic a piece of fiction. Fiction overcomes
fact in the story as love casts out fear, or sexual desire the
instincts of repression. And it must be that Kipling, or his
'daemon' intends this. The reader is right to be shocked, or
even to think it 'the wickedest story in the world'.

But what we can do is to move right away from the story
and the tableau it presents. Then indeed we shall see it in a
different perspective, and that is where its apologists came
into their own. Like many of Kipling's most remarkable
stories it has a completely dual nature. I have remarked on
this in the case of 'The Strange Ride' and 'The End of the
Passage', where the real story is accompanied by a
melodramatic yarn with which it is in effective alliance. With
'Mary Postgate' the case is different. Kipling indulges
himself and the reader in the full experience of Mary, and the
indulgence is so complete that the reader is fully persuaded
some 'bloody pagan' of a German airman has indeed dropped
a bomb on a defenceless village, killing a little girl; that he has
then himself fallen to earth and has lain helpless, unsuccoured
by a woman, Mary Postgate, who has seen the dead child, and
who enjoys as '*her* work – work which no man . . . would ever
have done', the revenge of waiting for and enjoying his death.
That is the way bloody pagans should be treated.

> A man, at such a crisis, would be what Wynn would call a
> 'sportsman'; would leave everything to fetch help and would
> certainly bring It into the house. Now a woman's business was to
> make a happy home for – for a husband and children. Failing
> these – it was not a thing one should allow one's mind to dwell
> upon – but . . . *But* it was a fact. A woman who had missed these
> things could still be useful – more useful than a man in certain
> respects.

'*But* it was a fact.' The italic insists on it, though these are
the thoughts going through Mary's mind, and the 'fact' of the
wounded German airman has been cleverly merged with the

fact that it is her job as an English woman to let him die as he deserves. Kipling has pulled off his main coup, which is to persuade the reader that these are Mary's actual experiences, and to identify himself with her sense of loss and her desire for revenge. These things – the random dropping of bombs from German planes and Zeppelins – had actually begun to happen in 1915, and to a public quite unaccustomed to the idea it indeed seemed unbelievable – in the story's words, 'by its very monstrosity'.

The paradox of the successful short story remains: the more complete the art the more it arouses speculation. Only such a story – only one of Kipling's – could produce the effects that 'Mary Postgate' does. With the catharsis of the tale nearly complete, for Kipling and the war-time reader, an unexpectedly disturbing element is introduced right at the end. The horrible *It*, the airman who has killed the dead child, is the enemy whom – in the words of the poem which came after the story in the original collection – 'the English began to hate'. And they were right to hate him, as the story makes clear. The fact and justification of hatred remain as the vivid tableau it has set before us. But for the reader who has been spellbound by the facts of the tale, who has believed in and with Mary, there is an unpleasant shock to come. Not only is Mary, the childless spinster, doing a proper woman's work in seeing that the enemy airman dies, but she revels in 'the secret thrill of it', and finds it a source of acute sexual pleasure, which makes her look, after she has relaxed and had a bath, 'quite handsome'. Not only that, but it is clear that Kipling throws himself into this aspect of things with all the personal vigour which he spends on the Germans, and the inevitability of hating them. No wonder 'Mary Postgate' might be seen as 'the wickedest story ever written'.

That sounds a little like 'the Finest Story in the World'. It was certainly not Kipling's intention to write the wickedest story in the world, but if he came anywhere near doing so it was because of the way he combined calm authenticity with a shock effect in which his own emotions were fully involved. This is the key of the story, and the reason why only Kipling could have fashioned so unique a narrative compound. Norman Page is surely right to say that 'there are good grounds for believing that, nearly seventy years after the story's first appearance, Kipling's intentions are still not fully and generally appreciated'; but it might be still truer to say that he never intended them to be. The story writer like Henry James, whose intentions, ruminations and calculations are not only a part of his narrative itself but may also be available in his Notebooks, showing how he planned it, is at the furthest remove from Kipling, the paradox of whose art is that a palimpsest of possible effects and intentions only come obscurely into view after the reader has already been knocked down by the story, winded, as it were, by the whole-hearted viciousness of its punch.

It makes no sense, therefore, to ask whether the airman is or is not a delusion, a phantom luxury summoned up by a mind long inured to boredom and deprivation, and now defending itself against shock and grief – the shock of Wynn's death for which the Germans are responsible, and the sight of Edna's body, for which Mary longs to think the Germans must be responsible. If fact and delusion are so much at one – it never occurring to the reader to disbelieve at the time what he is told – then truth is indeed the first casualty, lost in the fog of war, and it is essential to the story's effect that it can never afterwards be established. The story – like Mary herself – wants to, needs to believe in the 'monstrosity', in order that it can defend and revenge itself by hatred. A detailed and intricate pathological outline emerges from all this, a map of reflexes and emotions, but it is a map of the artist himself, as well as of his character and his story. If Kipling were able to be objective and detached he would not be able to write a story like this one. Bonamy Dobree was surely drawing an unreal distinction when he suggested that in it Kipling is not telling us 'how people should behave; he is merely telling us "this is what happens".'

'This is what happens' may be an ideal for the short story writer, but it is usually a very misleading ideal. Kipling has not said or implied that this is what happens, but has managed to combine his own rage, shock and disgust with something more mysterious, something in the background, so that the crudity of his own emotions disappear into it. 'This is what happens' becomes more like: 'Something else was also happening', and this is likely to be a very much better formula for a story. The 'something else' is in our relation with Mary Postgate herself, who, whatever she does, remains a wholly sympathetic figure, as far as possible removed from a casebook study of gruesome and spinsterish oddity, sexual psychosis, and so forth. Nor could this happen if Kipling were really able to take a detached and humanitarian line, an understanding line, and say 'this is what happens'. The triumph of Mary is Kipling's close personal involvement in her own predicament and her own feelings. Revealed in himself they would be repulsive: revealed in Mary they excite in the reader not pity but interest and fellow-feeling, as if Mary were quite removed (as in a sense she is) from the events that occur, or seem to occur, in the story.

Mary's background, and the world she has lived in, is densely blocked in, as dense in the story as the Portuguese laurels down by the destructor; and this is characteristic of Kipling's best tales, in which the setting, as in 'The End of the Passage', speaks more eloquently than the events. We feel we have known Mary all her life, and Kipling is as unerring on the nature of the social scene she has to inhabit as Jane Austen (whom he had recently taken to reading in earnest) would have been. Where Jane Austen knew her village by involuntary experience Kipling had got to know it as he had once got to know the ins and outs of a social organism in India. It may be that his sense of Jane Austen keeps out of 'Mary Postgate' the odd facetious vulgarity and an outsider's lack of touch which is to be found in other tales of the village like 'They', 'My Son's Wife', and 'A Habitation Enforced'. Possible, too, that Kipling had at the back of his mind some such contrast as that between the village community of Jane Austen, relatively undisturbed by the wars that were going on, and the village of 1915, engulfed in the trauma of Mons and violated Belgium, Zeppelins and the Boches.

However that may be we seem to have lived with, and to be living with, Mary Postgate, as with a Jane Austen character: one more proof of how Kipling can exploit the innerness of the short story form at its best. We are at home with Mary without sharing in her delusions – if they are delusions – and seeming to stand rather helplessly by if they are real, as it

might be a friend whose phobias and fixations do not disturb
the placidity of daily intercourse, and need not be enquired
into. This situation seems natural, but it supplies the mystery
at the back of the setting. Mary's inner consciousness might
have remained in that fairly comfortable area of obscurity if it
had not been for the war, the death of Wynn, the death of little
Edna Gerritt. Mary is perfectly at home with death, as any of
Jane Austen's characters would have been, and her relatives,
as she once told Miss Fowler her employer, have had the
knack of dying under 'distressing circumstances'. There was
'dear papa in the late 'eighties; aunt Mary in 'eighty-nine;
mamma in 'ninety-one; cousin Dick in 'ninety-five; Lady
McCausland's   housemaid   in   'ninety-nine;   Lady
McCausland's sister in nineteen hundred and one . . .'

Jane Austen wrote to her sister, about a battle that had just
taken place in Spain, that it was sad so many brave fellows had
died yet it was a mercy that one cared for none of them. That
robust view is held, tacitly, by most of us, and for most of us a
lifetime's experience may do nothing to disturb it. The steady
catalogue of years and deaths in its time brought real grief to
Mary, stoically accepted as the normal way of things. But now
within two days the young man whom she has loved since he
was a boy has been killed, and so has a little girl in the village.
Unlike her relatives, Wynn has died in a way horribly novel to
the imagination, falling from his plane from a great height.
More significant still she has seen the body of the little girl,
wrapped in a table-cloth, cut to pieces. Jane Austen's
brothers may well have seen in their ship men dismembered
by enemy shot, but they would not have mentioned it to her,
nor would it have made them hate the French: it was all in the
day's work. Mary, like Jane Austen, has read 'horrors out of
newspapers' in the family circle. The story is uncomfortably
close to us in the distinction it does not bother to make, where
horrors are concerned, between what we merely apprehend
and what we actually experience.

This is not to say that Mary Postgate behaves and imagines
as every woman might: Jane Austen, for one, would not have
done so. The 'secret thrill' of her nature, never self-admitted,
is sado-masochistic, connecting both love and hate with
suffering; and it makes her simultaneously a very ordinary

woman and the mysterious priestess of a new and barbaric cult. The most powerful thing about the story is that Mary does not 'fantasize' consciously, as anyone might do: her delusions go much deeper than that. She does not know she is in love with Wynn, even though she lifts 'her lean arms' in the dawn at the window, when she thinks she hears his plane overhead; and what Miss Fowler calls the 'deadly methodical way' she sets about burning his possessions does not include any sense of herself as 'burning her heart to ashes'. Her delusion about the German airman is pathetic in one sense, because she has to supply him with the conventional apparatus of anti-Boche repulsiveness out of reports and newspapers. He speaks like a stage German, and his head 'was as pale as a baby's and so closely cropped that she could see the disgusting pinky skin beneath'. The heads of our young flying men, whom she had met at Wynn's funeral, are of course quite different – 'dark & glossy'. This in itself shows that what she sees is made up in the depths of her mind, which can only deal in popular clichés, second-hand materials. And yet in the act of burning, of suffering and inflicting imaginary suffering, she becomes a priestess, possessed by the new god of war, and almost literally so, for her sexual response and its aftermath of satisfaction is quite real. The first-hand knowledge of death, which was an inevitable sadness in the slow tempo of her quiet life, has now become a part of the unreason of hate, and its detestable reward.

And yet Mary remains human and almost a friend. It is one of the feats of the story's construction and its division into seemingly unrelated parts, as unrelated, on the top level, as are the continuities of the older England and the new horrors of war. 'Mary Postgate' is emphatically not a horror story, and shows how the best in its genre can never be assigned to any special category of effect. Although we can see – after the event – Kipling having things both ways – working out his own hatred and at the same time creating a strangely sympathetic figure on whom to project it – the knowledge does not disturb a full appreciation of the story, just as our awareness of Mary's sado-masochistic interior life does nothing to alter the heartrending poignancy of the love she feels for the young man she has looked after in the role of mother.

The same poignancy fills another brief war-time story, 'The Gardener', in which a real mother has had to pretend for years to her illegitimate son that she is only a surrogate mother, an aunt. When he is killed in the war Helen Turrell goes after it is over to visit his grave, still keeping up the fiction that he was her nephew. Kipling served on the War Graves Commission and knew what the cemeteries were like: their overwhelming presence is another example of a story's setting bulking larger in its total effect than the plot. No one has ever been told about Helen Turrell's situation, and for her the lie has closed up completely, so much so that when another woman at the hotel near the cemetery breaks down and confesses that 'her' grave is not what it is supposed to be ('*You* don't know what that means. He was everything to me that he oughtn't to have been – the one real thing – the only thing that ever happened to me in all my life; and I've had to pretend he wasn't. I've had to watch every word I said . . .') she is unable to reciprocate and console by means of a similar confession. Kipling brings out very effectively here the self-centredness of grief: the woman whose lover was killed has no suspicion that she may be talking to another in the same boat. When Helen visits the cemetery in the morning she sees across 'a waist-high wilderness as of weeds stricken dead' a man putting in young plants in the more finished part of the cemetery. He asks her, 'without prelude or salutation', whom she is looking for.

'Lieutenant Michael Turrell – my nephew', said Helen slowly and word for word, as she had many thousands of times in her life.

The man lifted his eyes and looked at her with infinite compassion before he turned from the fresh-sown grass towards the naked black crosses.

'Come with me,' he said, 'and I will show you where your son lies.'

When Helen left the cemetery she turned for a last look. In the distance she saw the man bending over his young plants; and she went away, supposing him to be the gardener.

This is a very good instance of Kipling's dualistic technique.

The heart of the story is the cemetery itself, and the associated fact that in this anonymous mass loved ones themselves are not necessarily what they seem to be. On this the gardener, his significance, and the echo from the gospel words, are superimposed like the comfort of a finished headstone. 'Comfortable' is an important word in the story. Kipling, whose own son's body was never discovered, must have got the idea on one of his visits, joining the image of the gardener to some scrap of gossip he had heard about the people who came there to see their dead. As in 'Mary Postage' we cannot get behind the illusion the story offers, implying that in the interior area of stress and secrecy there is no division between what is illusory and what is real. The story gives no hint that Helen was startled by the gardener's words, which could easily be the result of a language misunderstanding, or an obvious but wrong assumption; but its best stroke lies in the fact that Helen remains in the permanent solitude of her practised deception. No miracle occurs; she is not freed or redeemed from her lie, only comforted by being shown the grave, as Mary Postgate was comforted by a kind of physical ecstasy in the aftermath of her grotesque delusion.

The marrying together of a setting and a sensation is a tried Kipling formula, and in the best of these stories it triumphs over his use of them as indulgence of hatred or grief. The evidence for that is all the clearer from the tight-lipped style, or perhaps rather the quiet absence of tight lips, which gives these stories their air of unstudied calm. Kipling's reticences can indeed be loud, but only in relation to his tricks and devices of narration and report, which in these stories are absent. They recur in a post-war story called 'A Madonna of the Trenches', a singularly misleading title even by Kipling's standards, except that mothers, or the notion of mothers, always exercised a powerful hold over his imagination. There was a deep romantic streak in him, too, about the nature of sexual love itself; and the idea that the more hopeless it was, the more powerful. This came partly from the literary climate of the 1880s and 1890s, Kipling's formative time as a writer, and partly from personal experience, the unhappy experience that lies at the back of his early novel, *The Light that Failed*. In 'A Madonna of the Trenches' the gist and point of the surface story is Kipling's frequent and didactic one about healing, more especially the healing powers inherent in a social organization like that of the freemasons, made up of a fraternal equality between all sorts and conditions of men. It is a post-war story. The young man who breaks down at a Lodge meeting is suffering from some inner horror which, under interrogation by a sympathetic doctor, appears to be caused by memories of life in a trench in mid-winter which has been revetted with the frozen corpses of French *poilus*. It emerges, however, that his real trouble is something quite different. His uncle, an elderly platoon sergeant, has been asphyxiated in a dug-out by the charcoal braziers he had carried in to warm himself, and the young man knows that he killed himself deliberately for love of the young man's aunt, an elderly married lady with whom, as we learn, he has only been alone once in his life before.

Before – that is – she appears to the sergeant one evening, in a quiet part of the trench system, stretching out her arms to him. The young man witnesses this apparition, and sees the sergeant withdraw into the dug-out talking to it, and bidding it join him inside. Corny as it may sound, the sense of eeriness achieved in the story is remarkably genuine, perhaps because the author himself seems deeply and emotionally involved. He also makes the reader feel the state of inner desperation to which the thing has reduced the young man, to whom the notion of normal courting and marriage has, as a result, become insufferably banal. The oddity, and the success, of the story consists in its reversal of the usual Kipling pattern. The setting – both that of the trenches in France and the south London masonic lodge – is not very convincing, having the air of a well-painted backdrop, but the invisible love affair, and its consequences, is conveyed with remarkable power.

The dual effect, whichever way round it is, seems necessary for Kipling to get the best out of a story's theme. In 'The Eye of Allah' the medieval back-drop, and the 'moral', are all there is, and the story is singularly lifeless in consequence. What one would expect, in 'A Madonna of the Trenches', to be purely melodramatic, is in fact both moving and mysterious, and all the more so because it seems so totally withdrawn from and alien to the atmosphere of the rest of the story. A deep and tragic love that never found expression is the last thing one would think Kipling would be able to find expression for, and yet it is the *donneé* of some of his best stories, from 'On Greenhow Hill', one of the soldier stories, 'The Wish House' and to 'Dayspring Mishandled'. One of the best, because least insistent, is a story which has frequently puzzled Kipling fans and caused a good deal of controversy among them: 'Mrs Bathhurst'. Published in 1907 it has nothing directly to do with the war or the political situation, but there is about it a strong and perhaps unconscious aura of disintegration and farewell, of the spirit that really prevails in 'Recessional', behind its emphatic disclaimer of imperial hubris.

> Far called, our navies melt away,
> On dune and headland sinks the fire.

The story is set outside Simonstown, the naval base at the tip of South African which Kipling knew well from his visits at the time of the Boer War. The sailor and the sergeant of marines, Pyecroft and Pritchard, who occur in some of the later stories, encounter the first-person narrator with his friend, a railway inspector, in a broken-down carriage beside the surf. The story starts with some of Kipling's most aggressively vivid description – references to the Greek traders and Malay fishermen who scrape a living in this imperial outpost – and a great deal of anecdotal bonhomie. But as this is going on the story begins to reverse all the normal Kipling tricks, even while it suggests them, by employing a new tactic of receding narration, which adds to the build-up of anticlimax. The inspector is about to tell the narrator a bizarre railway incident, authenticated by the false teeth he has in his waistcoat pocket, when Pyecroft and Pritchard arrive, and are soon launched into reminiscence of their own about 'Boy' Niven, a young sailor who once led his seniors on a wild goose chase round an uninhabited island in Vancouver archipelago by pretending his uncle had a farm there, on which they could all settle in pastoral content. 'We believed,' says Pyecroft; and the teller of tall tales, now 'Mr

Niven', a warrant officer, appears, after a little unpleasantness occasioned by this incitement to desert, to have made a success of his life. Not so 'Click' Vickery, whom the subject of desertion now brings into his shipmates' minds. Called 'Click' for his false teeth (here the inspector steals a hand again to his waistcoat pocket) Vickery had been a friend of Mrs Bathhurst, who kept a little hotel at Hauraki in New Zealand.

The question of what Mrs Bathhurst was 'like' now comes up among the four. At the end of a page or so of reminiscence from the sailors she seems to be taking her place in the gallery of Kipling's meticulous unbelievables, as 'one who would never scruple to help a lame duck or to set her foot on a scorpion' (which Kipling tells us in *Something of Myself* he once heard applied to a woman in New Zealand, and which gave him the germ of the tale). The inspector says, 'I don't *see* her yet somehow,' and yet the reader begins to see her very clearly, in spite of the oracular comments of Pyecroft and his friend. 'Some women'll stay in a man's memory if they once walk down a street, but most of 'em you can live with for a month on end, an' next commission you'd be put to it to certify whether they talked in their sleep or not, as one might say.' This will hardly do, but Kipling – as we shall see – has been remarkably cunning in keeping the idea of Mrs Bathhurst herself clear of what the unreliable narrators have to say about her, strong as was the impression she made upon them, and touching in their own way as are the nice things they find to say about her.

From this chat among self-assumptive experts, though they are chivalrous and comparatively innocent experts, the inspector gets the point, whether or not he can yet *see* Mrs Bathhurst. The reader may be doing so, from a point picked up from the marine sergeant, who in the course of an anecdote illustrating the young widow's thoughtfulness to all the patrons of her little hotel, remarked on the 'blindish way she had o' looking'. To the kind but unremarkable proprietess of a small haven for men who are themselves betwixt and betweens – naval warrant officers from all over the empire which covers the world – Kipling is assigning the blindness of the fates in mythology, as he was to imply the role of priestess

and mistress of the war god to Mary Postgate. And such
heavy-handedness pays off, at least on these two occasions,
because he so well combines the idea of something strange,
even portentous, in the image of the title character, with a
background as domestically detailed, as effectively 'seeable',
as that of a Jane Austen heroine.

Kipling may be heavy-handed, but he manipulates here
with great cunning and complete lack of emphasis. The bifold
nature of the image exactly suits the scale and technique of his
short story, as they might also have suited Conrad's. But
Conrad had no power of conveying the reality of women in his
stories; and when he attempted it, as 'Because of the Dollars',
or 'Freya of the Seven Isles', the result was uneasy, defensive,
verging on facetiousness. Even the impressive young woman
in 'Falk', with her hair plait as thick as a club, is a convenient
ancillary and makeweight in what is certainly a serious tale,
but has no room for her as a serious person in it. Mrs
Bathhurst is a serious person because of the mythological
weight, verging as usual on melodrama, which Kipling puts
into the telling of the tale and into the narrators' responses to
her. The marine sergeant remembers his own heavy-handed
gallantry when she puts aside for him some bottles of a
particular kind of beer that he liked. ' "This is my particular –
just as you're my particular." (She'd let you go *that* far!)'
When he visits again, five years later, ' "Sergeant Pritchard,"
she says, "I do 'ope you 'aven't changed your mind about
your particulars".' To such encomiums the inspectors retorts
that 'My mother's like that for one', and Pyecroft comments
on the number of women he and his shipmate must have 'been
intimate with all over the world'.

The impudence with which Kipling brings the word
'mother' together with 'intimate' and 'particular' is so
discreet as to be hardly noticed; and the reader in any case is
sent off on another track by the inspector's 'slow answer' to
the sergeant's rhetorical question about what happens to a
man who 'gets struck with that kind o' woman'. 'He goes
crazy – or just saves himself.' It is remarkable, once again,
how the story manages to save itself both from the heavy-
handed worldliness of these observations, and from the
melodrama that is to follow: the latter, of course, particularly

relished by the narrators themselves. The almost uncanny
success of 'Mrs Bathhurst' as a short story – and it is
something only the genre could produce – is the way in which
all the author's most vulgar and knowing sentiments,
messages and methods serve to bring out something beyond
them, the actual identity and fate of the young widow herself,
which makes her a figure even more memorable than Mary
Postgate.

She seems in some way to have fallen for Vickery, the
'superior man', the senior petty officer with the false teeth,
and his shipmates are unanimous that what followed could
have been no fault of hers. All we find out is that Pyecroft at
Cape Town went to see one of the early biographs, which gave
silent newsreels – 'home and friends for a tickey' (a South
African threepenny bit) – which gave such simple scenes from
home as ships in harbour, soldiers on parade, and trains
arriving at the London stations. A shot of the latter shows the
Plymouth express coming into Paddington, and the
passengers getting out, amongst them Mrs Bathhurst. 'There
was no mistaking the walk in a hundred thousand. She came
forward – right forward – she looked out straight at us with
that blindish look which Pritch alluded to. She walked on and
on till she melted out of that picture – like – like a shadow
jumpin' over a candle.' Vickery sees the show every time he
can, insisting on Pyecroft getting drunk with him after it, and
after a few days is in such a state that he goes to their ship's
captain. No one knows what happens, but the 'owner' seems
to have been an understanding man, because Vickery is
ordered right up country, to entrain some ordnance stores at a
disused warehouse. There he deserts and disappears. At this
point the inspector has some information to give. Way up in
Rhodesia the line runs straight through a solid teak forest –
'seventy-two miles without a curve'. Beside a rail siding two
black figures had been found standing, killed by lightning or
the forest fire it caused. 'They fell to bits when we tried to
shift 'em. The man who was standing up had the false teeth. I
saw 'em shinin' against the black. Fell to bits he did too, like
his mate squatting down and watchin' him, both of 'em all wet
in the rain.'

So much for the information the partial narrators can give.

The identity of the dead tramp is clinched by his tattoo marks, known to Pyecroft. In deference to the feelings of his two new aquaintances the inspector never brings out the object in his waistcoat pocket, over which his hand has hovered several times in the course of the tale. As the little gathering prepares to break up a picnic party walks past up the beach singing 'The Honeysuckle and the Bee'. The desultory, untidy nature of the tale, as of bits of newspaper blown from everywhere, is concluded on the same note by a comment from Pyecroft that after seeing Vickery's face every evening after the biograph show he feels it's just as well he's dead.

T. S. Eliot, an admirer of Kipling, and of the pleasure of meeting in him 'a mind so different from my own', once spoke of the 'meaning' of a poem as being rather like the bit of meat the burglar threw the guard dog while he got on with robbing the house, or, in this case, working on the reader. 'Mrs Batthurst' provides a melodrama in the form of a conundrum, and provides it through the reminiscence of narrators who thoroughly enjoy the lurid aspects of the affair. The success of the story, in the sense that T. S. Eliot was thinking of the success of a poem as something beyond its meaning, comes from the way in which all the narrative possibilities it contains run away into nothing, leaving only the image. Like the distant princess, Mrs Bathhurst is far removed from the comments of those who have known her, or of those who listen, like the railway inspector, with sympathetic scepticism. The latter's 'I don't *see* her somehow' is a direct challenge to the story, which is taken up by the image of Mrs Bathhurst getting out of the Plymouth express and walking down the platform at Paddington until she melts out of the picture 'like shadow jumpin' over a candle'.

That is the image the reader retains, and it is associated with an extraordinary pathos, the pathos of space, the defencelessness of time suddenly caught and repeated by the new invention of the cinematograph; the great distances and the tiny units of community, imperial outposts, ships, boarding houses, with their memories and desires and muffled dramas, smouldering on at intervals until extinction. In this aspect Mrs Bathhurst is both a symbolic image and an idea of human goodness, though in neither manifestation is she anything more than shadowy, touched with the pathos and absurdity of human preoccupations seen at a great distance.

But people love stories which seem to give shape and meaning to uncertainties and vanishings; and the idea of 'the story in it', which Kipling may have picked up from James, is played with by the background of the tale, which leaves all such stories behind as it diminished to the clarity of a single microcosm. The various leads implicit in our narrators' recollections burst like matches into lurid flame and flicker out like the same shadow jumping over the candle. The hints and speculations of the narrators give the old thrill of a mystery to themselves and to the reader, but it is a mystery which is self-absorbing and self-generating, removed from the real *donnée* of the tale, but, as in the case of many of Kipling's, necessary to the total effect. 'Mrs Bathhurst' is by a long way the most subtle of these compound stories, for the melodrama has an excitement of its own, and curiosity and suspense are played off against each other. The story tacitly allows the reader to discount much of the graphic 'terror' which the narrators, naturally enough, delight to summon up amongst themselves; and yet at the same time the reader is held by something at the back of all this, something awful enough in itself, and doubly so, touchingly so, from its unawareness of how the narrators will make the story up. Mrs Bathhurst is a long way from her own story, as far as New Zealand from Paddington, and whatever happened to her she will never know that for the narrators she has become the story that she is. Kipling's genius in the genre has contrived that she will not be her story, in the sense that Conrad's Amy Foster is her story, and still more, of course, such famous heroines as Eugenie Grandet or Tess Durbeyfield, or Isobel Archer.

But, apart from that, what *does* happen to her; what are the facts of the tale as far as they go? Kipling is using variations of the same technique which he would use later in 'Mary Postgate' and 'A Madonna of the Trenches': only here there is no question of a ghost or a delusion, but of a figure seen on the screen of an early cinematograph, a figure which repeats itself endlessly, coming blindly forward before the viewer's eyes in each performance. Kipling is anticipating the power of such images to produce infatuation, to become a secret part of the lives of those who see them, as in the case of the early film stars and Greta Garbo. There was nothing phantasmal about the potency of the silver screen, nor was Kipling merely being clever, as he is in his story 'Wireless', written about the same time, which shows us a young chemist with TB making up some rudimentary lines of a poem he has never heard of – Keats's 'The Eve of St Agnes' – while under the influence of the Marconi transmissions his friend is experimenting with upstairs.

Mrs Bathhurst on the screen must however be connected with Mrs Bathhurst in the flesh. She followed Vickery from New Zealand to England, either because he married her or made her a promise, or because her feelings for him could not be satisfied with anything less. Her unconscious participation in the newsfilm, as the Plymouth express reached Paddington, suggests that she had been down to see Vickery and failed to get anywhere with him, perhaps because he had told her, for the first time, that he was a married man whose wife was pregnant. From Vickery's words to Pyecroft, before he leaves the ship at Cape Town, we know that 'my lawful wife died in childbed six weeks after I came out'. This might indicate that Vickery has missed enjoying a lawful love with Mrs Bathhurst through a piece of diabolical mistiming, that he has – as Kipling says of Punch in 'Baa Baa Black Sheep' – 'missed heaven after a glimpse through the gates'. It might equally indicate that the married Vickery, back in his own country, has simply sent Mrs B about her business, giving her to understand that their affair – whatever it was – is over; and that in consequence the sight of her in the newsreel on Paddington station has caused him to have terrible pangs of conscience, all the more bitter because his own wife has just died.

Such explanations, as Kipling well knew, are inevitably banal in real life; and how much more so in terms of a story. Whatever has happened, of that kind, must not be allowed out. And yet still more banal would be any sensational explanation which might account for the almost catatonic state to which Vickery is reduced when he is watching the shadow of Mrs Bathurst on the screen every evening and getting drunk with Pyecroft, a state which Pyecroft describes with sage relish to the little circle of narrators and listeners. This is where the many close critical decipherings of the story, and its clues, run into trouble. Because Pyecroft has remarked of the look on Vickery's face, after the first film show, that it was like things preserved in bottles – 'White an' crumply things – previous to birth as you might say' – it does not help to interpret it as an indication that Mrs Bathurst has had an abortion; or to assume from Vickery's behaviour that he knows she has done away with herself.

As a ghost story or sensational tale the whole point is simply that she has come to find him, and that she is the last person one would expect in such a role. This incongruity is what really matters, pointing up, as it does, the goodness of the woman and the pathos of her in such a situation. Kipling's sense of melodrama had always enjoyed the idea of the Demon Lover, and he used it in a story in *Plain Tales from the Hills*, with the demonic figure also cast as an unlikely individual – a gentle and chivalrous civil servant who comes up to Simla to see his love for the last time, and dies on the way. The verse epigraph to that story made the point plain.

> When the Earth was sick and the skies were gray
> And the woods were rotted with rain,
> The Dead Man rode through the autumn day
> To visit his love again.

And in death he is almost as memorable an apparition as Mrs Bathurst on the cinema screen. 'Sitting in the back seat, very square and firm, with a hand on the awning-stanchion and the wet pouring off his hat and moustache'. Even such a dead man would be a less arresting phenomenon in a Kipling story than a live woman – if that woman happened to be Mrs Bathurst. But Kipling himself has again given the clue in the epigraph to the story – a laboured piece of pseudo-Elizabethan play headed 'From Lyden's "Irenius"'. Kipling enjoyed fashioning such squibs, probably more than we enjoy reading them, and a couple of sentences in the little farrago tell what he had in mind. 'She that damned him to death knew not that she did it, or would have died ere she had done it. For she loved him.' Being the good woman she was Mrs Bathhurst would never have dreamed of reducing Vickery to the state he is in, as a result of accidentally seeing her coming to try to find him. (Or at least that is what he thinks she is doing). His own original feelings can only be guessed at, but it seems likely that he fell in love with her, as she with him, and either married her bigamously or renounced her because he was a married man, with a wife at the other end of the world. Possibly he could not, or did not, bring himself to tell her this. Perhaps she came after him in good faith, thinking it an opportunity to visit 'home', perhaps to see him again. She would have believed him in any case, being, like the sailors in the 'Boy' Niven story, 'lovin' and trustful to a degree'.

As regards the specification of the story, a critic like Todorov would consider all these queries beside the point. Kipling's project is to realize Mrs Bathhurst, whom we never meet, as a remarkable woman, a good woman, in terms of the effect she has on others, and notably, of course, on the unfortunate Vickery. 'Blindish' as the fates, she drives a man mad without knowing it, although – a final turn of the screw – she herself loves him too. It is a fine idea, which might have found a place in Henry James's notebook, but like so many of Kipling's bright ideas it might have been spoilt by overemphasis, a too nudging insistence. What makes the story such a success is the bewildering effect that Kipling manages to build into it at every level, the queries and speculations which are so integral a part of it; and yet which *never* threaten the central image of Mrs Bathhurst – the good woman – with her blindish look, walking towards us down the platform, and disappearing like a shadow jumping over a candle.

James would not have got this particular effect, for, as Todorov implies, James does not leave a story under a cloud of speculation, like a swarm of bees, but settled for a solid and as it were a magisterial ambiguity. It was his specification to create an exact effect. Kipling, more dangerously, prefers here to create an extremely inexact one, made up of impressions that must not be allowed either to dominate or to be discounted. The situation must remain impenetrable, but at the same time must not be presented as a deliberately impenetrable situation. And Kipling cannot resist giving a final twist to the screw which completes the effect of melodrama, and has also exercised the critics as much as the figure of the German airman in 'Mary Postgate'. It is essentially the same device, which might be termed that of the highly suggestive impossibility.

Just as there is no question that the first readers of 'Mary Postgate' assumed that Mary behaved in the way she does to a real German airman, fallen from the sky; so Kipling's readers, however bemused by the way the story was told, would certainly have supposed that the second tramp, the blackened figure found with Vickery's in the teak forest – 'squattin' down lookin' up at 'im' (a detail twice repeated) – must be Mrs Bathhurst herself. Certainly Kipling's illustrator must have believed so, when he drew the picture for the story's first appearance in the *Windsor Magazine*, for he showed the second tramp, looking up and watching, as an obviously female figure.[1] The notion nicely rounds off the tale, and its absurdity is not betrayed by the *tone* of anything in it. At the same time Kipling is meticulous in not making any overt connection, other than that there were two tramps, and their pose in death. The suggestiveness of this itself gets through to Sergeant Pritchard, who 'covered his face with his hands for a moment, like a child shutting out an ugliness', and says 'to think of her at Hauraki!'

It is possible to labour inordinately at the detail of 'Mrs Bathhurst', for the story's success depends only indirectly on the cunning of its narration and technique. Its inner dimension is less obviously intriguing but more satisfying in the long run. As so often with Kipling it depends on effect by association, though associations much less melodramatic than that which at first suggests to the reader that Vickery and Mrs Bathhurst have been literally united in some mysterious holocaust in the heart of Africa. The fires of passion are genuine enough, but even they are not what really count. So artfully cavernous is the story's perspective that it takes time

1. C. A. Bodelsen points this out in *Aspects of Kipling's Art*, an excellent investigative study.

even to realize something to which the not very tasteful mock-Elizabethan epigraph, about the love of queens and princes, gives a clue: that Kipling's customary didacticism is at work even here, his finger pointing at a truth he wished the reader not to miss – that a *grande passion*, with all its tragic consequences, is not to be found only in the upper reaches of society. By the time we come to the war and to 'A Madonna of the Trenches' that truth will be taken for granted, but Vickery and Mrs Bathhurst are unobtrusively proffered to the reader in the light of what would nowadays be called 'ordinary working people'.

We can discount that; but the fact is that they are uniquely memorable characters, and with something of that air of mystery about them which remains a very great literary achievement, even though it may be partly secured by narrative trickery. The banal platitude that ordinary people *are* basically mysterious is here given real meaning and poignancy. Kipling of course learnt much from Dickens, but Dickens' 'ordinary people' possess nothing of this quality, which probably could only be suggested within the boundaries of a short story and would not survive treatment in a full-length novel. In the same way, and for the same reason, Mrs Bathhurst herself becomes a full-blown character, subject as such a character should be to every variety of speculation; and also a single disturbing and unforgettable image, walking with her blindish look on the biograph screen. Something in 'Mrs Bathhurst' takes its place with Keats' vision of the two lovers in 'The Eve of St Agnes', which has all the qualities of a great short story in verse. Perhaps the shadow jumping over a candle was suggested by Madeline's taper, whose 'little smoke in pallid moonshine died'; a line characteristically misquoted by Kipling in 'Wireless', which rubs its hands over the Wellsian idea that great poetry may be forever free on the waves of the ether, until received through some suitable human transmitter. Where anything to do with art is concerned, Kipling can sometimes rise to heights of myopic vulgarity, as he does over Jane Austen in the 'The Janeites', and over Surtees and the culture of The Yellow Book in 'My Son's Wife'.

But the art on the inside of 'Mrs Bathhurst' has nothing to do with this. It is Kipling's most uninsistent and therefore his truest vision of the way in which empire and commonwealth are made up; function; work obliviously in all sorts of anonymous ways; suffer their own obscure kinds of breakdown and entropy, their own unspectacular relaxations and easements, dooms and decays. The whole story is filled with a restless disquiet. The ghost of anticipation on the widest scale. Association, so hypnotic in the case of Mrs Bathhurst and the second tramp, works similarly to weave a sense of doom and tragic fulfilment out of the seemingly genial chat of the two naval 'characters', the railway inspector, their interlocking complacencies, worldly wisdoms, glimpses into darkness, the idyll of 'The Honeysuckle and the Bee', a sweetly sentimental song in which the girl 'answered "yes," and sealed it with a kiss'. Like all good stories of the kind this one has its own unique sort of poetry, some of the most persuasive that Kipling wrote. And like all good stories it leaves unsaid, but within the wide area of creative tension its formal limits set up, a great deal more than it utters. It is a more subtle story, with more dimensions of meaning, than another story symbolically involved with the break-up of a society – Hawthorne's 'My Kinsman, Major Molineux' – but it transmits, though much more unexpectedly, a similar atmosphere of strange disquiet.

CHAPTER FOUR

Hemingway's wives, it seems, picked up his idiom and spoke like characters in his stories. When he wanted to go to the races – and whatever he wanted to do was the story in which all took part – his loyal wife Hadley announced that she would 'make good sandwiches'. As a reviewer of the Hemingway memoirs commented, if she had made bad sandwiches it would have been something. The story, that is to say, would have taken an unexpected turn. Hemingway himself was perfectly conscious of his need for an exact verbal scenario, matching the will of the plot. He could even make a joke about it, representing his third wife as saying, 'You use such original adjectives' when he told her the sea was 'good' that day.

Hemingway's idiom symbolizes the need of many stories for an exactness commensurate with the precise individual effect that they will upon the reader. Even Kipling, in 'Mrs Bathhurst', sets his scene with characteristic precision and superb verbal painting, as does Conrad at the opening of 'The Secret Sharer', although Kipling does not say that the sea was 'good' but 'seven-coloured'. The adjective probably conveys, and with reasonable discretion, the impression of imperial society and its many races that lurks inside the story; while the opening of 'The Secret Sharer' hints of puzzles and compartments and identities doubled or reversed. In 'Mrs

Bathhurst' the glittering enamel of the opening description fades and dissolves into smoke and shadows, odds and ends of dialogue and fragments of gossip like newspaper scraps; and with this fade-out goes a dissemination of significance, settling out into separate and powerfully enigmatic images.

The willed precision of the Hemingway idiom generates, as I have observed, a total and immediate effect which can be repeated with each re-reading, though probably with lesser impact, but not greatly expanded or modified. Similarly, in a story like Katherine Anne Porter's 'Pale Horse, Pale Rider' – her masterpiece – the very strong memory of a unique reading experience will possibly not survive a later re-reading, which will tend to disestablish the individuality of the story, turning what had seemed a strong confident idiom into one that seems more commonplace. What seemed the certainties of effect in the tale become themselves a source of weakness, like a figure seen to be held erect by a stiff suit of clothes. The dissolution of Kipling's story, though equally willed, is much more successful in seeming to contradict its own stylish assertiveness, producing after-images and meanings of a quite different kind.

The verbal exactness and precision of effect that are characteristic of a certain kind of short story are certainly not to be found in the work of Chekhov. On the contrary, Chekhov's 'flow' has a diffidence about it, in structure and syntax, which takes away all potential either of emphasis or understatement. Chekhov is the opposite of Hemingway: he seems to have no idiom at all. This can be a source both of strength and of weakness. Hemingway, Kipling and Conrad are alike in exercising supreme power over their verbal idiom, however much more craftily the latter two writers use their skills to give effects of uncertainty and forbearance. But Chekhov, when he is not on form, can be very limp, as genuinely limp as a newspaper or a magazine article. When he is on form the 'flow' is magical: clear, transparent, unerring in its own simplicity. But considering how many stories he wrote his masterpieces are relatively few. One could not say he has been overrated, but his great and his inferior stories were once hailed with equal rapture by his admirers. Today, available at last in a good translation by Ronald Hingley, many of them are chiefly interesting for the comedy of their factual detail about all levels of Russian life and society, and the sense they give of what those facts meant.

But others are, so to speak, real stories, and among the best ever written. Near the end of his life, an invalid from the tuberculosis which killed him, Chekhov wrote one of his finest, 'A Lady with a Little Dog' – the indefinite article probably gives a better sense of the Russian title than the definite 'the'. Russian does without the article, and the implications of this can themselves be an aspect of style. The story is pervaded with Chekhov's characteristic comedy, some of which is clearly difficult for non-Russian speakers to appreciate; even to be sure in what sense comedy is present. 'A Lady with a Little Dog'? (Russian again does without the adjective, having only a diminutive – 'doglet'.) Does that phrase, as title and theme, express something different from the same phrase used at the end of the second paragraph? The two are identical, but whereas the first is like the title of a picture, the second seems both impersonal and familiar, with a slight leer in it, so that it might be rendered, as Hingley does, as 'the dog lady'. *Nikto ne znal, kto ona, i nazivali ee prosto tak: dama s sobachkoi.* 'Nobody knew who she was, and spoke of her simply as "the dog lady".' Between the two phrases there is a difference which spreads throughout the story: their sameness is only on the surface. And the same thing seems true of the story as a whole. It is both, if you like, a cynical tale, and a pathetic and beautiful, a touching and heart-rending one. It never decides, or needs to decide, which is which, because like so many of Chekhov's stories it breaks off, not with a self-conscious air of remaining 'unfinished', but for the opposite reason: that life goes on, bearing forever entwined within it the two themes, two possibilities, neither of which can be defined while the characters remain alive, and which can never be resolved into a single solution. There will always and inevitably be, as it were, a lady with a dog and the dog lady, interfused but never the same, like art and life.

Chekhov wrote the story at the resort of Yalta, where he was living as an invalid, and the locality seems to come alive as itself, to a much greater extent than in his other stories, where place is usually indeterminate. This story arrives at indeterminacy by other means. To mention 'Cat in the Rain' – that fixed, vivid, memorable little tale – would be to show how large the area of indeterminacy is. What is this thing which the story is all about, which Gurov and Anne feel for each other? Is it love? Sometimes it seems like it and sometimes not: the word forfeits its sense while at the same time the thing itself gains immensely in possibilities of feeling and interpretation.

Indeterminacy goes with an almost dramatic precision. 'It was said there was a new face on the promenade: a lady with a dog.' The opening sentence repeats and re-emphasizes the title. The second introduces a name. 'Dimitri Gurov, who had been staying in Yalta for a fortnight and was now quite settled in, had begun to take an interest in new faces.' Like a Boudin seascape, the picture is already complete. For what reason? For a pick-up? No one knew who she was: she was just referred to as 'the dog lady'. It is after this sentence that we have the first movement of consciousness in the story. 'If she has no husband or friends here,' reflected Gurov, 'it mightn't be a bad idea to get acquainted.' The same thought must have occurred to others, and to the lady herself. Gurov reflects that 'this must be her first time ever alone in such a place, with men following her around, watching her, talking to her: all with a concealed purpose which she could not fail to divine.'

So the first 'positive' aspect of the story to go is that of the experienced seducer and innocent victim. Anna Sergeevna (it seems likely this recalls the famous Anna of Tolstoy's novel) is no more innocent than Gurov himself. Like him she wants to 'live', but living for her – 'fully living' – naturally enough means something different. It means love, though the word is not mentioned by her. Having been married at twenty to a worthy but tedious creature – a bit of a 'lackey' is how her words in Russian describe him – she comes to feel there must be 'more to life'. She tells her husband she's off-colour and needs a change, and comes to Yalta.

The seduction scene is quickly over. Both go through it as if it were something that has to be done, with Anna's awkwardness giving him the impression of someone taken aback, as if by a sudden knocking on the door. It is very hot.

Afterwards she sits deliberately pensive and despondent, like an old-fashioned picture of the 'Woman Taken in Adultery'. Gurov sees a water melon on the table, cuts himself a slice and eats it 'without haste'. They sit silent for 'at least half an hour'.

The picture here, which might be by Steer or Degas, in spite of Anna's more traditional pose, is arranged to contrast with the indeterminacy which is beginning to take over the whole. Gurov and Anna instinctively adopt their positions, as they had instinctively gone through the motions of seducing and being seduced. As he is about to make love to her in her hotel room the experienced Gurov reflects on his other affairs: the women who were honest and simple about it and glad of a little brief happiness; the ones like his wife who always implied that 'this was neither love nor passion but something more significant'; the rapacious ones who pretended the thing was more intense than it was, as if 'to snatch more from life than it can give', and whose sexual charms became repulsive to him, the lace on their underclothes 'like a lizard's scales'.

Anna's responses are not like these, and yet in one sense they are equally conventional. She is ill at ease and frightened that he will 'lose respect for her', no doubt all the more worried about this because of his calm and taciturn behaviour after the event. She is not upset about deceiving her husband but deceiving herself: what has happened seems no proper correlative for her longing that there should be 'more to life'. All these 'positive' things that she longed for, and that he is accustomed to seek and enjoy, seem to have disappeared, gone underground in their story.

But as the story, like life, continues, we see they are still there, unnoticed because transformed, part of the involuntary acceptance of things. There is no longing for 'more to life', but an intimacy which neither has expected, which does not correspond to either's desires or wishes for more, and which goes with the sound of the sea, and its unconcern. The gentle and sudden simplicity of the story's sentiments here, its unembarrassed openness, are very moving. Gurov and Chekhov become unashamedly one, a tactic not uncommon in Lawrence's tales but scrupulously avoided by most short story writers. Sitting peacefully on the seat with Anna, in the dawn, Gurov–Chekhov reflects, tritely enough, that it will always be the same old sea, booming away.

> This persistence, this utter aloofness from all our lives and deaths ... do they perhaps hold the secret pledge of our eternal salvation, of life's perpetual motion on earth, of its uninterrupted progress? As he sat there, lulled and entranced by the magic panorama ... Gurov reflected that everything on earth is beautiful really, when you consider it – everything except what we think and do ourselves, when we forget the lofty goals of our being and our human dignity.

This is commonplace in a way that Chekhov can do with perfect naturalness and without any sense of bathos; like a little piece of dull music leading the way to a motif which, though over in a second, strikes a sudden chord of response in the listener.

> Someone, a watchman probably, came up, looked at them, went away. Even this incident seemed mysterious – beautiful, too. In the dawn they saw a steamer arrive from Feodosiya, its lights already extinguished.

The watchman, and the reassurance his silent arrival and departure bring, are in their small way essential to the story's being, but they have an effect the very opposite of Kipling's gardener at the end of the story, with his look of 'infinite compassion'. Some mysterious blessing seems to have been conferred on Gurov and Anna, and they become more tranquil and intimate as a result. But their instinctive separate responses still continue. 'Disturbed ... by the fear that he did not respect her enough, she kept repeating the same old questions.' He goes on kissing her, complimenting her, soothing her, with his own private feeling inside that she is making a fuss which requires this kind of treatment. Then a letter arrives from her husband, who was to have joined her, saying he isn't well and asking her to come home. Even at the moment of parting her old reflex is to the fore, as she says 'Don't think ill of me.' But this is set aside by the way she asks him to look at her one last time, and the way she says: 'I'll think of you, I'll remember you.' Gurov's own slight constraint and embarrassment can be felt but is not mentioned. It disappears after she has gone, because he can now reflect in a troubled way, but freely, on 'this young woman whom he would never see again'. He had done his best but he must have seemed rather patronizing – this sense of himself as inevitably betraying 'the rather crude condescension of your conquering male' corresponds to her fixation that he won't respect her, will secretly despise her. 'She had kept calling him kind, exceptional, noble, so obviously she hadn't seen him as he really was, and he must have deceived her without meaning to.'

Nothing is more noiselessly and acutely perceptive in the story than the way Chekhov conveys the inevitability, and the irrelevance, of 'deceit'. Doing his best to be nice, as he really wishes, Gurov creates what seems to him a false impression: but for Anna it is a true one. Similarly her nervous obsession with what she feels may seem to him the shameless way she has behaved, touches him deeply, becomes the thing that 'gets' him about her. Behind the inevitability of deceit there is something else, growing up from their parting; and besides, it is the ways each react in and to themselves which unknowingly move each about the other.

It was the way Chekhov described their parting, and its aftermath, which probably struck Ivan Bunin, the Russian writer who did that most difficult thing – *really* learning from Chekhov – where Chekhov's foreign admirers and imitators merely tried to be 'Chekhovian'. In Bunin's story 'The Encounter', a young army officer – 'just the usual lieutenant' – meets a young woman on a Volga steamboat, and they have an immediate affair in the hotel at the next stop. She has to go off in the morning to meet her husband, and he remains in the room. What Bunin concentrates on with great force and brilliance is the lieutenant's sudden realization that he loves her – loves her passionately – and that he will never see her again. This is the 'story' as it remains with the reader, and as it is intended to do. Bunin takes up what is obscured in the indeterminacy of Chekhov's story – the theme of the casual Don Juan who is suddenly 'hooked' – and gives it a powerful and effective local emphasis. (He does the same sort of thing in his much better known story 'The Gentleman from San

Francisco'.) As it happens, this theme has a venerable history in Russian literature, for it is the leading idea in one of Pushkin's little 'tragedies of investigation', as he called them – *The Stone Guest.*

There Don Juan has genuine love and affection for all his 'conquests' but falls deeply and irretrievably in love with one of them, the pale, subdued, invalidish Donna Anna, widow of the Commendatore whom Juan has killed in a duel. Like our Anna Sergeevna – the dog lady or lady with a dog – Donna Anna is full of gloom, sorrow and remorse, convinced that she is a worthless woman, but secretly quite overcome by her love for Don Juan, just as he is overcome by her cold timid passivity. I should say there was no doubt that Chekhov, perhaps unconsciously, followed the same theme in his story. A key passage distantly echoes the exchange between Don Juan and Donna Anna.

'... now I'm just another worthless vulgar woman whom everyone feels free to despise.'

Gurov was bored with all this. He was irritated by her air of naiveté, and the unexpected, uncalled-for remorse. If it was not for the tears in her eyes he might have thought she was joking or pretending.

'I don't understand,' he said quietly. 'What is it you want?' She hid her face on his breast and clung to him.

'Please please believe me,' she implored, 'I long for a good and moral life. I really hate the sin of it – I don't know what I am doing myself. The common people say the "Evil One" tempted them, and now I can say the same – I was tempted by the Evil One.'

'There, there,' he muttered, 'That's enough.'

He looked into her staring, frightened eyes, kissed her, spoke to her softly and gently. She gradually relaxed and cheered up again; and both of them began to laugh.

Gurov is quite surprised to find that 'Anna', this 'lady with a dog', had her own special view – a very serious one – of what had happened, but of course in time it gets to him and becomes an important part of what he feels for her and the way she haunts him. But this is the second 'positive' aspect of the story to go (the first was the theme of experienced seducer and innocent victim). It disappears into the background, into the indefinability of them having fallen in love; although a Russian formalist theorist, Vladimir Propp, would no doubt have counted Chekhov's story as one of the examples of this particular story motif – among the 96, or whatever it was, possible motifs that a short story can have.

In formalist terms Propp is no doubt right, and it is in any case obvious that Chekhov's story follows a tradition in Russian nineteenth-century literature since Pushkin, in which Donna Anna and Anna Karenina both figure; just as Chekhov has also observed for himself how Russian woman behave. For, as in all the best short stories, background and behaviour are intensely localized, though without any trace at all of national or ethnic self-consciousness. Miriam Quarterman, in James's story, is in this sense, however, completely the product of a time and place, as are the characters in early Hemingway stories, Kipling's Mary Postgate and Mrs Bathhurst, Chekhov's lady with a dog. To a far greater degree than longer fictions the short story can combine the universal and particular in a short space, so that each enhances the other; and each lends the other, for the reader's benefit, an immediate authority of recognition. Without knowing the background we none the less *know* Miss Quarterman to be the new England girl of her time, just as we know Chekhov's Anna Sergeevna to be the Russian provincial one.

In his enthusiastic review of the first French translation of Anna Karenina Matthew Arnold remarked on the fact that an English woman would not have 'fallen' as rapidly and impetuously as Anna did. Whether or not this is true it indicates a kind of passion in the Russian character which the Russian writer takes for granted, and which Chekhov suggests with inimitable skill in his account of how Gurov and Anna first make love. They have been watching the steamer come in, and Anna peers through her lorgnette 'as if looking for someone she knew', she clumsily drops it. She has been talking animatedly, and then suddenly stops talking and sniffs her bouquet. When Gurov suggests driving out somewhere for the evening she does not reply.

Gurov gives her a quick stare and then embraces her. As an

old roué he recognizes the symptoms. Chekhov's cunning consists in showing how completely she invited her fate, just as she had come to Yalta in the first place to 'live', but at the same time she is not at all 'that' sort of girl. She behaves both wholly naturally and wholly uncharacteristically, and this again gives us an inkling – like the many indeterminate inklings in the tale – of what 'love' is about. To the man in the street, the unsympathetic observer, the person who is not reading the story in fact, she might indeed have seemed to behave at this moment like a pick-up, that 'dog lady' looking for an adventure.

Chekhov's reticence is part of the way in which he gets the appearances, the seaside picture, and the mystery of her other being. Most other writers as naturally frank as he would mention that they continued to go to bed together in Anna's hotel room, would even describe a little their behaviour there. Chekhov says nothing at all except that they were inseparable, they kissed ardently but surreptitiously in quite public places, they drove out to look at local beauty-spots, and that 'these trips were invariably a great success'. Perhaps they never made love again, after that first time? Again love – even physical love this time – is withdrawn into the area of the indeterminate.

Their parting is so moving that the story can be braced up a little after it. Gurov accepts but is saddened by the fact he won't see her again, which makes him want all the more to get away. 'It's time I went north. High time.' (At this point Chekhov even skirts, with a certain insolence, a point he has been keeping out of sight: Why was Gurov, with a wife and young family, all on his own at Yalta in the first place?) But the main thing is that winter has come; everything is different; he plunges back with zeal into his old cheerful routines. But then he realizes that the lady with the dog is still there. He longs for someone to talk about the affair with, but 'What was there to say, anyway? Had he really been in love?' He made vague ponderous observations about women, upon which his wife 'just twitched those dark eyebrows, and told him that "the role of lady-killer doesn't suit you at all, Demetrius".' (Gurov's wife, whom we never meet at first-hand, is a small miracle of economical characterization.) But what makes

Gurov suddenly decide to see Anna again, if he can, is the casual remark a friend throws after him as he leaves the club. 'You were quite right just now – that sturgeon *was* a bit off.'

Gurov has a sudden vision of the awful vulgarity of life. The casual comment is infinitely memorable, and meaningful. It suggests that Gurov himself is as deeply embedded in the routines of vulgarity as his friend, or anyone else; and it is this realization which infuriates him. Moreover the suggestion of fish being a bit 'off' has a specific sexual suggestiveness, reminding us of Anna's tears and her conviction that she had disgraced herself by behaving like a loose woman. Did the affair itself have the same physical vulgarity as his daily life in Moscow seems to have for Gurov? It is this maddening thought which seems to impel him to find out, to discover whether the love affair really had been so magical, so 'different'. With great gentleness and cunning the story plays with the idea of two worlds, as so many such stories do – one gross and palpable, the other mysterious and far away.

The second is the world of love. But is there really any difference between them, or is the happiness and the mystery just illusory?

> ... it would all suddenly come back to him: that event on the pier, the early morning with the mist on the mountains, the Feodisiya steamer, the kisses. He would pace the room for hours, remembering and smiling until these recollections merged into fantasies: until, in his imagination, past fused with future. Though he did not dream of Anna she followed him everywhere like a shadow, watching him. If he closed his eyes he could see her vividly – younger, gentler, more beautiful than she really was. He even saw himself as a better man than he had been back in Yalta.

For the story the indeterminacy of love is the elusiveness of memory and desire, and the illusions they produce. But there must be something there; there must be a way out, a solution. In his strange and moving story 'The Bishop', which Chekhov wrote two years later, near his own death, the dying bishop feels that 'all his past had escaped him to some infinitely remote place, beyond all chance of repetition or continuation.

' "And a very good thing too", he thought.' But, for Gurov, repetition and continuation, the possibility of this other life, of memories going back and reaching blindly forward, has become obsessive, a symptom of love. And it is a torment too. It is a highly accurate touch that he does not dream of Anna, but she pursues him everywhere like a shadow, watching him. We may remember the torment of Vickery, watching every night the shadow of Mrs Bathhurst approaching down the platform, and no doubt having his own memories, which we know nothing of. Kipling's story and 'The Lady with the Dog' were both written at the turn of the century, within a few years of each other, and have an oddly comparable resonance, although Kipling's theme is characteristically mixed with trickery and melodrama, and Chekhov's story is done with tact, taste and understanding. But it is singular that *Traffics and Discoveries*, the collection in which 'Mrs Bathhurst' appeared, consists mostly of inferior work, journalistic sketches of the time, and in that sense comparable to the kind of story which Chekhov, too, produced in large numbers. Both stories have the air of exceptions.

Never exactly a conscious and bracing affair, Chekhov's style became increasingly unemphatic in his last stories, though its effects are as simple and delicate as ever; and phrases like *kak-to* (somehow) lend their own kind of effectiveness to the difficulty of solution or definition. Even anti-climax does nothing to clear things up. After Gurov has resolved to travel to the provincial town where Anna lives, with the hope of seeing her again, he finds the house and sees the dog, but is then stuck in an awful hotel room, and grumbles to himself: 'So much for your romance with ladies with dogs – now you're stuck in this dump.' But then the plan of going to a first night theatre occurs to him, and he does see her, and it is just as wonderful as ever, and she loves him just as much, and takes to coming to Moscow to visit him in a hotel. But there again the sequence of repetition and difference occurs, with Anna crying and Gurov ordering tea in the hotel room and drinking it while she stands with her back to him, facing the window. ' "Let her cry", he thought, "I'll sit down for a bit".' But he knows they have become inseparable in their own way, just as Anna know that her husband 'believes her and doesn't believe her' when she tells him she is going to Moscow to consult a doctor about a female complaint (Gurov has children but we infer that Anna has none, a significant loading of the dice by Chekhov, who may have been thinking of Anna Karenina, torn between her lover and her little boy). They believe and don't believe in a solution; and Gurov reflects on the stasis which must occur in every life, lodged perpetually between what he does in the open and what goes on in secret. 'Each individual life is based on mystery, which is perhaps why civilised man makes such a neurotic fuss about having his privacy respected.'

Their affair is doomed to go on as life goes on, in its duality between what might be and what from day to day actually is. The philosopher Leon Shestov, a profound critic of the inner workings of the Russian novel, observed that Chekhov's wish is to get his characters into a situation from which they cannot possibly escape; and that their vitality, their interest, their Chekhovian 'literariness' as we should say, proceed from this insolubility. This is probably an exaggeration, for in the social aspect of his stories Chekhov is a meliorist, who can point reasonably to all sorts of ways in which things can get and are getting better. If only war and revolution had not prevented them from getting better in Chekhov's way ... But it is true that some of his stories, and 'The Lady with the Dog above all', encapsulate, almost allegorically, the human predicament as both a philosopher and a connoisseur of life's banality might see it. *Zhivaya zhizn* – 'living life' – predicates an impossible situation that is none the less the only possible one. The story ends with the verbal form *nachinaetsya* – 'beginning' – which is like a sigh of despair and recommencement.

And yet the story would not be the masterpiece if it were intended to convey some metaphysics of this sort. Its joy is in its unerring simplicity, its capacity to move the reader, above all in the extraordinary quantity of precise information which it unobtrusively dispenses – about Yalta, about Moscow, the provincial town, the wife, the husband, the two lovers, even the dog. Its method depends on this spare saturation, just as that of 'Mrs Bathurst' depends on scattered hints and speculative exchanges. But the main thing is the simplest of all: that a brief seaside affair has turned into a lifelong passion which can no more be got away from than the conditions of life itself. In the theatre, when he sees her but has not yet spoken to her, Gurov realizes that Anna now absorbs his whole being; that she is, now, (the repetition is significant) 'his grief, his joy, the sole happiness he wants'. Chekhov makes us completely believe in this – a hard thing to do when we think how other love stories fail to make us do so.

Like all great stories 'The Lady with the Dog' has its sense of inner mystery, of one thing hidden inside another; but here the pattern or progress towards the wholly individual effect, which can only be defined by reference to itself and its particular achievement, is turned, as it were, inside out. The mystery is quite simple: a love affair that went on; that became fixated, permanent, instead of following one of the many variants of a beginning to ending course, a course that would itself constitute the pattern of a ready-made narrative. So that, instead of a 'story', we have a 'love'. And in pondering on this we see why most love stories *are* unconvincing: because the element of the story is more important than the fact of the love. By comparison with Chekhov most short story writers, even James and Kipling, are telling 'love stories', of a moving and ingenious kind, in which the 'love' element is the one thing the reader has to accept as a given datum and take on trust. By contrast, the indeterminacy of Chekhov's tale finally produces one thing which cannot be got rid of, which sits unmoving in the path of the story and stops it in its tracks.

Chekhov may have felt just the same about his own problem at the time. He wrote the story at Yalta, where tuberculosis had forced him to settle permanently, and which bored him to distraction. He missed his little estate near Moscow, his friends, the theatre. He was in love with the actress Olga Knipper, from whom he had to endure long periods of separation even after they got married in 1901, though she was with him when he died in Germany two years later. There is thus a lot of 'life' – his own at the time painfully distracted and discontented life – in the story, as well as the feeling that his art is bringing to its creator some kind of relief or compensation. And this impression of a peculiar kind of

directness between life and story, as if the genre could
exercise its own special form of autobiography, is a fact very
much to be reckoned with where the masters of the genre are
concerned.

James's stories disclose it in their own way; so, and much
more obviously, do Hemingway's. But the writers whose
consciousness has a special relation to their stories, in a way it
does not have to their novels, are Hardy and D. H. Lawrence.
Both appear to use the story, in their own ways, as a kind of
safety-valve, for things in their mentalities which demanded
direct and even crude expression. The novel, with all its
greater resources and relative demonstrations, negated this
kind of reductive process. The story lets it out, drastically and
simply. The *sureness* of Lawrence's stories, a merry confident
sureness, at once derisive and tender, seems to come from the
fact that the form releases something in him, while the novel
form commits him to repetitiousness, overstatement,
bullying. Not all his stories are entirely direct: the best have
an inside to them, a cryptic quality. But behind the events of
the story, many of which, like the characters, are taken
straight from life, we can feel the sureness of what Lawrence
wants, and what he is, as he arranges everything for his own
benefit. His famous remark about trusting the tale, not the
teller, is true in one sense: the tale is so wholly the teller's
instrument that it is like an extension of his will, an expression
of desire which could not be formulated in any other way. In
this respect Hemingway's best stories are very similar,
though without the equivocation which is so human and
fascinating in a Lawrentian tale.

For Lawrence's manipulation of the tale and participation
in it is both calmly underhand and at the same time
shameless, as if he were making a great joke. He puts himself
and his desires into the tale in exaggerated form – as Maurice
Pervin in 'The Blind Man', Henry Grenfel in 'The Fox',
Lewis in 'St Mawr', Hepburn in 'The Captain's Doll', Alan
Anstruther in 'The Border Line' (a demon-lover story), even
as the mysterious Indians in 'The Woman Who Rode Away'.
This confident indication of what he is and wants gives the
stories their hypnotic, as if predestined, power and vividness.
They depend upon the opposite of that indeterminacy – the

unanswered question – which has so many variations as a story formula.

In her well-known story 'Bliss', Katherine Mansfield made the fatal error of coming under Lawrence's spell, in terms of literary influence, without realizing what its true significance was. The result is a story which is half-way between Chekhov and Lawrence, but lacking the being of either and unable to find one of its own. Its chief fault, oddly enough, lies in its attempt to be dispassionate, cool and objective; in the absence in it of the determining Lawrentian figure of power. And it is satiric, or would-be satiric, where Lawrence's syntax in the stories seems constantly trembling with suppressed amusement at the expense of somebody or something or other – a very different thing. This agile gaiety goes with his lordly conviction, which in the stories is never insufferable or boring, as it can be in the novels. In 'Bliss' the author's handling of her heroine is, by contrast, merely pert. And her sympathy makes the narrative tone waver uncertainly. Husband and wife seem equally fatuous, and the husband's pursuit of the other woman of no significance. The innerness of the story depends on its suggestion of a lesbian attraction between the heroine and the other woman, who seems prepared to have a rather vulgar intrigue with her husband; also on the wife suddenly feeling physically attracted to her husband, whereas before their relation has been that of 'good pals'. The story bids for pathos here, in the image of the happy young wife who is secretly worried about her lack of response, images which are manipulated to converge on that of the husband's face, alight with the pleasure of his own intrigue, and the pear-tree motionless in all its blossom. These are the proper ingredients of a good short story, but just because here they are so too emphatically they fail to come entirely alive, remaining fixed only in a striking pose. Elements that are vulnerable and interesting in the story – the undercurrents of lesbianism, the inner consciousness of the wife – remain detached from this pose, free-floating as if helplessly, as if in the stream of a Virginia Woolf prose: and she, of all writers, is least by nature a composer of short stories.

Some of Lawrence's best tales, and the ones that seem most

to ease his own instincts and desires, employ a device which has a curious affinity with Kipling's use of delusion, as in 'Mary Postgate' or 'Mrs Bathhurst'. In those stories the reader is as much deluded as the character, and in the same way. Tacitly, the ring of narrators all feel that the second fire-blackened tramp is, in some sense, Mrs Bathhurst, and the reader involuntarily feels it with them. Lawrence uses the delusive event for a different purpose: to correspond with the real wishes of the character who embodies the dynamism of the tale. Its events have one hidden among them which can only have happened in the fantasy area of the hero's will, such as the defenestration of Mrs Hepburn in 'The Captain's Doll', and the death by a falling tree of Banford in 'The Fox'. If the hero of 'The Fox' were a real murderer, who had engineered the girl's death deliberately to make it look like an accident, the story would have no significance. The point is that Henry *is* a murderer, in his own mind and desires, as Lawrence himself certainly was, and no doubt many of us are: a man who is quite ruthless in getting what he wants at the expense of other people, who, like Banford, can be felt to have no 'real' existence. The lack of a proper Lawrentian existence in the frail and querulous Banford means that actual existence can be terminated as an act of the will by the hero on behalf of the author.

The disconcerting thing is that this makes no difference to the quality of the story and its mesmeric effectiveness. Perhaps indeed it is part of the 'joke', on which many stories of Lawrence's mature period seem to be based. Their seriousness is often involved in their not taking themselves all that seriously. And an odd consequence of Lawrence's sly use of delusion, or 'imaginary event', is that the tales in which it occurs always seem dramatically brief, whatever their comparative length: 'St Mawr', which works much more like one of the novels, seems by contrast even longer than it actually is. Even blindness, in 'The Blind Man', is created by Lawrence as an imaginary, an exploratory, situation. Blinded in the war, Maurice Pervin enters 'a new way of consciousness', which gives him a mysterious authority and domination, the kind of authority Lawrence himself possessed over others, or wished to possess. His imagination of the state of blindness is as uncannily vivid and delicate as his imagination of the state of being a fish or an animal, and yet at the same time, and for the same reason, it is a situation in his own mind and created for his own will, as Hepburn in 'The Captain's Doll' seems to create the death of his wife, who falls out of the window; and young Henry, in 'The Fox', actually does engineer the death of Banford, by planning how the tree he is chopping down will fall on her. These events seem to make, as it were, organic stories, as if their protagonist were creating action or situation in the same way that the author does in creating the tale.

Many are variations on the same theme: Lawrence's simple assertion of how he wants to be. In 'The Blind Man' the hero, Maurice Pervin, achieves domination over Bertie, his wife's friend, by asking to touch him. Bertie 'suffered as the blind man stretched out a strong naked hand to him'. The marvellously apt word 'naked' suggests the extremeness of the transposition. Blindness is nakedness, the condition of sexual intercourse. But in such situations Lawrence always achieves the saving incongruity, the suggestion of a joke.

> Maurice accidentally knocked off Bertie's hat.
> 'I thought you were taller,' he said, starting. Then he laid his hand on Bertie Reid's head, closing the dome of the skull in a soft, firm grasp, gathering it, as it were; then, shifting his grasp and softly closing again, with a fine, close pressure, till he had covered the skull and the face of the smaller man, tracing the brows, and touching the full, closed eyes, touching the small nose and the nostrils, the rough, short moustache, the rather strong chin. The hand of the blind man grasped the shoulder, the arm, the hand of the other man. He seemed to take him, in the soft, travelling grasp.

It is one of the most erotic passages in Lawrence, much more so than anything in the novels. The joke about the hat is succeeded by the soft caressive passage, full of the hesitancy of commas, which explores the body until the final moment of 'taking', and the strength of the 'soft, travelling grasp'. The character of Bertie is based on that of J. M. Barrie, the playwright, whom Lawrence had met through Lady Cynthia Asquith, and who combined great kindness and sympathy with a horror of any sort of physical intimacy. He was also a very short man.

Lawrence's imagination of the encounter combines a joke with a very intense realization of his own desires. There is something very funny, which Lawrence was no doubt well aware of, in the idea of the two men standing in this involuntary togetherness, but it is also a matter he took very seriously. Maurice clasps the unfortunate Bertie's hand.

> 'Oh, my God,' he said, 'we shall know each other now, shan't we? We shall know each other now.'
>
> Bertie could not answer. He gazed mute and terror-struck, overcome by his own weakness. He knew he could not answer. He had an unreasonable fear, lest the other man should suddenly destroy him. Whereas Maurice was actually filled with hot, poignant love, the passion of friendship which Bertie shrank from most.
>
> 'We're all right together now, aren't we?' said Maurice. 'It's all right now, as long as we live, so far as we're concerned?'
>
> 'Yes,' said Bertie, trying by any means to escape.

In these remarkable stories the element of comedy, almost of farce, itself constitutes the inner dimension of the story, its mystery almost. 'The Blind Man' is a particularly vivid example of this. Maurice has never previously got on with Bertie, the great friend of his wife Isabel, and this was a source of distress to her. But now he is blind, Maurice can claim the physical authority over Bertie which he has always wanted, and Bertie has to put up with it. There is an obvious resemblance to Lawrence's male friendships, particularly that with Middleton Murry, but here it is transformed by humour and art, and by the pressure of the imaginary event. The pair go in to the wife, and Maurice says 'We've become friends', standing with his feet apart, like a strange colossus. 'I'm so glad,' says Isabel, 'in sheer perplexity', and she darts a glance at Bertie, who meets it with 'a furtive, haggard look'. And the story ends with swift abruptness. 'You'll be happier now, dear,' she says to her husband, as if soothing some strange little boy, and she knows that Bertie has 'one desire – to escape from this intimacy, this friendship, which had been thrust upon him.'

Sometimes the joke is so elaborate and prolonged that it runs away with and deceives the reader, rather as Kipling's delusory skills do in the cases of 'Mary Postgate' and 'Mrs Bathhurst'. I think this is what happens in the case of 'The Woman Who Rode Away', which is usually regarded as a case of solemn Lawrentian absurdity and mumbo-jumbo with race consciousness. It seems to me that this comes from the fact that Lawrence is enjoying the joke too much, throwing himself into it with a sort of sensuous abandon. The weight of the novel form in *The Plumed Serpent* means that he cannot do this, but the art of the story allows it, however equivocal the effect may be. Two key points come very early. The apparently cynical and experienced traveller, Ledermann, who asks scornfully 'What's wonderful' about the Indians and the mountains, 'in fact felt some of the vulgar excitement at the idea of ancient and mysterious savages'. And the woman herself is 'overcome by a foolish romanticism more unreal than a girl's.' 'She felt it was her destiny to wander into the secret haunts of these timeless, mysterious, marvellous Indians of the mountains.'

Lawrence, in fact, is very cunning at having it both ways. He gets in his own way the duality, the inner and outer selves, of which there are so many variants in our type of narrative. As a story 'The Woman Who Rode Away' is both deliberately vulgar and inwardly mysterious: the woman herself a person of silly ideas and restless dissatisfactions, who none the less finds a 'true destiny'. Her sacrifice by the Indians is one of Lawrence's imaginary events, like the killing of Banford or the defenestration of Mrs Hepburn; but here it is dignified by that most fundamental of Lawrentian laws for women – the complete and voluntary submission to a will stronger than her own. This is the inner point of the story, and not the Indian mumbo-jumbo, about which Lawrence himself is secretly a little derisive, as is shown by the tone of the conversation the woman has with the young Indian in the hidden village.

This swift narrative equivocation, quite absent in the portentous longueurs of *The Plumed Serpent*, is found in several stories and often takes the form of sardonic paradox. In 'The Border Line' it is the ghost of the heroine's husband, killed in the war, who is *warm* ('the warm, powerful, silent ghost had come back to her') while her present husband, whom she married out of affection and pity, is cold and clinging, and actually dies of cold. The story, usually censured or passed over in censorious silence by critics who take Lawrence himself very seriously, is in fact a brilliant and humorous *tour de force*, like most of the 'imaginary event' stories. The triangle of Lawrence, Frieda and Middleton Murry as lovers, with its accompanying jealousies and hatreds on Lawrence's part, is transformed by his story-telling art, which exploits ambiguity and his own peculiar sense of fun, as well as reiterating what he requires from women and from men.

As the ghost is warm and the lover cold in 'The Border Line', so in 'The Princess' the 'Sheikh' figure – Romero – who carries off and seduces the princess, is feeble and doomed, while she is contemptuous and untouchable. Lawrence has fun with his inversion of the vulgar and popular 'Sheikh' mythology of the 1920s, in which modern woman is swept off her feet by masterful and primitive man. He himself seems present in the tale in the broodingly vivid picture of the trees and the Rocky Mountains. He emphasizes their 'ponderous involved mass', all 'kneeling heavily', and 'the strange squalor of the primitive forest', all things beyond the will of the princess, who none the less has intense desire to reach the top and look into the 'inner chaos' of the mountains, among their 'lumpish peaks'. The story makes explicit what is already implied in 'The Captain's Doll' and 'The Woman Who Rode Away' – mountains bulking ambiguously in the body of the stories. They are, after all, the first works of art to convey with such power that mountains and 'scenery' are a nothingness beyond the human will, and having no connection with it. With considerable skill and malice Lawrence brings together the 'squalor' of primeval nature ('what a tangle of decay and despair lay in the virgin forests') and the squalid emptiness of sex itself, as forced on the princess by the vacuous rather than mysterious Romero. Romero's sullen 'I'll make you like it' echoes the popular determination to 'like' nature, to find mountains, forests and beaches beautiful and accommodating. There is no Lawrentian symbol in the story as there is in 'St Mawr': it is entirely bleak but extremely bracing. Lawrence never achieved with such effective economy a sense of the contrast between ordinary human consciousness – wanting this and that – and the outside world. Among the mountains the princess in her pretty clothes – orange and yellow and buff – 'felt quite in the picture'.

> From her saddle-pouches she took the packages of lunch, spread a little cloth, and sat to wait for Romero. Then she made a little fire. Then she ate a devilled egg. Then she ran after Tansy, who was straying across-stream. Then she sat in the sun, in the stillness near the aspens, and waited.

The syntax is parodic, but also merrily spontaneous. The princess is as busy as a chipmunk or the consciousness in a Hemingway fishing story. In the next few paragraphs we hear the echo of the word 'then' against the word 'nothing', as a pair of Indians ride out of the trees, 'swathed like seated mummies in their pale-grey cotton blankets'. The Indians have nothing, mean nothing. Twice one of them laughs 'his little meaningless laugh'.

But the story is careful not to stress the contrast too much. It is full of moments of lightness, and the sense of death and vacancy is no more emphasized than it is in 'The Lady with the Dog', at the quiet moment when the lovers sit and hear the boom of the surf below them, Gurov reflecting that it was there before and will continue afterwards. Temperamentally Lawrence is as different from Chekhov as could be, and in the stories that temperament comes glinting out in all its shameless simplicity, identifying with its victims. Lawrence knows the extent to which he is the princess, or 'The Man who Loved Islands', even the Woman Who Rode Away. A derisive part of him enjoys identifying with her vigorously earnest Germanic romanticism (Frieda's) and likes the idea of being held down by dark muscular men and sacrificed. He mocks American restlessness, but is himself the most restless of men, and knows it; and that knowledge permeates all his stories with a kind of liberating joy. So does his knowledge of his own sexuality, with its dependence on women and its desire for men. Dependence on his victims is indeed a striking feature of the stories, as if he knew that they could not be created without those victims, and without his identification with them.

Victims they are, none the less, for the sadistic impulse in Lawrence's character gets free rein in the stories. Yet there is something in the story form, and in his mastery of it, which associates victim and author in a kind of comradeship. In the little story called 'Smile', Matthew, an obvious portrait of Middleton Murry, travels to a convent in Italy to see his sick and estranged wife, much as the real Middleton Murry paid his last visit to Katherine Mansfield at the Gurdjief Institute near Paris. Lawrence catches to a tee Murry's priggish-naive responses, and his desire for ritual suffering and repentance – Matthew sits up all night in the train when he might have slept in a *wagon-lit* – but he also exhibits the shameless element in Murry's nature which must have held the two men together. When the Mother Superior shows him his dead wife, and lifts the veil of lawn from her face, 'something leaped like laughter in the depths of him, he gave a little grunt, and an extraordinary smile came over his face'. At the sight of it the three nuns begin to smile too, and he feels the dead woman digging him in the ribs, to make him smile. It is an extraordinary tribute to something in Katherine Mansfield's nature which Lawrence discerned, and to Murry himself: the paragraph describing the nuns, and their three different smiles, is one of the most delicious and disarming in his prose. The smile is wholly spontaneous. But Matthew does not want to smile; he wants to wear the look of 'super-martyrdom', and to say '*Mea Culpa*'.

> They hovered in fascinating bewilderment. He ducked for the door. But even as he went, the smile began to come on his face, caught by the tail of the sturdy sister's black eye, with its everlasting twink. And, he was secretly thinking, he wished he could hold both her creamy-dusky hands, that were folded like mating birds, voluptuously ...
>
> The three women left behind in the room looked at one another, and their hands flew up for a moment, like six birds flying suddenly out of the foliage, then settling again.

Lawrence's own fascination with the idea of the nuns mingles with his rapid, bird-like analysis of the strange difference in

Murry's nature (but perhaps no stranger than in those of our own) between spontaneous movements and desires and those which their owner thinks proper and suitable, and owing to himself. Just as spontaneous as his desire to smile is Matthew's agitation at the end of the story when he finds that he has lost his hat. When the nuns spot him again, in the cold distance at the corridor's end, 'the Mother Superior suddenly pressed her pace into an appearance of speed'. He sees them bearing down on him, 'these voluminous figures with framed faces and lost hands', and 'never was man more utterly smileless'.

The innerness of the story contrasts vividly not only with a merely vulgar attempt at a 'portrait' of Murry, like Aldous Huxley's of Burlap in *Point Counter Point*, but with Lawrence's own horrible letters to and about Katherine Mansfield and Murry. The story has turned all that to delicacy, gaiety and understanding. And something of the same sort happens in 'The Fox' and 'The Captain's Doll', two of Lawrence's most masterly tales, even though the 'imaginary event' in both is the willed death of an inconvenient character; inconvenient, that is to say, to the working out of the hero's fantasy of what he wants for himself.

Although the tales are quite different in manner their inner statement is the same. The man is free to do as he wishes, to get what he wants. To an unsympathetic woman 'he's bossy, and he's selfish through and through'. But to a receptive woman the authentic male is fascinating, and beyond judgement. The aristocratic young German women in 'The Captain' Doll' (Frieda and her sister) laugh at the captain and mock at him between themselves, and make a doll to burlesque his most fetching masculine attribute – his long legs in their tight trousers. Their purpose is to tame and enclose him in their own way, as he has already been caged to suit her own style by his wife, who pays for the emasculated little *ménage* she has set up by falling out of the window. Both Captain Hepburn and young Henry in 'The Fox' aim to break into and break out of the feminine enclosure, and get what they want from the women in their own way.

But down inside the stories are already secretly moving in another direction, stealing like the fox; slipping past like the

Germans on the ice slope in 'The Captain's Doll', who 'were scrambling like crabs past our hero, doing better than he'. The reader can feel that Lawrence is perfectly well aware of this contrary direction, and that it gives him pleasure, as an artist and as his own man. The women who seem to give in, like March in 'The Fox', or who cheerfully engage in the sex war, like Hannelel in 'The Captain's Doll', are alike in their inner female confidence, a confidence not shared by bossy women like Banford and the captain's wife. So that while the man is getting what he wants in his own way, the woman is doing the same in hers ('But he isn't,' says March quietly, when Banford accuses her of letting young Henry think he's the master) and the stories use the inbuilt ability of the short narrative form to illustrate in their depth the secret criss-cross process. In 'The Lady with the Dog' Chekhov does something very similar, showing the wholly different expectations and responses of Gurov and Anna, on which their intimacy grows.

An extremely funny scene in 'The Captain's Doll' reveals the difference in farcical terms. Hannele and Hepburn converse on a bus by screaming at each other in order to be heard above its noise. (Its driver, as he sets it vindictively in motion, silently rejoices that 'another beastly trip was over, another infernal joyful holiday done with'.)

> 'In fact,' he shouted, 'I realised that, as far as I was concerned, love was a mistake.'
> '*What* was a mistake?' she screamed.
> 'Love,' he bawled.

Male pomposity is compelled to explain its most cherished notions in this ridiculous fashion. And they were indeed Lawrence's own notions – his extreme dislike of 'love', of being adored, of the woman who wants you to adore her. All these are commonplaces of his attitude, but the story gives them subtle and original play; revealing too, with unexpected humour and sympathy, Lawrence's sense of 'Germanness' with its own nuances of derision and enthusiasm. (It is significant that Chekhov's originality deserts him on this point in 'The Lady with the Dog', and he makes Anna's husband Von Diederitz conform to the sterotyped fictional model of a Russian of German extraction.)

But in both stories the most subtle effect remains unspoken, a looming presence towards their conclusion, indicating that a story is never self-sufficient and self-insulated; that for the artist life goes on, as in 'The Lady with the Dog', continuing the problematic situations which the story has explored. Young Henry, in 'The Fox', has got what he wanted, but 'the blue flower' of happiness still eludes him. We can feel the same situation awaiting Hepburn in 'The Captain's Doll'. The search in some sense has been in vain, for the unspoken target – male friendship – remains below the horizon of achievement, making it less than satisfactory, and even diminishing 'the imaginary event' – the fantasy deaths of the women who get in the way – which had seemed the key to that achievement.

Lawrence remarked that the great thing about the novel form was that it was so 'incapable of the absolute', incapable, that is, of clear-cut statement and metaphysical conclusions. It must live, like its characters and situations, in a relative world. The same is true of his short stories, but with an important difference. The explicit fantasy on his own life problems is left hanging in the air, with a certain irony which is itself part of the story's formal effect. 'The Woman Who Rode Away' breaks off before the sacrifice of the woman takes place, as if Lawrence were shrugging his shoulders, dismissing a fantasy which he knew to be self-willed. No doubt there appealed to him the notion of a tiresome, pseudo-romantic woman, living on vulgar female dreams and illusions, who finds herself in the grip of true and genuine male powers, rituals and necessities. Thus in creation he both amused himself and took revenge on silly bossy women like Frieda, on whom he none the less knew he depended.

Hardy, too, can give the impression of using the short story as a means of easing his most direct and elemental urges and emotions. Some of his tales, like 'Barbara of the House of Grebe', to which T. S. Eliot so vehemently objected, saying that it portrayed 'a world of pure evil', are actually designed by Hardy as anecdotes circulating in a world no more good or bad in itself than is any community, but intended to appeal to its connoisseurs of the macabre. Where his audiences were concerned Hardy was a shrewd psychologist, concocting in the collection called 'A Group of Noble Dames' a traditional mixture of horror and class, the Gothic fantasy and the aristocratic background. His sense of fact, of the humdrum nature of things, informs the gruesome twists and turns of anecdote and gives them at times the peculiar kind of staid repulsiveness which Eliot noted and deplored. Hardy took more than the average pleasure in nastiness, and his temperament was passively sadistic in a manner quite compatible with real pity for the lot of humans and animals, as with all kinds of humane views and responses. But, more than that, his own experience and feeling come straight and precisely into a tale in the same way that Lawrence's do, and inform his creative powers in a fashion at once more direct and more underhand than they do in his novels.

Hardy's little collection of stories provides a singularly clear instance of the difference between anecdotes, told in an effective and craftsmanlike manner, and the short story in which the writer himself is deeply involved, and in which the element of explorative fantasy gives the form its special individuality and perspective. Two of the stories – – 'The Withered Arm' and 'The Fiddler of the Reels' – have been much admired and anthologized, but there is a dead quality about them: they have all the faults of Hardy's fiction and few of the virtues. The same is true of 'The Distracted Preacher', 'A Tragedy of Two Ambitions', and even of 'The Son's Veto', the story which Hardy himself said he thought the best of. It is easy to see why. The story contains, and in a very intense form, the ruminations on sex and society which he had brooded on all his life; his awareness of the various kinds of implacability which society showed towards marriages ill-assorted in terms of class; probably even his own long experience of a wife who declined to have any social relation with his mother, and a mother who maintained her own isolation in regard to his wife. Hardy, who acquiesced passively in whatever social arrangements had befallen him, and who found consolation in a sedulous pursuit of the London *beau monde*, nourished his own kind of secret resentments, and keenly observed the pains and sacrifices to which class consciousness gave rise.

But here is the source of the trouble. The indignation in the tale of 'The Son's Veto' is too clearly self-indulged. The author is proud of having, or at least of showing, the right feelings. There is no underlying honesty in the story, of the involuntary kind which is essential to the form at its best. Hardy's real interest is, quite naturally, in the woman he portrays, but only as a woman, a creature of his own observation and reverie, not as the wife and mother who is the story's pathetic victim. Sophy Twycott has been the vicar's parlourmaid; has married the vicar; has found herself transported in consequence from the pleasant Wessex country to an ugly south London parish, for her husband knows quite well that he commits 'social suicide' in marrying her, and has exchanged to a parish where nobody knows him. Sent to a grand public school, her only son comes to feel ashamed of her, and at last fiercely forbids her, when she is left a widow, to think of marriage with her old sweetheart, now a prosperous greengrocer. The story ends with Sophy's funeral procession, and her son, 'a young smooth-shaven priest in a high waistcoat', looking blackly at the tradesman who has ventured to attend it.

The point is too plain, and so is the intention of pathos. The story may suggest to us that the best in the genre, although they are set in a specific period and culture, and may indeed call a special kind of attention to it, are none the less independent of the particular local object lessons and emotions connected with it. Hardy's pity for the mother and indignation at the son are in this sense not fundamentally true emotions, where art is concerned, but localized by his intentions towards the reader of the time. In 1930 the young Evelyn Waugh published in the *Evening Standard* an article called ' "Tess" as a Modern Sees It', in which he commented that 'the trouble about the pessimism of *Tess* is that it is bogus'. That is a very shrewd perception in its day and age, for Waugh intuited that Hardy's pessimism in the novel, like his sentimentality about Tess herself, were Hardy's way of expressing and exploiting a fashion of the time. The success of *Tess* shows how well he did it, but the truest and most intimate parts of the novel are Hardy's vision and day-dream of Tess herself, and not the way in which he exploits and moralizes her fate at the hands of society.

The same thing is true of 'The Son's Veto', and the small scale of the story makes it more obvious. Hardy's gloomy denunciation of society, and the son who is its representative, is, if not bogus, mechanical enough to create that fatal air of predictability which no good short story can afford. As in the case of Tess, what really matters for Hardy's imagination, and thus for his reader, is the woman herself. And here the story contains some remarkably engaging and characteristic instances of Hardyan viewpoint. It must be almost the only fiction which opens with the heroine being seen from behind; more precisely, from the back of her head. Hardy the voyeur has approached, as it were, from an unexpected angle.

> To the eyes of a man viewing it from behind, the nut-brown hair was a wonder and a mystery. Under the black beaver hat surmounted by its tuft of black feathers, the long locks, braided and twisted and coiled like the rushes of a basket, composed a rare, if somewhat barbaric, example of ingenious art. One could understand such weavings and coilings being wrought to last intact for a year, or even a calendar month; but that they should all be demolished regularly at bed-time, after a single day of permanence seemed a reckless waste of successful fabrication.

That opening very exactly conveys both the virtues and the limitations of the story. Like all good short stories it is told in 'glimpses', but Hardy bears down too hard on the method itself, and draws attention to it instead of allowing it to seem natural. (A page or so further on he says of the heroine: 'The next glimpse we get of her is when she appears in the mournful attire of a widow.') At the same time, the opening glimpse of Sophy Twycross's hair is a brilliant stroke in term's of the story's atmosphere, for as we should expect this emphasizes the unnaturalness of the whole life and society with which the story is concerned. Sophy marries the parson instead of her old admirer the gardener, later greengrocer; her son grows up ashamed of her; she spends hours a day on her coiffure. When the parson dies he is buried in a 'well-packed cemetery' in south London, where if all the dead had awakened and stood up live, no one would have recognized him. This was the worst thing possible for Hardy, for whom one of the most important things in life was to lie dead at last with friends, family, and fellowtownsmen beside you. It should not be forgotten that his social pertinacity during the London season, and in high society, was not just snobbishness: it was instinctive for him to live in and be accepted by a community, and his anomalous position at Dorchester isolated him almost in the way that Sophy Twycross was isolated by her unnatural life in south London, with a husband and son from whom her background makes her essentially estranged.

'The Son's Veto' carries a social 'message' in a way that was becoming fashionable for short stories at the time it was written: Hardy had read de Maupassant and the other French writers whose method had been influenced by the social side of Flaubert's stories and by *Madame Bovary*. Even Robert Louis Stevenson, in distant Samoa, was to take pride in having written a story, 'The Beach at Falesa', in which he felt that he had been pioneer in realizing and embodying the feel of a new kind of society, and how things already went wrong in it. As in *Tess*, Hardy is concerned in 'The Son's Veto' with what he calls in the story 'a woman of pure instincts', but his own view of her, as of Tess herself, is not especially pure, and the hidden life of his glimpses and reflections seems separate from the social views of the story, making them seem weaker and more strident. In the scale of *Tess* as novel these separate ingredients get on better together, but the story compresses them, and at the same time reveals Hardy's hidden life much more frankly than the novel does. The truest and most spontaneous things in 'The Son's Veto' are Hardy's own glimpses not only of his heroine, but of the country quietly stealing into the town in the early hours of the morning, when green produce goes by up to Covent Garden, and the sleepless Sophy is comforted by the sight of it, and even by the 'aged nighthorses' who plod along pulling the carts. Hardy's pity is itself complete and natural here, as he watches Sophy watching the nightly procession of vegetables.

In the earlier story 'A Mere Interlude' there is the same curiously intimate collusion with the heroine, which at the same time leaves her a stranger to Hardy and to the reader. It

is as if the story method contrived to bring us close its
heroine, but only in the sense tht we seem to follow her by
stealth. This occurs in spite of the fact that there is a notional
narrator, a 'traveller in school-books', who has made a
'confidential study' of her, so that the frame of the narrative
seems cool and judicious. Hardy likes the idea of still waters
that run deep, and of an impassive young woman who has
agreed to marry an older man, has suddenly met a former
admirer and agreed on the impulse to marry him instead; has
lost him by drowning within twenty-four hours, and has
returned quietly to her native place to wed her original suitor.
In our 'feminist' times it is interesting to see that Hardy was
perfectly well aware of the secret independence of women's
feelings – feelings which the social conventions of the age kept
well below the surface – and was fascinated by them. The
heroines of his stories are not expanded and romanticized by
sentiment, as happens in varying degree in the novels, but are
presented laconically, almost brutally. Of course, that does
not prevent Hardy having his usual tenderness for them; or
from both identifying with them and looking at them like a
voyeur.

In 'An Imaginative Woman' Hardy plays with the idea of
the brief encounter – the one glimpsed who might have been
all in another fate or in a different life – but he also gives it, as
he does in many of his poems, a local dimension and a sad,
penetrative humour. Hardy's better stories specialize in
something missing – something from his own life – which he
transposes into the mood and setting of a tale. The humour of
'An Imaginative Woman' lies in the fact that not only does the
woman never meet the man she adores from having read his
poems, but that Hardy has got inside her to the extent that he
makes the poet a genuinely romantic and elusive figure, seen
as he is through the eyes of the imaginative woman; while at
the same time the reader is aware of him as a commonplace
young man whose poetry is not much above the average in the
fashion of the age.

The story is both heavy and naive, and yet its very
artificiality enhances the effect of something infinitely
touching and vulnerable. The story's form and emotion is
supremely banal, but has nothing of the care and

sophistication with which Flaubert or Joyce would have built up the idea of banality. As he might do in a poem, Hardy makes the very silliness of the narrative move the reader deeply; making the story seem like 'life', as it does in the case of 'The Lady with the Dog', and at the same time portraying with great insight the absurdity of daydream, and its hold over a helpless consciousness wholly pinned down by the conditions of life. The heroine's sense of her poet as 'nearer my real self, more intimate with the real me' than is her husband, even though she has never seen the poet, is conveyed with complete conviction by Hardy in a manner which only the story form could lend to the most secluded part of him. Here it is the ideal mask for intimacy. The heroine, who finds herself living in the poet's seaside lodgings, while he is staying a short distance away, and who is always just about to meet him but never quite succeeds, even finds herself lying in the bed he occupies and deciphering his pencil scribbles on the wall beside it.

> . . . no doubt the thoughts and spirit-strivings which had come to him in the dead of night, when he could let himself go and have no fear of the frost of criticism . . . And now her hair was dragging where his arm had lain when he secured the fugitive fancies; she was sleeping on a poet's lips, immersed in the very essence of him . . .

No doubt Hardy himself sometimes composed in this way, temporarily oblivious of the critics, who might have raised their eyebrows at the word 'dragging', whose rightness, in a Hardyan context, seems to sum up all the pathos and vulnerability of the tale.

'On the Western Circuit' has the same theme of isolation, of a longing for love and the communication of love, but it is a far more simple and natural story, without any of Hardy's pleasure in, and frequent dependence on, the grotesque. It is indeed something of a masterpiece in its own way; at least comes as near to being one as Hardy's use of the story form, for his own particular sort of emotional need, can take him. In 'An Imaginative Woman' there is the not unfamiliar contrast, where Hardy's fictions are concerned, between the truth and power of the feelings displayed and the gaucheness of the story's contrivance. In a sense the two get on perfectly well, but an impression of something coarse remains – coarseness and delicacy having a curious relationship in the texture of Hardy's stories – which is more muted in the texture of 'On the Western Circuit', and subtly effective where it exists, rather than the reverse.

'An Imaginative Woman' uses absurdity almost in the manner of an Elizabethan play – after the coincidental failure of all her efforts to get in touch with her poet, and tell him how she loves him, the heroine hears he has committed suicide in a fit of despondency after a severe review of his volume of verses entitled 'Lyrics to A Woman Unknown'. Her grief is absurdly but totally moving, caused as it is by her forlorn sense that had she met him she could have touched him, comforted him, given him love. Hardy is remarkably – if probably unintentionally – successful in distinguishing this longing from any sort of erotic feeling on his heroine's part. But he provides one of the endings he was apt to fancy: his heroine dies in childbirth, and her husband, to whom she has revealed some of her feelings about the poet, finds a lock of hair among her possessions when he is about to remarry, two years later, and looks at the child with a sudden conviction that it is the poet's, and not his own.

No such contrivances are necessary to the story 'On the Western Circuit'. The title refers to the hero's occupation: that of a junior barrister who comes to the town of Melchester – Hardy's Salisbury – in the course of the legal year, and meets at a fairground the young woman, Anna, an orphan from a lonely village on Salisbury Plain, and now the servant and protegée of Mrs Harnham, the wife of an elderly wine merchant. The story opens with two touches characteristic of Hardy, and suited to the subdued accuracy of its events. 'The man who played the disturbing part in the two quiet feminine lives hereunder depicted – no great man, in any sense, by the way – first had knowledge of them on an October evening, in the city of Melchester.' That first sentence is echoed by another at the end of the second paragraph. 'Thitherward he went, passing under an arched gateway, along a straight street, and into the square'. Charles Raye, the young barrister, has been gazing at the cathedral, 'the most homogeneous pile of architecture in England, which towered and tapered from the damp and level sward'. He then decides that the fair in progress in the market square is the greater attraction, and Hardy's method cannot resist sober accuracy, detailing how he gets there by a route that anyone who has been to the town can still recognize. This accuracy, a feature, of course, of every one of Hardy's narratives, has a natural affinity with the comment thrown off in the first sentence, that Raye is no great man in any sense – merely one of the humdrum denizens of the nineteenth century's last decade, a 'middle-class male'. Prosaic truth goes with ordinariness. More important, we are seeing here in this Hardy story a very decided feature of the most effective modern short stories, which we shall meet again in Joyce's masterpiece, 'The Dead'. The 'ordinariness' of their characters is not only evident but is strongly emphasized by the writer in various ways, overt or concealed: and it is contrasted with the epiphany of the story – to use Joyce's phrase – which gives a flare of uniqueness, illumination, apotheosis, to a humdrum background.

In Hardy's story an epiphany of this sort is the first event; and it marks his usual sense of things in life taking an entropic form. If anything good occurs what succeeds is likely to be less so. So Charles Raye passes under the arched gateway of the close, and down the straight street to the square where the fair is in progress. There he sees a pretty girl seated on one of the horses of a merry-go-round, so absorbed in the pleasure that her features are 'rapt in an ecstatic dreaminess'. 'She was absolutely unconscious of anything save the act of riding'. It is this total happiness which so strongly attracts him, full of 'vague latter-day glooms and popular melancholies' as he is.

The epiphany is effortless, and like all its kind it is for the moment – the moment in life, the moment of a story – complete. Hardy makes this perception itself a question of contrast: his noticing of the roar and glare of the steam machinery, and its decorations, in conjunction with the effortless smoothness and silence of the mechanical horses' rise and fall. I do not think either Hardy or his reader make the connection, to which a more modern story writer would draw attention in some way or other, between this riding on the merry-go-round (though of course the young woman would be riding 'side-saddle') and the idea of sexual bliss. What concerns both narrator and reader is rather the inevitability, once the young man has smiled on and spoken to the rider, of a love sensation between them.

> Each time that she approached the half of her orbit that lay nearest him they gazed at each other with smiles, and with that unmistakable expression which means so little at the moment, yet so often leads up to passion, heart-ache, union, disunion, devotion, overpopulation, drudgery, content, resignation, despair.

Metaphorically the reader rubs his eyes for a moment, and feels inclined to say, 'Well, really, Mr Hardy'. The tone of the tale has changed. The quiet, mature knowledgeability of the opening ('no great man, in any sense, by the way') has suddenly given place to this excitable, show-off manner, worthy of a young man's debating society. From affecting to be old and wise, the fifty-two-year-old author has suddenly plunged back into the expression and outlook of a very young man. And this expression, and the way it comes about, seem highly spontaneous, as if the writer had come, unexpectedly and involuntarily, to *identify with the persons* of his tale – the very young man, the very young girl, and 'the lonely, impressionable' young married woman who is her employer, and very little less warm and impulsive than Anna herself.

This identification is very different from anything that takes place in 'The Son's Veto', or in any of the other stories. There is nothing bogus about it, as there might be said to be between Hardy's identification with Tess, and the ponderous apparatus of pessimism and indignation with which he surrounds her. Hardy, as he was well aware, remained immature in many ways till the end of his life; still childish, as he confided, in middle age, and only just beginning to have the balanced outlook of a fully grown-up person when he had one foot in the grave. A susceptible, precocious, but ingenuous youth lurked always behind the façade of the writer, who became so used to cultivating concealment and disingenuousness on behalf of his official self. (Even that account of his own development has something disingenuous about it.) His art, no less than his circumstances, could suddenly thrust him back into all the sensations of being young, shaking his fragile form at eve, as his poem puts it, with throbbings of noon-tide.

It is this intimate but customary process which the story so perfectly encapsulates, with a concentration which neither the poems nor the novels can show. It is a story wholly convincing and touching in itself, without any of Hardy's zest in laborious contrivance, but beyond that it has a hidden dimension still more touching: Hardy's own response to it and to the situation it reveals. He must often have heard of illiterate girls, like Anna, who managed to get some trusted friend to write love-letters on their behalf; he may even have done it himself for such girls, as the novelist Richardson is supposed to have done in the previous century. Certainly when he lived in town 'monotonously' as a young architect, in rooms 'enclosed by a tawny fog from all the world', he must often have thought of girls, notional or actual, in the country near Bockhampton.

So completely does Hardy identify with the feelings and situation of his youthful trio that he takes for granted what is common in their situation, and criticizable in the case of the young man. Charles Raye is 'no great man, in any sense'; few in his situation are, as Hardy was well aware in his own feelings and sense of himself, and in his feeling with his hero. He was familiar with Raye's wish to hear from a girl he intends only to see again in a carefully delimited manner, and with the masculine complacency which comfortably anticipates in such a letter 'its terms of passionate retrospect and tender adjuration'. Raye, in fact, is writing the letter himself, in his imagination of Anna's simple charms; and is all the more surprised when, after half an hour or so of pleasure in its expected contents, he gets around to opening it and to finding how unexpectedly 'sensible' and 'human' it is.

Part of Hardy's youthful identification with his hero Raye is a young man's world-weary sense of things, expressed in that sudden burst of jejune eloquence about 'union, disunion, devotion, overpopulation, drudgery, content, resignation, despair'. How pleased a very young fellow would be with that overview of the human situation, to which he suddenly found himself unexpectedly and disconcertingly committed. The mastery of the story lies in the compression with which it brings together the warm helplessness and bliss of love, akin to Anna's ride on the merry-go-round, with the lover's own equally spontaneous feelings of superiority to this sensation, coupled with a tender envy for the one – Anna – who is unconscious of such a dual response. In all this Hardy immerses himself with abandon, but he retains his own artist's detachment from it too. The secret paradox of the story is that commonplace youth has its own detachment, into which Hardy enters with his own 'youthful' sympathy, while at the same time he is creating his story with the true artistic detachment of the great writer. 'On the Western Circuit' perfectly illustrates – putting it, as it were, in story form – the nature of the truth caught at by Hardy's candid friend Edward Clodd, who is said to have observed after Hardy's death that he had been a great writer, but not a 'great man'.

One does not have to be a great man to experience Charles Raye's moment of 'love and its ecstasies', as Hardy put it in one of his happiest poems, followed by a lifetime of comparative disillusion. Hardy had experienced much the same thing himself, and at the time he wrote the story, in 1891 or thereabouts, his marriage was at its nadir. That is less important, however, than the way in which Hardy throws himself, where the story is concerned, into the commonplaceness of its characters; and this comes about through what seems an involuntary and spontaneous contrast in style between the disillusioned older author, who writes with cool dismissiveness of his hero as 'no great man, in any sense, by the way', and the young man who plunges into the tale with the same hectic absorption as his characters. There is a considerable contrast here, as we shall see, with Joyce's story 'The Dead', in which the author is cunningly withdrawn from full participation in what he writes, whereas Hardy seem to be fully at one with the very ordinariness of his characters.

This is the more evident from the way in which the tale engrosses him in oblique wish-fulfilment. Anna and Mrs Harnham, between them, represent the combination of his youthful dreams: a 'young thing' capable of being 'absolutely as happy as if she were in a paradise', and 'an interesting creature' who writes him human and sensible letters and feels with him in her culture and background. In his early infatuation Charles Raye assumes that 'the pink and breezy Anna' is the letter writer in fact, and resolves to marry her on that supposition.

But this would be nothing in itself. A more important part of Hardy's youthfulness, for the story, is its identification with the two women. The only dream specifically mentioned is not Raye's, who does not know that his vision of Anna has utterly misled him, but that of Mrs Harnham, who has been writing to him on her maid Anna's behalf until she has fallen in love with him, and come to think of Anna's situation – she is pregnant by Charles Raye – as virtually her own. After Anna's condition has caused her to be exiled back to her village on the Plain, Edith Harnham promises to continue the correspondence, 'under no supervision by the real woman, with a man not her husband, in terms which were virtually those of a wife, concerning a corporeal condition which was not Edith's at all'. There is a curious tenderness even in Hardy's getting himself into the physical side of the situation, emphasizing Edith Harnham's marital solitude – 'that contract had left her still a woman whose deeper nature had never been stirred' – and her forlorn sense of the sole bond between Raye and his Anna. ' "I wish his child was mine – I wish it was!" she murmured. "Yet how can I say such a wicked thing!" ' Like Raye himself in regard to Anna, who seems enchantment in the flesh and a soul-mate in her letters – letters she could never write – Edith has a dual vision of Raye as the man she loves: the man she can fulfil her soul in writing to, and the man by whom her maid is pregnant. 'That he had been able to seduce another woman in two days was his crowning though unrecognised fascination for her as the she-animal.'

The Imaginative Woman also has that side to her nature – 'What sly animals women are,' her husband thinks – and Anna herself, while Edith and Raye are talking after the wedding, appears 'an animal who humbly heard but understood not'. Hardy's identification with his characters, body and soul, extends to the degree of their self-deception. When all is over, and Edith Harnham has come home to her house in Salisbury, she crouches down on the floor of the drawing-room. ' "I have ruined him!" she kept repeating. "I have ruined him because I would not deal treacherously towards her".' Hardy gives no suggestion that this is not quite the case: that she did it for herself, as she admitted to Raye; but his sense of their separation is overwhelmingly poignant. The sweetness of love returned, the dreariness of being married, goes deeply into him, and into the story. As Edith crouches in the dusk the door opens and a figure appears. She starts up, saying 'Ah – who's that?' 'Your husband – who should it be?' said the worthy merchant. Both women have had their moment at the beginning of the story: Anna when she rides on the merry-go-round and a lover comes to her there; Edith Harnham when that same lover takes her hand in mistake for Anna's, and gently presses two fingers inside her glove. For Edith the letters have after that been everything, and at the end she accompanies Anna to the wedding 'in a last desperate feeling that she must at every hazard be in at the death of her dream'.

The 'something behind' in a story as good as this is not of course the same as any further possibilities it may suggest to the reader at its ending. In 'The Lady with the Dog' Chekhov makes his hero's sense of what may be to come a part of the specification of the tale. Hardy in a sense does the opposite, putting all his feeling into the desolation that awaits the newly-married pair and the married woman who travels back to her barren home. As Edith says with forced gaiety she is to go up to Anna's wedding 'to see the end of her'; and the end of her is the end of the story – the death of the dream. But the story's atmosphere is not quite like that: Hardy's awareness of things – the archway, the straight street, the market square where the fair is held – going with the tale's embodiment of the littleness and ordinariness of things, combine to make the reader feel that life does go on, and that dramatic misery is as temporary and self-deceptive as lyric joy. The wine merchant may yet become a father; Anna will be happy with her child; Raye may obtain a fascinating brief. All three may meet again, the process of 'keeping up' with old friends replacing their long-gone 'story'. All that is present in the tone, even at her worst moment, of Edith's 'forced gaiety'. 'To see the end of her' is an affectionate phrase which, in general use, signifies the opening of a new kind of relationship.

CHAPTER FIVE

Like so many of the best short stories 'On the Western Circuit' is not homogeneous in style and approach. It is full of instabilities, which pull it now towards an ironic overview ('no great man, in any sense, by the way') now towards an almost feverish identification with the predicament of Raye and Anna and Edith Harnham. Anna is passionately desirable because she is *not* a writer; because she is illiterate, and her emotions immediate and absolute – something that no literary sense of things can achieve. Edith Harnham, on the other hand, has all the attraction of a potential soul-mate, with whom feeling can be explored and shared, in whom and with whom a story can be born, or be constructed. Raye, like Hardy, feels the allurement of both. Hardy identifies with Raye in the very syntax of his simple – indeed crude – response to his first glimpse of Anna.

> . . . by and by the observer's eyes centred on the prettiest girl out of the several pretty ones revolving.
> It was not that one with the light frock and the light hair whom he had been at first attracted by; no, it was the one with the black cape, grey skirt, light gloves and – no, not even she, but the one behind her; she with the crimson skirt, dark jacket, brown hat and brown gloves. Unmistakably that was the prettiest girl.

This rapt selection in its turn gives way to an overview again;

in many respects a more subtle one than is usual in the novels, and also more concentrated: bringing together as it does the prison atmosphere of class and sex, but also overcoming them with the powerful forces of instinct and individuality. Ordinary as they may be, there is nothing doomed or dumb about the human actors in the story. At the same time, the story depends on a deep latent pressure of protest – much the more effective, in terms of the genre, for never coming to the surface – which gives it a remarkable similarity to other outstanding examples in which protest is embodied but not stated, such as Gertrude Stein's story 'Melanctha', in her collection *Three Lives*. There, too, the growing realization in a narrative of a social situation which has forced individuals to correspond emotionally to its patterns, is dealt with in such a way that it becomes all the more meaningful and prominent.

The syntactic imitation of young Raye's consciousness, as he eyes the girls on the merry-go-round, comes naturally to Hardy in his own experience and pleasure as voyeur. In James Joyce's stories, *Dubliners*, the process is used in a far more deliberate and sophisticated manner. To complete our study of the theory in the short story I shall take two examples to examine in detail: the last and most famous story in Joyce's *Dubliners*, 'The Dead', and Elizabeth Bowen's wartime story, 'Mysterious Kôr'. Both are remarkable examples of the formula that I proposed earlier: the incompatibility between the story's art, and its mystery, must become the story's own justification. Both show the direction taken by the best and most subtle examples of the genre, which puts them in contrast with the ordinarily 'effective' story, as it has been developed from models mostly French – Flaubert and de Maupassant – and as it has been practised by a great number of talents, from Katherine Mansfield to Karen Blixen and to Mary Lavin, from Scott FitzGerald and Edith Wharton to Flannery O'Connor and Eudora Welty (whose stories Elizabeth Bowen much admired).

Young Raye's awareness of the girl on the merry-go-round leads him in time to the hard social fact of the story: the incompatibility between the educated and the illiterate, the gulf between the classes which the attractions of love can do nothing to close. Although this fact is not what gives its secret structure to Hardy's story it is none the less deeply inside it. Raye is not exactly a modern Don Juan, but he behaves in a manner in which Don Juan always has behaved, and is then betrayed by the logic of seduction: however mutual the spirit of the event, the seducer is then compelled to find out what his partner victim is really like. This fact in Hardy's story becomes a feature, almost a preoccupation, with the literature of the new age, and was cunningly turned into brilliant comedy by Shaw in *Pygmalion*. Shaw was himself greatly struck by one scene in an amateur play sent him by a very minor writer, James Elroy Flecker, and wrote to the author that 'it is one of the best I have ever read, it is in fact a stroke of genius.' Making allowance for Shaw's Irish kindness, one can still see why he was so impressed. Flecker never managed to finish his play, *Don Juan*, which was to be a study of the figure in a contemporary setting, and eventually put it aside to write *Hassan*, which was to become popular as a theatrical extravaganza after his death. But the figure of Tisbea in his *Don Juan* does stand out. She is a fisher girl who helps Don Juan, and they fall in love; a love which makes them seem equal in their intimacy; but when she appears later in the play she has become what she naturally is – a timid, dumb and submissive peasant, from whom he recoils in pity and disgust.

Both the play and the novel could come seriously to grips with the class-consciousness of the new age, even when it is handled awkwardly and sententiously, as it is by Flecker in his play, or by E. M. Forster in *Howard's End*. But the short story at its best never has to 'confront' such an issue. It remains on the outside of the tale's secret interior, as it does in 'On the Western Circuit'. Although the stories that make up Joyce's *Dubliners* are alive with social as with national questions, these have their effective being as part of the density of the tales, and above all as part of their calm sense of omniscience. With his genius drawn naturally to the parodic, Joyce delicately calls on a great variety of the tones conventionalized by the short story form, and these combine to make an impression of imperturbable neutrality.

There is a theory behind it, of course. As we know from his correspondence Joyce was much taken with the idea that in true modern literature 'beauty' must be avoided. His art, in the stories that he was writing, must bring a new kind of beauty into the world. 'Beauty', in the old literary sense, was in the same kind of category as social and moral issues in art. The story must act as a kind of melting-pot, in which all such things would be dissolved into a new medium of words. And it is significant that this involves the presence in these stories of something beyond; something impalpable which constitutes the atmosphere of the tale, and to which Joyce's new concept would discreetly point. What is 'beyond' in a Joyce tale involves misunderstanding in its most aesthetically seductive form; the misunderstanding, that is to say, which lies at the root of human intercourse, and extends to our reception of the story itself. We take things in different ways, and Joyce's flattering idiom persuades us, through the intercession of blankness or puzzlement, that we perceive what is forming in the story where its denizens naturally do not. They cannot be in at the death, any more than other readers can be who have given the story up, or have formed ideas about it which misunderstand those which we have formed ourselves.

'The beauty that has not yet come into the world' is naturally something that the characters themselves are dead to, unconscious of: even though they embody it, and their speech gives it expression. Mary Jane, the middle-aged niece of the two elderly sisters in the story, observes at the end of the party that she has 'read this morning in the newspapers that the snow is general all over Ireland'. As he lies in bed on the edge of sleep, Gabriel Conroy remembers the phrase.

> Yes, the newspapers were right: snow was general all over Ireland. It was falling on every part of the dark central plain, on the treeless hills, falling softly upon the Bog of Allen and, farther westward, softly falling into the dark mutinous Shannon waves.

Mary Jane's remark symbolizes the new style of 'beauty' which Joyce was set upon capturing. She is quite unconscious of it, and so is Gabriel himself, for all that he is a teacher and writer, a sentimentalist and a bit of a poet, who enjoys remembering a phrase he has written about Browning's 'thought-tormented music', and the thought that his wife's 'household cares had not quenched all their souls' tender fire'.

Joyce himself was fully aware of the incongruity between the new 'beauty' he was trying to create, and the old 'music of words', the cadences and the Celtic music to which he was so strongly attached. His sense of the incongruity is embodied in the division he was subsequently to make, in *Ulysses*, between Bloom, the newspaper man, an artist in his own way and an involuntarily cosmopolitan figure, and Stephen Dedalus, the old-fashioned young intellectual and wordsmith, attached to the past and to its traditions of verbal poetry. Yeats was to change his style deliberately, forsaking the Celtic twilight for what he felt to be a tough new idiomatic simplicity. Joyce is much more subtle, and 'The Dead' shows how he can use the short story form to bring the two sides together, in mutual ignorance, but also in the totality of a new atmosphere. The passage that begins 'Yes, the newspapers were right,' is, so to speak, not Gabriel's thought, but Joyce's own celebration of the two halves of his literary being, his own complex awareness. The story embodies these in the moment when Gabriel, on the edge of sleep, sets out 'on his journey westward', reconciling in himself and for the story the two styles, his sense of marriage and of his wife's early romance, his complacency and his knowledge of his own fatuity, the image of living and the awareness of death.

But the working of this reconciliation appears only late in the story, as what might be called – using Joyce's term – its secret epiphany. Until then there is no reconciliation at all between the new world 'beauty' Joyce is bringing into being, and the old conventional one. The new style is one of banality and fragmentation, of reading in the newspaper that 'snow was general all over Ireland', and the snow in Gabriel–Joyce's own sense of it 'falling softly . . . and softly falling . . . falling faintly through the universe, and faintly falling, like the descent of their last end, upon all the living and the dead.' The epiphany is one of a final peace between style as the sense of how we talk to ourselves and think of ourselves, and style as the Other: the way other people appear to think and behave.

Throughout the story the expectations of the old style are continually brought up against and baffled by the incursions of the new. The first sentence tells us that 'Lily, the caretaker's daughter, was literally run off her feet.' Joyce's intention in using the solecism here is unmistakable, for in an earlier story in the collection, 'Counterparts', he used the same word with pointed accuracy. The hero pawns his watch and chain, and is offered five shillings by the clerk. He holds out for six, 'and in the end the six shillings was allowed him literally. He came out of the pawn-office joyfully, making a little cylinder of the coins between his thumb and fingers.' After this first sentence the opening two pages of 'The Dead' are told more unobtrusively in Lily's style, until the arrival at the Miss Morkans' annual dance ('Never once had it fallen flat. For years and years it had gone off in splendid style, as long as anyone could remember') of Gabriel Conroy and his wife Gretta. There follows the first of the unexplained hitches in the narrative, hitches which signal to the leading figure of Gabriel, and through him to the reader, the divided, incomplete and essentially meagre nature of experience, which art – and specifically the art of this short story – cannot overcome if it is to remain true to itself.

Lily, the caretaker's daughter, who is letting in the guests at the party, and helping the men off with their coats, is greeted with kindly patronage by Gabriel as he comes in out of the cold. He brings his style with him, in the way he is described as well as in the ways he reflects and talks.

> A light fringe of snow lay like a cape on the shoulders of his overcoat and like toecaps on the toes of his goloshes; and, as the buttons of his overcoat slipped with a squeaking noise through the snow-stiffened frieze, a cold, fragrant air from out-of-doors escaped from crevices and folds.
> 'Is it snowing again, Mr Conroy?' asked Lily.
> She had preceded him into the pantry to help him off with his overcoat. Gabriel smiled at the three syllables she had given his surname and glanced at her.

But Gabriel receives a shock when he says archly to Lily, 'I suppose we'll be going to your wedding one of these fine days with your young man, eh?' Glancing back at him and speaking with great bitterness she says that 'the men there is now is only all palaver and what they can get out of you'.

Gabriel is discomposed by this bitter and sudden retort, which seems directed, if not intentionally, at his own image of himself as a man. It is the first of the shocks he will receive in the course of the evening, and the virulent cliché in it suggests that he is himself a man of 'palaver', fancy talk, uplifted sentiments which are themselves no more than the higher cliché. There are strong suppressed feelings inside the story which surface momentarily and are no more heard of, but contribute none the less to the web of tension setting against the hilarious satisfactions of the grand evening.

The most evident is Gabriel's encounter with Miss Ivors, a nationalist who wants him to join some of them on a holiday in the west of Ireland, one of the benefits of which would be to keep in touch with the Irish language – 'your own language'. Gabriel observes that Irish is not his language, but Miss Ivors continues to tease him and call him a 'West Briton' as they dance through the movements of the Lancers together. Gabriel sees a way of getting even with her when he makes his speech at supper, by referring to the older generation, with its 'qualities of hospitality, of humour, of humanity', which is lacking in 'the very serious and hypereducated generation which is growing up around us.' His plan is frustrated, however, by Miss Ivors' abrupt departure before the supper is served, a departure which disconcerts all her hosts, and not only Gabriel, although she seems to go away in high good humour, bidding them goodnight in an Irish phrase. As she goes away laughing Gabriel stares after her, 'blankly down the staircase', and Mary Jane, niece of the two elder Misses Morkan, also gazes after her, a moody and puzzled expression on her face. The tensions between language and expression, and the differences they denote, seem to be growing. Gabriel has already had a little tiff with his wife over the west of Ireland holiday project.

> His wife clasped her hands excitedly and gave a little jump.
> 'O, do go, Gabriel,' she cried . . . 'I'd love to see Galway again.'
> 'You can go if you like,' said Gabriel coldly.
> She looked at him for a moment, then turned to Mrs Malins and said: 'There's a nice husband for you, Mrs Malins.'
> While she was threading her way back across the room Mrs Malins, without adverting to the interruption, went on to tell

Gabriel what beautiful places there were in Scotland and
beautiful scenery. Her son-in-law brought them every year to the
lakes and they used to go fishing. Her son-in-law was a splendid
fisher. One day he caught a beautiful big fish and the man in the
hotel cooked it for their dinner.

The banalities of the party are soothing to Gabriel, and set up
a musical interchange with the sudden chords of tension.
Aunt Julia sings her song 'Arrayed for the Bridal,' and 'to
follow the voice, without looking at the speaker's face, was to
feel and share the excitement of swift and secure flight'. It is
succeeded by the stuttered congratulations of Freddy Malins
–

'I was just telling my mother,' he said, 'I never heard you sing so
well, never. No I never heard your voice so good as it is tonight.
Now, Would you believe that now? That's the truth. Upon my
word and honour that's the truth. I never heard your voice sound
so fresh and so . . . so clear and so fresh, never.'

– and by the kind of unexplained discord that only a story as
good as this can handle. Aunt Kate suddenly bursts out at her
sister Julia going at six o'clock on Christmas morning to slave
away in the church choir, and turns fiercely on her niece when
the latter says smiling that it's all for the honour of God. If so,
why has the Pope turned the women out of the choirs and put
little boys in their places? That's not just and not right. Mary
Jane acts as peacemaker. Her aunt's indignation will give
scandal to Mr Browne, 'who is of the other persuasion'.

Aunt Kate turned to Mr Browne, who was grinning at this
allusion to his religion, and said hastily:
  'O, I don't question the pope's being right.'

Supper is the next restorative, and its solidity and order lie in
magnificent reassurance beside the vaporous hubbub of the
conversation, caught at the pinnacle of platitude.

. . . two little ministers of jelly, red and yellow; a shallow dish full
of blocks of blancmange and red jam, a large green leaf-shaped
dish with a stalk-shaped handle, on which lay bunches of purple

raisins and peeled almonds, a companion dish on which lay a solid rectangle of smyrna figs, a dish of custard topped with grated nutmeg, a small bowl full of chocolates and sweets wrapped in gold and silver papers and a glass vase in which stood some tall celery stalks. On the closed square piano a pudding in a huge yellow dish lay in waiting, and behind it were three squads of bottles of stout and ale and minerals, drawn up according to the colours of their uniforms, the first two black, with brown and red labels, the third and smallest squad white, with transverse green sashes.

This solid phalanx, uniformed, arranged in compact blocks, makes a contrast – possibly an intentional one – with the array of sweetmeats Porphyro brings forth from the cupboard in Madeleine's room in 'The Eve of St Agnes'. That was poetry in the old sense, prelude to a hushed romantic consummation, with the snow and the cold outside and the lovers' warmth diminishing in the final stanza towards their still far-off death.

Joyce makes his own use of the snow, the warm interior and the dance; alternating without pause the layers of experience as they impinge swiftly on the actors; are come and gone. ' "I love the look of snow," said Aunt Julia sadly.' The contradiction, in all passivity, foretells her death, as later perceived by Gabriel, but records more effectively the alternation of response which affects them all and bears them on helplessly through the evening. 'The Dead' would be a lesser story if a climax were visible in the offing, implied in the mode of narration; or if the symbol of death lay with irony on the living and their merry activities; or if (as some critics have claimed) the story is making the deadpan point that these solstitial activities – the speechifying, the banal reminiscences, the aimless chat – show that the company are as good as dead already.

The escape of the story's mystery from all these explanations, themselves sufficiently banal, is pointed by a sudden pose, that in which Gabriel perceives his wife Gretta, as she listens to the notes of an air sung upstairs.

There was grace and mystery in her attitude as if she were a symbol of something. He asked himself what is a woman standing on the stairs in the shadow, listening to distant music, a symbol of. If he were a painter he would paint her in that attitude. Her blue felt hat would show off the bronze of her hair against the darkness and the dark panels of her skirt would show off the light ones. 'Distant Music' he would call the picture if he were a painter.

It is not just that all the 'literature', the romance and meaning in the story, are gathered into Gabriel's consciousness, leaving the story itself outside them. The story's mystery resides precisely in what its central participant, who stands so close to Joyce himself, cannot grasp. Joyce himself was well aware of his own tendencies where romance was concerned. His tenderness, his self-indulgence, his pleasure in his own love-phrases, come out in his letters to his wife Norah, in the same breath and spirit as the intimate little obscenities and simple talk. His style and consciousness needed both. In 'The Dead' both are on the outside of the story while its interior remains enigmatic. That interior, the texture of life in the story, is come to about as close as can be in a phrase used about Freddy Malins and his mother. Freddy drinks too much and is inclined to arrive 'screwed' at parties. But now Mrs Malins has been told that Freddy has come and that he is 'nearly all right'. The atmosphere of life, as 'The Dead' reveals it, is 'nearly all right'.

Joyce does this far more effectively, in terms of the story form, than his disciple Samuel Beckett. The fact that life is 'nearly all right' damns it far more effectively, if damning is in question, than do Beckett's theatrical gestures of despair, played straight. Beckett's humour is obvious – Joyce's far more subtle. Although 'The Dead' is in a sense a large and elaborate joke – the distillation of the Anglo-Irish sense of humour – it eclipses the fact with its poignancy, its warmth, its unpretending strangeness. The joke is funniest in that it ceases to be one. But the bundle of its ends protrudes, sticking out in all places. Gretta, with 'grace and mystery in her attitude'is like a symbol of something. In Nathaniel Hawthorne's notebook of ideas for stories he sketches an event which could be 'a symbol of something'. On that a story would be built, but for Hawthorne his symbol would be a serious matter.

Gretta is not posing: her symbolic air is suggested by her real concentration; and yet it is the prelude to the reader's touched awareness of self-deception, in herself no less than in her husband. Unlike Hawthorne, Joyce needs no symbol in his story, nor the kind of meaning which the symbol is there to express. In no sense is the story 'about' self-deception; yet it is clear that towards its climax there is a sort of collision between the imagination of himself and his being that Gabriel needs to have, and the corresponding shape of his wife Gretta's. It is a part of her inner life that a man has 'died for her'; and this essential, dormant in her years of marriage and child-bearing, is suddenly revived at the end of the party by a few notes from the song he used to sing, *The Lass of Aughrim*. Poor Michael Furey, the 'gentle boy' with whom she used to go out walking, and with whom she was 'great' at the time, could hardly be said to have died for her, since he was dying in any case of tuberculosis; but because he stood out in the rain hoping to see her, and told her that he did not wish to live, his act took on the image of self-sacrifice, and an idea of love which has lived in her secretly for years.

Carried away by the self-satisfaction of his desire for his wife – a desire which parodies the romantic feelings of Keats' Porphyro for Madeleine – Gabriel fits her into the idiom which most ministers to that self-satisfaction, imagining them running away together 'with wild and radiant hearts to a new adventure'. The comedy of connubial lust first rendered diffident and then totally extinguished, by the unawareness of the partner at whom it is aimed, is suggested by Joyce with wonderful delicacy, with that 'friendly pity' which Gabriel comes to feel for his wife as she lies asleep beside him, after telling him the tale of her romance with Michael Furey. Equally true is the way in which Gabriel gets over his moment of 'shameful consciousness of his own person', the 'fatuous fellow' whose face he had glimpsed in the mirror. (It is a very Joycean face, with its 'glimmering gilt-rimmed eye-glasses', and an expression that always 'puzzled him when he saw it in a mirror'.) He gets over it by placing Michael Furey, like Gretta, in the pale of his own idiom, and by joining them together in the spell of language. ('Better pass boldly into that other world, in the full glory of some passion, than fade and wither dismally with age'.) In that area of recovery and reconcilement sleep comes as the snow falls.

Technically, Joyce's feat in 'The Dead' is to call attention to his own verbal fastidiousness, which, like all emphatic fastidiousness, has its fatuous side, and yet in no way compromise the 'friendly pity' with which the story is told. This is realized through Gabriel himself and Joyce's relation to him. In the course of *Dubliners* Joyce moves from narrative in the first person about the narrator's childhood ('The Sisters', 'An Encounter', 'Araby'), which because it is so conventional a form receives in his treatment of it a faintly sardonic whiff of parody, to impersonal sketches from which a narrator is absent. In 'The Dead' he returns to a close relation with his hero, now grown-up and confirmed in all the habits and mental customs of maturity. Joyce is more intimate with Gabriel than with any other of his Dubliners, and through him can express such evident divisions as the wish for solitude – in the snow, along the quays – and the simultaneous pleasure in company. Gabriel throws himself into the party, entirely reassured and happy in his expert carving of the goose, anxiously wondering about the nuances of his after-dinner speech, but he is also easily upset and disconcerted – by the nationalistic Miss Ivors, the threat of Freddy Malins' drunkenness, even by the words of Lily the caretaker's daughter. Like a real writer he is absorbed by society while dwelling, in himself, in solitude. At the same time Joyce can project on to Gabriel the comedy of his own verbal fastidiousness, coarsening it into Gabriel's separate though related idiom. Gabriel is, however delicately, the butt of Joyce; but such a butt can accommodate all the most ardent and indulgent of his creator's impulses. We know, too, that his wife Norah did confide to Joyce an experience similar to Gretta's, and that it made a great impression on him.

It seems likely that the best short stories always exhibit, in some degree, a sense of the world as made up out of the different versions which individuals require in order to live in it. A communal world exists, but it is overlaid by the worlds as conceived and expressed by the writer's characters. At the same time the writer must set up a strong counterpoint with the actual neutrality of things, a neutrality which the writer need not – probably should not – endorse as his own view of the world, but which retains a status of plain truth in the groundwork of the story. No good short story writer can be a 'realist' in the sense that novelists are, or have been; and it is probably significant that the form of the short story has come to define itself most perceptibly in relation to the solid qualities of the novel, and the individual version of the world which each novelist creates.

Thus 'The Dead' is a kind of work quite different from *Ulysses*. The latter, in spite of all its trimmings, is essentially a realistic novel of a kind well understood in the nineteenth century, and Joyce, to whom I suspect the short story form came more naturally than the novel, has paradoxically secured the 'realism' of Ulysses by giving it a robust framing of myth, a frame which secures the same extended fictional effect as a story in chapters or instalments. At the same time there is a short story inside *Ulysses* which is not so different from that of 'The Dead', and which depends in the same way upon the different versions of life which individual consciousness weaves for itself, making its own poetry of. Bloom and Molly have a good deal in common with the Conroys.

And the way in which the Conroys are short story people is also the way in which the same is true of the couple in 'The Lady with the Dog' and in 'A Landscape-Painter'. Mary Postgate, and the inhabitants of 'Mrs Bathhurst' also live in a world in which it is hard to say where their consciousness ends and external reality begins. Kipling is deliberately exploiting this aspect of the short story for a particular purpose – a didactic purpose – and in 'A Landscape-Painter' Henry James uses the new short story atmosphere of different consciousnesses to construct an old-style *dénouement* of mutual deception. Later practitioners of the art, we might say from Joyce onwards, use the materials for the picture of itself which a consciousness creates, as if they were a form of poetry, touched with the pathos or irony which poetry shows when enclosed by a form different from itself. This is true of some of Elizabeth Bowen's best stories, like 'Ivy Gripped the Steps', and 'Mysterious Kôr'.

Elizabeth Bowen's Anglo-Irishness relates her to Joyce,

and her style is as distinctive as his, though more intrusive. Its friendliness is equally unsentimental, and she constructs her stories with the same instinct for combination between the interior need of the character and its relation to the outside world. Kipling, whose stories she greatly admired, was at his best as good as Joyce in giving a mastery of detail – in Kipling's case hypnotically vivid detail – to that outside world, in order both to attach it and distinguish it from individual consciousness. All these stories' writers make their characters 'ordinary', unaware of whatever 'poetry' surrounds them, and of which their need is unconscious. The pioneer in such things, Joyce draws distinctions with delicate clarity, as if he were himself faintly amused by his own specification for the poetry in the tale, and the way it is divided between the traditionally poetic, and that involuntary poetry of common utterance he is himself exploring. Joyce is both deeply involved in, and amused by, the feelings and experiences of youth, when the name of a friend's big sister 'was like a summons to all my foolish blood'. 'My body was like a harp and her words and gestures were like fingers running upon the wires.' The emotion is real, the expression of it at least partly quizzical. Eveline, in the story of that name, reflects on her childhood in a different way, and in Joyce's simplest idiom: 'Still, they seemed to have been rather happy then.'

Between the two tones Joyce moves as if playing an instrument, and with an instrumentalist's dispassion. The highly equivocal man the two boys meet in 'An Encounter' at times 'spoke as if he were simply alluding to some fact that everybody knew, and at times he lowered his voice and spoke mysteriously, as if he were telling us something secret which he did not wish others to overhear.' Joyce's own tone has a touch of that, but in 'The Dead' the two merge gravely and gently, less perceptibly. And there is one aspect of its romance to which Joyce draws no attention at all. That is his use in it of space, of the physical dimension. Again he may have had unconsciously at the back of his mind a memory of Keats' castle in 'The Eve of St Agnes', which the reader comes to know with a similar intimacy – its passages, ballroom, bedrooms, lower and upper landings, entrance hall . . . And outside the country tranced and gripped by the frosty night. Keats' is a curiously homely castle, though the setting for a night of romance; and the Misses Morkans' establishment 'in the dark, gaunt house on Usher's Island, the upper part of which they had rented from Mr Fulham, the corn factor who lived on the ground floor', seems to swell and enlarge as the story goes on, till it has more and more rooms and staircases, space for guests who are present where story and dialogue are in operation, and for others who are heard in other rooms. While Gabriel is making his speech at the supper, leaning his 'ten trembling fingers on the tablecloth', the piano outside is 'playing a waltz tune and he could hear the skirts sweeping against the drawing-room door'. And yet 'all the guests' are assembled; and 'people, perhaps, were standing in the snow outside, gazing up at the lighted windows and listening to the waltz music. The air was pure there.'

The 'studious meanness' (as Joyce himself once referred to it) in the prose of that last sentence does not hide his reliance on the dimension of old world romance. Gabriel's after-dinner speech, every word of which is given us, emphasizes the old-world traditions, the 'princely failing' of Irish hospitality, dwelling on these qualities from the 'spacious days' of the past – the adjective suggests the phantom spaciousness in the house itself, in which the same party has been held for so many festive seasons – and the speech is also, like many such utterances, an act of melodious propaganda against the 'new generation growing up in our midst'. Miss Ivors, who had discomposed Gabriel earlier by her references to him as a 'West Briton', has already gone away, although in apparent good humour, so that Gabriel's intention of getting even with her in his speech, by his reference to the courtesy of former days, loses its target, in the manner of so many after-dinner speeches.

The whole performance is reassured and lightened, however, by the harmony and precision of its commonplace, and by the asides throughout it. When Gabriel refers to the three ladies as 'the three Graces of the Dublin musical world', Aunt Julia vainly seeks an explanation of what he has said from her neighbours, and, not understanding, none the less 'looked up, smiling, at Gabriel, who continued in the same vein . . .' A chorus of 'For they are jolly gay fellows' greets the speech's end, the guests turning towards one another, 'as if in melodious conference', while they sing 'Unless he tell a lie . . .'. Reassurance is complete, sealed by the occasion's sweet banality, and by the extraordinary amount of Dublin information, of a minor kind, which Joyce has woven into the progress of the tale. Facetious episodes at the supper table occur 'amid general laughter', and the discussion about singers of the past and present is resolved by Aunt Kate's impressive reference – 'for me there was only one tenor' – to the mysterious Parkinson, whom no one has heard of, and who is too far back even for Mr Browne. 'A beautiful, pure, sweet, mellow English tenor,' Aunt Kate concludes with enthusiasm. A more lugubrious subject, the ascetic habits of the monks of Mount Melleray, is similarly buried when Aunt Julia invites guests to the port and sherry, as prelude to Gabriel's speech.

The title of 'The Dead' is not its mystery, which accompanies the statement in the title to the most subtle effect. As in 'The Eve of St Agnes', the story brims itself again and again with all the enchantment of life – enchantment for Joyce being the new 'poetry', in its entire and banal comfort – and this total reassurance is shadowed by an equally total menace: the snow, the sadness in Aunt Julia's voice, the passing of the years, the coming of death. The dead are in the midst of life, and it is *life* which the story mysteriously celebrates, all the more from the presence of death inside it; a presence which is not confirmed but comfortingly evaded by the tranquil sleep into which Gabriel sinks beside Gretta in their room at the Gresham, with the snow falling in the dawn lamplight outside. Sleep and death are *not* near neighbours, as everybody knows, for sleep is the most confirmatory and restorative aspect of life. This invisible humour brings the great story to its peaceful and melodious close.

The threat is in it there, none the less; a streak of melodrama displayed by some of the best examples of our genre, as if a touch of the melodramatic was an earnest of the mystery. Kipling's stories, and 'Mrs Bathhurst' in particular, are the obvious case of it. But Joyce also understands it well, and the movements to and fro, anxious or ebullient flittings

and peerings into other rooms or down the stairs, create an
atmosphere which would do credit to the kind of highly
charged film sequence anticipated by certain narrational
aspects of 'The Dead'. The isolation of Aunt Julia, even as she
takes her part in the domestic bustle, is one of these.

> As the piano had twice begun the prelude to the first figure Mary
> Jane led her recruits quickly from the room. They had hardly
> gone when Aunt Julia wandered slowly into the room, looking
> behind her at something.
>   'What is the matter, Julia?' asked Aunt Kate anxiously. 'Who
> is it?'
>   Julia, who was carrying in a column of table-napkins, turned to
> her sister and said, simply, as if the question had surprised her:
>   'It is only Freddy, Kate, and Gabriel with him.'

The figure of death is not present, even in suggestion, here,
except in retrospect. It is only Gabriel 'piloting' Freddy
Malins, who is 'nearly all right'. Later Aunt Julia will sing
'Arrayed for the Bridal', to great applause – the occasion of
her sister's denunciation of the church choir which has
exploited Julia's durable voice over the years – and it is only
when he is lying in bed that Gabriel recalls the haggard look
on her face, and realizes that he will soon be hearing the news
of her spousality in death at last. The warning is of the
dissolution of the house on Usher's Island, glanced at by the
accidental verbal echo of Poe's melodrama. At that point
Gabriel himself has already confronted the adversary his
wife's behaviour has conjured up, saying she thinks that
Michael Furey died for her.

> A vague terror seized Gabriel at this answer, as if, at that hour
> when he had hoped to triumph, some impalpable and vindictive
> being was coming against him, gathering force against him in its
> vague world.

Melodrama is an excuse, a concealment, a kind of substitute
for the truth in a story; and yet although it is not the true thing
it points towards it, giving a presence to what in a masterpiece
of narrative must necessarily be intangible. In 'Mysterious

Kôr', a title which is quite blatant in the way it commandeers the melodrama a great story must have, the status of a masterpiece is none the less achieved, although it is far from easy to say how. Elizabeth Bowen's use of melodrama – she was a great admirer of Le Fanu's creepy novel *Uncle Silas* – can be excessive in some of her stories, and too brisk, short-circuiting any chance for the story to reveal a true inner dimension. In fact in most Bowen stories there is no inner dimension, any more than there is in the stories of Eudora Welty; although, like hers, they are usually masterly specimens of the genre. But 'Mysterious Kôr' has the quality found in 'The Dead', and in most of our other examples: the quality of a completeness that travels on indefinitely, so that the reader may feel, as Gabriel does when his wife has finished and is sleeping, that 'perhaps she had not told him all the story'.

And yet nothing could be less like 'The Dead' than the tone of this story. Its brilliance, like that of the moon itself, begins by shouting itself at you; stridently, but also intimately, as if moonlight were both searching inquisitively in the individual face, and yet also in the highest degree impersonal. The MOON! – that is what it is all about; and the moon will take the significances of a story anywhere, as everyone knows. The full moon makes the story appear overwhelmingly public; while the title, and what the title is found to mean, carry it in the opposite direction, into a dimness and silence of indeterminacy: not quite like sleep, not quite like the future, but with the provisional nature of both. These two extremes are like those of 'The Dead', where the strangeness of living contrasts with, and yet is part of the utter banality of life; but they also have a more local application, one expressed with extreme force. In the war the communal pressure towards survival, victory, the end of it at least, grapples with the desire to escape into whatever can be found of the personal, the vague but unchanging needs that keep out of sight and disappear into secret places.

It is a story very much with a place and a time, that of the dead middle of the war: after the excitements of the Battle of Britain, and the early bombing; before the exhilaration of the final campaigns. For anyone old enough it recalls the sense of London at that time of the war better than anything else; for others it may create an atmosphere – as Joyce's story does – which is authentic of any time, and yet which gives a powerful sense of an epoch and a history.

> Full moonlight drenched the city and searched it; there was not a niche left to stand in. The effect was remorseless: London looked like the moon's capital – shallow, cratered, extinct. It was late, but not yet midnight; now the buses had stopped the polished roads and streets in this region sent for minutes together a ghostly unbroken reflection up.

Those first two sentences impress the war-time setting. The remorselessness of the moon is like the war itself – a stagnation of glare, and of menace, although 'the Germans no longer came by the full moon'. The effect is that of blue unshaded light beating down, on a prison compound, on refugees huddled together in an underground shelter. But nothing like that comes into the story; an impression of such things is purely indirect, as is uncanny melodrama in the plain Joycean idiom of the third sentence. What is happening is that the moon, like the war, is exerting its total and impersonal insistence, pressing down its publicity upon every aspect of life.

> This day between days, this extra tax, was perhaps more than senses and nerves could bear. People stayed indoors with a fervour that could be felt. The buildings strained with battened-down human life, but not a beam, not a voice, not a note from a radio escaped. Now and then under the streets and buildings the earth rumbled: the Underground sounded loudest at this time.

The moon reveals its own kind of blank humour. 'At this point, at this moment', three French soldiers trying to find a hostel pause in their singing to listen derisively to the waterbirds in the park, wakened by it and by the moon. Two ARP wardens, coming off duty, turn their faces, mauve in the moonlight, to look without expression at the Frenchmen. A few passengers come out of the Underground and 'disappeared quickly, in an abashed way, or as though dissolved in the street by some white acid, but for a girl and a soldier who, by their way of walking, seemed to have no

destination but each other, and to be not quite certain even of
that.'

The two are lovers with no place to go, except back to the
tiny flat the girl, Pepita, shares with her girl friend.
Overcrowding was a fact of life in the war, and so – at least
among the middle classes – was a kind of sturdy
respectability. People might say that all proprieties had
lapsed with the war-time crises, but on the whole this was not
so, nor did the young people wish it to be so. Arthur, the
young soldier, and Pepita are therefore doubling up with
Callie, the other girl, who will share her bed with Pepita while
Arthur has Pepita's usual sleeping place, the divan in the tiny
lounge.

The arrangement is not satisfactory, as all know, but would
not say. They put a brave face on it, as on other wartime
deprivations and discomforts. But the tiny flat becomes in
consequence as much alive as the Misses Morkans' home on
the Dublin quays, or the castle in 'The Eve of St Agnes'. The
place of the erotic in a short story is always in itself oblique.
Although a seduction takes place in 'The Lady with the Dog',
as indeed it does in 'The Eve of St Agnes', the event is
invisible: what matter is the atmosphere it generates and
which has brought it to being. Sex in 'Mysterious Kôr' is as
insistently present as the war, or the moon; but like them it is
as troubling and incalculable as unseen; waiting, as such
things do wait in short stories, for art to have done its work in
its own way. The most erotic event in 'The Dead' is an act of
love envisaged by Gabriel but unimagined by his wife, as by
the rest of the company; an act that never takes place. After
the satisfactions of the evening Gabriel can hardly wait to
make love to his wife, but his lust is displaced and eventually
chastened by the corresponding ardour with which she recalls
an event in her past, a young man whose eyes she can see 'as
well as well', a young man standing at the end of the garden
under a dripping tree. Such an image is more potent than any
physical act; and the story would not exist if there were one
now, or had been one then.

A similar abstinence determines the potency of
'Mysterious Kôr'. Arthur and Pepita stand in the moonlit
road, and she says 'Mysterious Kôr'. It is not a game they

have played before, although he remembers the book it refers to – Rider Haggard's *She*. But neither the novel nor its title is directly mentioned. It is a single image from it which compels Pepita, and which moonlit London now summons up; the image of an abandoned city, its towers, walls and stone steps lit up by the moon, empty and unchanged throughout centuries. This is her comfort, her safe place, her charm against life. Arthur immediately and automatically resents it; while consenting in a grudging masculine way, to play along. 'I thought girls thought about people,' he says; and Pepita vaguely blames the war and the crowding – the communality forced on them all. 'I don't know how other girls manage: I always think about Kôr.'

To share it with him is a pledge of intimacy, and a rather forlorn assertion of their status as a couple, even a couple with nowhere to go. 'But to think about Kôr *is* to think about you and me,' she says. 'In that dead place?' 'No, ours,' she rejoins, '– we'd be alone here.' It is a *solitude à deux* she wants, but he comes back, in a husbandly way, to the idea of community. Pepita cannot bear its homely expectations of sequence. 'I should not mind what you did, so long as you never said "What next?"' They would populate Kôr , he remarks; and she says: 'I suppose it would be all right if our children were to marry each other.'

Under the moon, as it were, the reader has a flickering sense of the obscure dualities of consciousness. Communion and the fruitions of time summon up their opposite: a ghostly city, in timeless arrest, where the heart can live alone, housed in a dream. But of course the heart wants a companion, and Pepita's last comment ('her voice faded out; she had been reminded that they were homeless on this his first night of leave') shows that human needs have to live together with each other in their incompatibility, in the solitude of the individual. It is a process as inevitable and as unsatisfactory as the communion of human beings with each other. In the lightness of the story the point is invisible, for the art of story cannot afford to make such a point; but it is implicit in the moonlight, the Kôr imagining, and the involuntarily close contact in the tiny flat. Pepita may be 'housed in a dream, at distance from the kind', as Wordsworth disapprovingly put it, but in practice she has to be all too close, positively huddled together with her fellow humans. No choice is involved, moral or otherwise; and there is no irony in the narrative either: the story is gentle as well as hard.

Such is life. But for the story the flat itself is the thing, and its contrast with 'the dazzling distance' of the streets outside. Chatelaine of the flat is Callie, the stay-at-home girl, 'not yet known to be home later than ten, who would now be waiting up, in her house-coat, to welcome Arthur. That would mean three-sided chat, drinking cocoa, then turning in: that would be that, and that would be all. That was London, this war – they were lucky to have a roof – London, full enough before the Americans came ...'

'That would be that, and that would be all.' It is like Joyce's 'Almost all right.' These are indeed the materials with which such a story – perhaps most good stories – work with to achieve what they do. Callie is guardian of ancient values, which are only seemingly contradictory – family, fertility, virginity. Her upright obtuseness is a bit absurd – 'she was more slow-witted than narrow-minded – but Pepita felt she owed a kind of ruin to her.' A kind of ruin, but not the old sense of 'ruin' in regard to girls. To the hint that she might try to find somewhere else for the night (' "But where would I go?" Callie marvelled when this was at last borne in her') she had had to say, laughing, that it wouldn't be proper to leave them on their own – 'I don't know what your mother would say to me.' But it is a part of the general atmosphere, the lethargy of wartime London, that there goes with this diffident sense of decorum a marked absence of enthusiasm, let alone of passion, on the part of the lovers themselves. Arthur, the unwilling soldier, is worn out. Pepita is off in her mysterious Kôr.

No story conveys more vividly a sense of waiting, and waiting in every sense; for the coming of the lovers, for the end of the war. All alone, Callie 'had come to that peak moment at which company should arrive, but so seldom does'. She has her few little objects around her, lares and penates. 'Callie recollected the fuel target and turned off her dear little table lamp, gaily painted with spots to make it look like a toadstool ... She laid her hand on the kettle, to find it

gone cold again ... Where are they?' Callie has to go to bed –
her share of the bed.

The tale is intimate with sleep, with the ways people sleep.
Pepita, as Callie apprehensively knows, is restless; given,
especially since her love-affair beginning, to 'broken-off
exclamations and blurred pleas, heard, most nights, through
the dividing wall.' Arthur, she also knows, 'as though from a
vision', will sleep 'with assurance and majesty. Did they not
all say, too, that a soldier sleeps like a log? With awe she
pictured, asleep, the face she had not yet, awake, seen.' As she
puts the bedside light out, she realizes, even through the
blackout curtains, that 'something was happening'.
Confronting the moon, she sees it shine on the mantelpiece of
the lost drawing-room, out of which the three little rooms of
the flat have been contrived, and on the photograph of her
parents, bringing out the thoughts with which they had faced
the camera, 'and the humble puzzlement of her two dogs at
home'. The moon's 'white explanation' also reveals
something – 'was it a coin or a ring?' – that glittered half-way
across the street. No matter how accidental, this divination by
moonlight gives the reader a sense of fortune-telling, like that
ventured on by Madeleine in her 'soft and chilly nest' on St
Agnes' Eve.

The return of the lovers wakes Callie up. The reader is
hypnotized by a sense of being present at this vividly
awkward scene, which, like the moon itself, reveals
everything, from the touching way in which Callie,
determined to get this over, asks 'Would Arthur like to wash
his hands?' – to the actual detail in which trips to the
bathroom are worked out. We seem to have known these three
all our lives: they have the overpowering thereness of a
family, in which the assault of differing temperaments is not
so much noticed as shut out. Yet this is art, which makes such
things compulsive as well as convincing.

Callie's good manners oppress the lovers, Arthur's sense of
her being none the less keener than it ever has been of Pepita,
whom in a sense 'he never *had* seen for the first time: she had
not been, and still sometimes was not, his type'. 'You might
say he had not seen Pepita coming: their love had been a
collision in the dark'. And so Arthur finds himself touched by

the 'grave good faith' of Callie's manners, and marks 'the strong, delicate arch of one bare foot, disappearing into the arty green shoe'. He and Callie, ironically, are made for each other, which is why there is instant sympathy between them but not desire or love. Arthur wonders, 'though he had once been told', how these two unalike girls had come to set up together, Callie, 'an unlit candle', with something votive in her demeanour, 'Pepita so small, except for her too big head, compact of childish brusqueness and of unchildish passion'.

Arthur instantly understands from Callie that the little flat is 'home' ('we'll make things ever so homey' had been one of her more unfortunate comments to Pepita when anticipating Arthur's coming to stay). Now Callie is the first to retire, thoughtfully shutting the door so that the lovers can kiss goodnight. Only child from a sheltered home, her father a country doctor, Callie dreads having to share her bed: it is a sacrifice she has made for them, and a paradox of her role as guardian of the household. Now, as they try to settle in the bed, Pepita vents upon the other girl her spite at the arrangement, replying 'Have you a screw loose?' when asked if Arthur's 'got all he wants'. Arthur intervenes through the wall – he can hear, he says, practically all they are saying.

> They were both startled rather than abashed. Arthur, alone in there, had thrown off the ligatures of his social manner: his voice held the whole authority of his sex – he was impatient, sleepy, and he belonged to no one.
> 'Sorry,' the girls said in unison.

Pepita makes some apology as she hears Callie crying silently into the curtains on her side, and is soon asleep. Callie awakes at four with swollen eyelids to hear Arthur attempting to light a cigarette. He gives a groan, and with movements 'soundless as they were certain' Callie hops over her bed-fellow to ask if he is all right. Instantly and easily they are in whispered talk, Arthur commenting how difficult the war makes things for a girl ('It makes me feel cruel the way I unsettle her') and referring gloomily to the general unsatisfactoriness of the evening, which had culminated in their playing at Kôr.

'Core of what?'
'Mysterious Kôr – ghost city.'
'Where?'
'You may ask.'

Although Callie is uncomprehending the two understand each other very well. 'And how's your moon?' he says.

'Mine?' Marvelling over this, as the first sign that Arthur remembered that she was Callie, she uncovered the window, pushed up the sash, then after a moment said: 'Not so strong.'
    Indeed, the moon's power over London and the imagination had now declined. The siege of light had relaxed; the search was over; the street had a look of survival and no more. Whatever had glittered there, coin or ring, was now invisible or had gone. To Callie it seemed likely that there would never be such a moon again; and on the whole she felt this was for the best. Feeling air reach in like a tired arm round her body, she dropped the curtains against it and returned to her own room.

Such as it was the epiphany is over; but Joyce's term does not really go with the humour of Elizabeth Bowen's (or of his own) story, and its vivid projection of felt and lived experience. Warmth has 'travelled between the sheets from Pepita's flank, and in this Callie extended her sword-cold body'. Pepita's untasteful gibe that she had better go in with Arthur to see that he's got all he wants has, in a sense, come true. Arthur has, in his own way, confided: with the result that Callie, as she prepares again for sleep, is touched with a feather of disillusionment, the loss of her own 'mysterious expectation, of her love for love'. The moon, 'not so strong', declines not only fortune-telling but the promise that kind Callie had cherished on behalf of Pepita and her young man. 'So long as you love each other' she had thought and said – love and its 'mysterious expectation' being the absolute in her consciousness that Kôr is for Pepita. Callie is less sure about it now she has listened to Arthur; but, virginal as she is, she is more capable than Pepita of adjustment to affection, and to its powers of recuperation, as of going blank.
    Her 'mysterious expectation' is as much a dream as mysterious Kôr, but it lacks the finality into which Pepita

escapes. Arthur has noticed that finality – 'funny the way she sleeps, isn't it? You can't help wondering where she is' – and he is resigned, even if barely so, to Pepita's disappearance into her own private being. The publicity of the war not only licenses such privacy but throws the appearance of it into strong relief. The word 'mysterious', happily indulgent in the use of the quotation about Kôr, is quieter – graver too – when it refers to Callie's expectation of what love brings for others, and perhaps for herself. Her startled, even bewildered new awareness, as the reader intuits, is that love may do in some case the opposite of what it is supposed to: it may force the participant back into an isolation in which all the gifts it brings seem questionable or merely upsetting. The warmth of Pepita's flank, as Callie creeps coldly back into bed, has only an impersonal friendliness. It should be a gift of love, but it has no proper recipient, and the donor is herself tenaciously far away in the territory of Kôr.

All these touches contribute to a complex situation, which the story throws off and leaves behind. As in all Elizabeth Bowen's stories there is a slight touch of brusqueness about this, brusqueness which in her other stories – most of which are primed and timed for a quick fascinated read and no more – is a standard part of the specification. Here it enhances the feeling of depth, of sympathy, experience realized; which none the less there is no point in lingering on and making too much of. The full sympathy of the story has a sensible lack of self-admiration about it. Pepita, tenaciously asleep in the story's last sentences, is for all their poetry a faintly comic figure: comedy is quite at home in the poetry of Kôr, as is the sadness of compulsive dream. In her dream Pepita needs Arthur – 'With him she went up the stairs down which nothing but moon came; with him trod the ermine dust of the endless halls, stood on terraces, mounted the extreme tower, looked down on the statued squares, the wide, void, pure streets' – but though he has surprised her into love, into a sharing of her dream, he cannot – in all the uncertainties of living in the war – give her the finality she longs for.

As the circumstances of war parody the changes and chances of life itself, so the 'finality' which Pepita craves glances at the nature of such a story itself. The story ends on its necessary note of finality but the situation it has brought into being continues to live in our consciousness. The two ends join, like the sleeping and waking life of the characters, a combination which produces the story's quite remarkable effect of close intimacy. In a preface to her stories Elizabeth Bowen wrote that 'the short story is at an advantage over the novel, and can claim its nearer kinship to poetry, because it . . . can be more visionary . . . I do not feel that the short story can be, or should be, used for the analysis or development of character.' As to poetry and the 'visionary', there is a great deal of both in 'Mysterious Kôr', and their power is all the stronger and more authentic for the understanding which the author shares with her reader that 'Kôr' itself – however compulsive and continuing its fascination for the youthful reader of Rider Haggard – belongs to the more self-indulgent world of fantasy and the poetic, rather than to that hard true world of poetic vision the story is creating. Kôr and its charms have something of the stalking horse quality which 'the vast hosts of the dead' and 'their wayward and flickering existence' have in Joyce's story. The impalpable life of both tales is their real mystery, which lives inexplicably beyond the satisfyingly mysterious ghost world they proffer. But that ghost world is necessary to the perspective of the narrative, its satisfactions of character and comedy.

For Pepita and Callie, like Gabriel, stand in a peculiar relation to their creator; a relation which only the story, and not the novel, can consummate. The novelist who uses himself does so in more involuntary ways, and he is justified as well as revealed by the whole sweep of his book, as George Eliot is, for instance, by her presentation of Maggie in *The Mill on the Floss*. Something of that comes into Elizabeth Bowen's own novel, *The Death of the Heart*, in which the reader intuits without difficulty, and with a pleasure he knows to be part of the pleasure the author plans for him, that she is herself both Ann and Portia: both, that is to say, the defensive adroit middle-aged woman, whose passions are battened toughly but insecurely inside her; and the young girl who cannot begin to handle the emotions she feels, and the sense of betrayal and desolation which goes with them.

Pepita and Callie stand in something like the same relation

to their author, but the story gives them a quite different status. Their extreme livingness is at least partly due to the fact that their author is not concerned with them as characters, but as persons seen and apprehended under a particular set of circumstances. She is intimate with them in the same immediate way that they are with each other: imprisoned together, that is, in the flat, the war, the moonlight. She is too much aware of them to be interested in them, or in long-term identification. Each of these stories, she wrote in her Preface of 'The Storm', 'Her Table Spread', 'Ivy Gripped the Steps', 'Mysterious Kôr',

> arose from an intensified, all but spell-bound beholding, on my part, of the scene in question – a fountain-filled Italian garden in livid, pre-thundery light; a shabbily fanciful Irish castle overlooking an estuary; an ivy-strangled house in a formerly suave residential avenue; or weird moonlight over bomb-pitted London. Each time I felt: 'Yes, this affects me, but it would affect "X" more. Under what circumstances; for what reasons? And who is "X"?' In each case the "X" I pondered upon became the key character in the resultant story.

Place comes before persons, but again we have the stalking-horse which seems to come into many of the best short stories; for the interior of the flat, which is in some sense the interior of the pair living in it, is more intimate with the mystery of the story than is the moonlight outside, or mysterious Kôr itself. In finding her 'X', or rather her two 'Xs', for Callie is no less important than Pepita, Elizabeth Bowen has also established an instant intimacy with them.

For her the process was close to poetry. Of Virginia Woolf she wrote: 'Sublimating personality into poetry, she had, as art, the chastity of the impersonal.' But though one sees what she means, her emphasis upon poetry is for the reader, perhaps, another kind of stalking-horse. Callie and Pepita are infinitely more alive – in one sense – than are any of Virginia Woolf's characters. More significant is the sense of place and person. If it could then be said that this is what poetry is all about, we should have to reply that in very many – the majority – of her stories her sense of the poetry of place, and of the X who lives there, gets in the way of the place's actuality,

and so that of the person as well. 'Mysterious Kôr' is one of
the few exceptions. That it *is* akin to poetry is clear from the
fact that it stands out as it does; in just the same way that a
certain kind of poet – Walter de la Mare, say – will produce a
few absolute masterpieces among a collection of poems which
are no more than characteristically graceful and well-made.

'The chastity of the impersonal' has a rather different slant
where such a masterpiece as 'Mysterious Kôr' is concerned.
The 'core' of the story is its toughness, its refusal to feel too
easily: to feel and to demonstrate feeling too easily is the
besetting sin of a certain kind of short story. The fantasy of
Kôr, and its poetry, is looked at with a quizzical eye, though it
is both moving and compelling as well. Remembering her
youth, and her fixation on Rider Haggard's *She*, Elizabeth
Bowen can do this with seeming effortlessness. As she puts it,
'the susceptibility is the experience', and the poet-storyteller
is using his own 'unique susceptibility to experience' – in this
case that of reading *She* at an early age. Rider Haggard is not,
to put it mildly, an entirely serious figure, and she is well
aware of that. One of the invisible jokes in her story is the way
she clings loyally to the spelling: what the circumflex on 'Kôr'
is doing is anyone's guess, but, as the original author was no
doubt well aware, it adds to the exotic dimension of his tale.

Elizabeth Bowen's sense is that of youth, and looking back
on youth. Pepita and Callie are young in different ways, and
she feels for both of them, feeling from the now impersonal
resources of her own youth, and her own maturity. The way
she can do this is the secret. She hated the idea of stories
'yoked to my personality. I am dead against art's being self-
expression'; and she comically lamented 'feeling young
persons writing feeling novels unless, absolutely, they must.'
It is probably true that the short story must eschew feeling, in
the obvious sense, as the novel need not. Certainly
'Mysterious Kôr' takes us back to a story in which feeling and
unfeeling are similarly blended into successful invisibility,
and that is Henry James's 'A Landscape-Painter'. James, too,
was close to his young painter in that tale; and yet equally
amused and distant; conscious, too, of the enigma in another
person – a female person – an enigma compounded by the
secret his hero is guarding inside himself. James knows all

this without the need for any self-expression; drawing only on his own susceptibility to experience, and above all – in that story – to place.

CHAPTER SIX

Most short stories today – good ones – are of what might be called the New Yorker type: sophisticated versions of the story with a sting in its tail as perfected by de Maupassant, and after him by Somerset Maugham. The New Yorker type story removes the sting, so to speak, and makes its absence itself the unifying and vivifying factor. The atmosphere of 'a story' substitutes for the presence of the story itself.

The best and most successful stories have effects related to this and yet essentially different. They work on the dual principle which has recurred many times throughout this study. Beyond the setting and subject, another story begins to take shape as we read, or after we finish reading. The graphic events of 'Indian Camp' hold our attention spellbound; but also working on us increasingly with each paragraph is a sense of the father and son outside the story, though momentarily revealed by it: the perspective of two lives foreseen and determined. The doomed father, sunk in his experience and knowledge of living and dying, rows his son across the still morning lake, a son whose innocence is shown to be totally intact after the events which the story has described. The concealed effect, about which Hemingway's art shows extraordinary percipience, is of innocence confirmed by experience. The boy Nick remains inviolate in a youthful Eden which was an inspiration to Hemingway, and on which he always looked back. His art remained preoccupied with it, and it is openly treated in one of his last books, *The Garden of Eden*, which has been published posthumously.

The same dual principle is also responsible for the success of 'A Landscape-Painter'. Its open subject is deception, with an effective suspense sequence and a neat *dénouement*; but its other dimension is again that of innocence, the idyllic Eden of the little sea village, and the practice of his art there, from which the young painter is expelled into a world of marriage and death. We might note that a story which fails to secure the coherence of such an inner dimension is Katherine Mansfield's 'Bliss', which substitutes for it an over consciously symbolic world, that of the flowering pear-tree seen by the heroine in her moments of bliss and of despair.

In Chekhov's masterpiece, 'The Lady with the Dog', a 'love story' has in its background the more curious and touching revelation of how two people with apparently incompatible ideas about what they want from love none the less come together, and remain together. The hidden irony is that they are indeed left together at the end of a story, which, like all conventional stories, has a beginning, middle and end. They are left outside their own story. And this points to something of importance in our reception of many outstanding examples of the form. They juxtapose a 'story' with what James would have called 'the story in it', or Joyce an 'epiphany'. The former we know how to read and respond to from our previous acquaintance with the genre of stories: the latter gives us a new and unique experience. Or to put it another way, we accept a 'story' without necessarily believing in it, or doing more than suspend our disbelief for the span of the narrative; while the inner dimension of a really good short story is both true and absolute, and like nothing else.

There can be an art in exploiting the two effects. A story, or 'tall story', which does not expect or require our belief, is used with professional cynicism by de Maupassant or Somerset Maugham. In 'The Necklace' Maupassant uses the already old anecdote idea of a fatal mistake or misunderstanding. The heroine borrows a necklace for a great occasion; loses it; buys another to replace it, and works like a slave for years to repay the debt; then discovers from the casual owner that it was only a paste one after all, and of no value. The story is not believable, but we believe it because it is a good story. Maugham takes up the theme and gives it a different twist. On a cruise a flashy young jeweller is asked as a party trick to value a lady's necklace, which he perceives to be far more valuable than she pretends. Suddenly realizing her reason for concealing its value from her husband and his friends, he accepts humiliation at their hands by admitting he has made a mistake: the apparent pearls are, he says, only cheap beads. The wife's secret remains undiscovered. In his late story 'Paste', Henry James himself takes up the theme, ingeniously using the implausibility of a valuable necklace supposed to be valueless to reveal the natures of three people: the mother who possessed it; her son who refuses to believe that his mother could, at some stage of her life, have been given such a valuable object; and the unattached girl, one of James's natural victims, whose scruples prevent her from accepting as a keepsake an object she suspects to be of great value. In all three stories the idea and the implications of 'value' are turned into contrivance, but the contrivance of a story is too strong to allow the growth inside it of a true inner dimension.

This is achieved however, and in the most unobtrusive way, by Joyce in 'The Dead'. The 'story' here is the one Gabriel's wife believes in, that a young man died for her. This is, as it were, her story, and becomes her story when she tells it to her husband, who fits it into the banal events of the evening. An exact balance is thus achieved between the meticulous non-significance of those events, their total truth, and the ambiguous tale of Michael Furey which they accidentally conjure into being. We are familiar with the genre of the story which Gabriel's wife invents by remembering; but the rest of 'The Dead' gives us the new and unique experience, the revelation and the moment. The two perfectly harmonize together, while remaining unobtrusively separate.

The same is to some extent true of Hardy's story 'On the Western Circuit'. As with most 'stories' it is not really credible that in this case the love-letters should act as they do, but it is a good idea which fits in to the tale's inner dimension: the moment, the dream, and the death of the dream. The power of the love-letters is that they do not exist except in terms of the 'story', for they are never quoted. In most of Hardy's tales there is no duality between a 'good story' and a true meaning, for the former simply takes over, as in the case of de Maupassant or Maugham. 'On the Western Circuit' is the remarkable exception. Kipling, as we should expect, shows the greatest virtuosity in combining an inner and outer dimension, the story with the meaning, contrasting the two most obviously in stories based on the enigma of a delusion, as in 'Mary Postgate' and 'Mrs Bathhurst'. The 'story' in Mrs Bathhurst requires that the heroine be found mysteriously immolated with Vickery in the Rhodesian teak forest, a melodrama *dénouement* which the participant narrators would like to believe in, and which is silently tolerated, as it were, by the true dimension of the tale. Kipling makes the most shameless use of any craftsman in marrying together a tall story with a true one.

The duality of a really good short story constitutes its expression of our human awareness that everything in life is full of significance, and at the same time that nothing in it has any significance at all. Every situation or event may have a story in it, but the short story's best art will also reveal an absence: the absence of its own meaning. The story's epiphany must also encounter and accept emptiness. To put it like that may sound a bit glib, but the effect is none the less basic to the developed short story. The tradition of the novel is quite different. It solves and settles its narrative, and belongs to an epoch in which solutions and explanations were taken for granted. Novels as different as *Wuthering Heights* and *Great Expectations* both end equally in restitution and fulfilment; emotional and financial matters have been cleared up; understanding, of some sort, has been reached.

That was in the nineteenth century. With the twentieth comes an age in which God has disappeared and solutions have ceased to be expected. From being – as with Pushkin and Merimeé, Scott or de Maupassant – a miniature novel, with a point and meaning commensurate with its concentration, the short story becomes the vehicle for the sense of life's unfulfilment, the momentariness of its experiences. It can preserve only short significances, temporary enlightenment.

And indeed novels themselves, like Virginia Woolf's, may begin to resemble the short story.

Although short stories borrow from anecdote, and use the conventional effects of fiction, they must in the end stand apart, using their 'story', if they have one, as a lure to draw the reader into their authentic selves. Their distance from other kinds of literary effect embodies their mystery, which often gives the impression of being removed in some way from the art of the story itself. Puzzles in a story can have their uses, as they do with Henry James, or with Kipling; they can thicken the mystery, but in terms of the story's effect they never offer a final solution. In this context Kipling takes the biggest risk. If he had revealed the exact relation between Vickery and Mrs Bathhurst the story would not only forfeit the silence into which it turns, but also the woman whose name as a title is the mystery of the story. Mrs Bathhurst as the victim of bigamy would be merely pathetic; as the woman recalled from all over by the men who have known and admired her, the woman seen on the newsreel, walking down the platform with her blindish look, and vanishing like a shadow jumping over a candle, she becomes an object of awe, a goddess or *magna mater*, whose creation in that role by the story contrasts with the reader's sense that there was nothing to it: that she was quite ordinary, quite attractive young widow who kept a small hotel in a New Zealand suburb. And yet the story need not separate itself from its author's intention, revealed in his fancy epigraph, to show that simple people have loves and lives of tragic sorrow and tragic mystery, of the kind only once thought suitable only for kings and queens.

Perfection, in the artistic sense, need not occur; the story can seem to do without it; just as it can offer simultaneously a touching mystery and an obscure triviality. We are aware of both, for as I have continually emphasized, the art of the short story must make us feel that the real subject has not been caught in the apparent one, or compromised by it. Mrs Bathhurst is free of any explanations about her. In the same way, and by an even more remarkable feat of art, Mary Postgate remains free of her experience with the German airman. There is no clinical suggestion, as there might be in a work of exploratory fiction about her, that Mary is defined by her experience, whether actual or illusory. On the contrary, the heart of the story is a sense it gives of monstrosity launched upon the world by the war, and yet in some way always immanent in the nature of the world itself: in the aggressive arrogance of young Wynn (a self-portrait, in some degree, of Kipling by Kipling) in the sacrificial nature of love, its hungers and its cruelties. The story is told with a kind of penitential care and reasonableness, as if the experience of Mary could not be understood but only recorded. And at the same time – as so often with Kipling – the feeling of his own personal hatred and outrage burns deep down in the story, like the banked fires in the incinerator. The same is even truer of 'A Sahib's War', in which the Sikh narrator, who has loved since his childhood the captain whom the Boers have treacherously killed, is incredulous that his British masters should insist on conducting the war in the gentlemanly way they do. Like Mary Postgate he has a vision, but it is the opposite of hers. When he is about to carry out his revenge against his captain's murderers he sees the captain coming towards him, 'riding as it were upon my eyes', forbidding him to continue. Apparitions in Kipling are the most natural things in the world, tokens of love and hate.

Both emotional men and good haters, Kipling and Lawrence are remarkably alike in their use of willed or imaginary events – as in 'Mary Postgate' or 'The Fox' or 'The Captain's Doll' – as if the short story form were a licence that gave these events their own sort of reality. Lawrence's 'warm ghost' in 'The Border Line' seems as true and as natural as the apparitions of 'A Sahib's War' or 'A Madonna of the Trenches'. They are parts of the short story, and the nature of the story makes it unnecessary for either author to admit any charge of fantasy.

The collision of meaning with unmeaning is at its most subtle in 'The Dead', where the evening party faithfully records the contingency of existence while at the same time mysteriously sublimating it. In 'The Lady with the Dog' Gurov has that moment of fulfilment and peace as he sits with Anna in the dawn at Oreanda, sees a boat with a light, hears the waves breaking on the shore.

... sea, mountains, clouds, the wide sky, Gurov thought of them as if, when you come to think of it, everything in this world is beautiful; everything, except what we think and do when we forget the high aims of life; when we forget our human dignity.

As with Gabriel in 'The Dead', Gurov's thoughts fall short of what the story seems to promise, and yet they deeply connect with it, giving a kind of humble assurance that the intangible world created by the story is true, even though the human agents in it can only express what it means in a lame and unconvincing way. Gurov's sensations and thoughts are in a way a parody of the real impression the story will make, but at the same time they are necessary to it, and to the authenticity of its mystery.

The short story form is hostile to definition, as to completeness. It is the hero of 'The Lady with the Dog', rather than the story itself, who has the sense that 'when you come to think of it, everything in this world is beautiful'. The same sort of feeling makes Gurov convinced, at the end of the story, that because he and Anna love each other everything will come right, must come right, sooner or later. The story knows better, though it does not insist on its knowledge. At the end of 'The Dead', as he drifts off into sleep, Gabriel has the comfortable and comforting conviction that it is better to die young, to 'pass boldly into that other world, in the full glory of some passion, than fade and wither dismally with age'. The story knows that he will fade and wither with age, though not necessarily dismally – that is Gabriel's own contribution to what he requires to be the positive side of things. Gabriel conceives of death as a romantic apotheosis, and the dead as figures of poetry and passion, and his impressions contribute to the story; but the story knows not about death but about sleep, which, like the banality of an evening party and its converse, has all the comfort of repetition and familiarity. The moment before sleep, a moment of significance which will none the less fade out and be repeated, is itself an image of the story.

A good story exhibits not so much restraint as a lack of curiosity. Its interior is revealed unawares, as if the story itself were not interested in it. Chekhov's excellent tale, 'The

Darling', is full of tenderness and humour, and also comes close to what I termed at the beginning an investigative anecdote. It very obviously began from an idea, or rather a perception, on Chekhov's part; the perception of a certain kind of woman, who throws herself totally into whatever her man is doing, becomes identified with him and his interests, and repeats the same pattern with another man after his death. Chekhov cunningly escapes predictability by his ending, which shows a little boy remaining immune to the 'darling's' attempt to identify with him and his world. But the tale takes too great an interest in the psychology of 'the darling' to be in the same class as 'The Lady with the Dog', or Chekhov's other late masterpiece, 'The Bishop'. 'The Darling' is too much its own subject, in whose interest it identifies itself too closely.

The same might be said of Kipling's autobiographical story 'Baa Baa Black Sheep', but here the reader has a queer sense, of the kind I have often referred to as significant where the true short story is concerned, that there is another dimension beyond the hurt and misery so unforgettably recorded. It has something to do with mothers, a subject on which Kipling is reticently obsessed, and which can also, as in his tale 'The Brushwood Boy', be rather embarrassing. The immediacy of the subject in 'Baa Baa Black Sheep', where Punch and his sister are deprived of their mother at the age of five and three, when they are sent home from India, is heartrending, physically as compulsive in its effect on us as so many such things are in Kipling. But it is also full of deception. In the loveless environment in which he grows up Punch becomes an accomplished liar, and when his mother at last returns to him in England, full of warmth and longing for her children's love, his first fear is that she will hear what a liar he has been. She does hear, from the unspeakable guardian, Aunty Rosa, but her love pays no attention. Behind the story it is clear that Punch's fear remains, none the less, and that it haunted the grown-up Kipling (where things like that are concerned nobody can exactly be said to 'grow up'). That fear is strangely audible in the tone Kipling adopts at the beginning of the story, when he describes the prayer of the mother about her children.

Mamma's own prayer was a slightly illogical one. Summarised it ran: 'Let strangers love my children and be as good to them as I should be, but let *me* preserve their love and their confidence for ever and ever. Amen'. Punch scratched in his sleep and Judy moaned a little.

Kipling was that rare thing among authors, a passionate lover of children. His own children of course especially, and he lost two of them in tragic circumstances. They haunt his work, as his mother does. But the 'illogicality' remains. How can love bear to renounce its object, to put other interests first? The story tells how strangers were not 'as good to them as I should be', a phrase in itself equivocal, and direly so in view of what occurs.

The story is full of a continuing and inevitable fear and resentment, looming behind the actual miseries it describes, though not in the least displacing them. The complexity and the need of love – and its unavoidable treachery – give the moments of separation and reuniting their special poignancy. In its way, and working with the same classic short story effect, 'Baa Baa Black Sheep' is very close to Hemingway's 'Indian Camp', in which an awareness of the father, the boy's hidden anxiety about and love for him, accompany the events the story describes and show them in a unique sort of relief. Because of the father the events in the story can be described in the way they are. Because Nick's curiosity has 'been gone for a long time' the story loses self-consciousness: the delivery of the Indian woman's baby, and the Indian woman's husband cutting his throat, become things that are not told for their own sake, and assume in consequence a dream-like significance, like the reminiscent smile of the young Indian when Uncle George looks at his bitten arm. As the pair row back across the lake the story conveys Nick's realization that his father is doomed, and his own corresponding feeling that he himself will never die. There sidles into the story both the power of love – Nick's acceptance of his father's protection – and its inability to protect the loved creature against the world. In both 'Baa Baa Black Sheep' and 'Indian Camp' the hidden epiphany is the boy's realization of the parent as a separate and vulnerable object, travelling towards death. The stories come into existence because in spite of the experiences undergone in them, the innocence of their heroes has survived, and they know they will 'never die'. The stories come into this realization by an invisible process, like their hero-inventors.

This renunciation of overt curiosity, intention, the will, is necessary to the best stories, which drift into being as if independently of their own craftsmanship. A sense of the will, and of her determination to achieve a given effect, is strong in Elizabeth Bowen's stories, but in her best, such as 'Mysterious Kôr', it seems to have slipped into abeyance, so that the intention of presenting the poetry of the feel of wartime London has become another and more intimate sort of poetry, burrowing as if involuntarily into lives observed and imagined, experienced in the author's multiple sense of herself. In Camus's *nouvelle*, 'L'Etranger', which has something of the feel of a good short story, the same intention is none the less too strong. As he said himself, Camus wanted to create a hero who cannot help himself feeling and speaking the truth, instead of going along with the shows and conventions of behaviour proper to civilized and social beings. This quasi-philosophical intention realizes itself in a brilliantly artistic style and setting, but none the less overreaches itself. Camus decides to drive his point home by having his hero commit an involuntary murder, and this improbable 'story' incident, the centre of the story, reveals far too great an insistence on its atmosphere and materials, materials that would otherwise fall naturally and easily into the flow of its meaning.

The effect is a little as if Kipling had insisted on the nature of Vickery's 'crime' in Mrs Bathhurst, or if Hardy, in 'On the Western Circuit', had actually quoted the letters Mrs Harnham wrote to the young barrister. Almost the final truth about the effect of a short story is that what goes on in it must not *seem* to tell the truth or 'see it happen'. A good story is part tale, part poem, part investigation, but the poem – the most reticent and least curious part – must predominate. And the poem in the story is itself telling another story.

The short story form today has reached a peak of popularity, and also of stylization. Would-be authors are taught how to do it, how to arrange all the effects I have been discussing, how to plan their epiphanies, play down their endings. A high degree of sophistication is reached, but inevitably the effects grow narcissistic, overcareful, a long way from the throwaway comedy of Hemingway's 'The Light of the World'. 'This is true, true, true, and you know it. Not just made up and I know exactly what he said to me.' One of the most accomplished short story writers today, Joyce Carol Oates, has recently published a book called *Marya. A Life*. Amongst other things, Marya is a writer of short stories.

NOTES AND BIBLIOGRAPHY

Foreword and Chapter One

Quotations in the Foreword are taken from the introductions to *The Art of the Tale: An International Anthology of Short Stories 1945–85*, ed. by Daniel Halpern (Viking, 1987), and *The World of the Short Story: A 20th Century Collection* ed. Clifton Fadiman. These large and comprehensive anthologies are good value, and include stories from a variety of · countries and traditions, opening with a useful commentary by the editors. Other general books and essays on the short story which may be of value are *The Lonely Voice* by Frank O'Connor (1936), *The Modern Short Story* by H. E. Bates (1941), *The Short Story: A Critical Introduction* by Valerie Shaw (1956).

Chapter Two

The best introduction to Henry James's short stories are his own *Notebooks*, ed. Murdock and Matthiessen (Oxford, 1947), recently republished in an enlarged and complete version, ed. Edel & Powers (Oxford and New York, 1987). These record the beginnings of his story themes in anecdotes told him by friends which he then develops or modifies.

In *The Poetics of Prose* by Tsvetan Todorov (Blackwell, 1977), Chapter 10, entitled 'The Secret of Narrative' puts forward a theory of James's narrational technique in his stories, which is claimed to be particularly true of those with a supernatural motif.

Chapter Three

A comprehensive and illuminating introduction to Kipling's stories is supplied by Craig Raine in his anthology, *A Choice of Kipling's Prose* (Faber, 1987). For a brilliant fictional comment changing the perspective of Chekhov's story, see Joyce Carol Oates's story *The Lady With The Pet Dog* (*Marriage and Infidelities*, Vanguard 1968, reprinted in *The Story and Its Writer: An Introduction to Short Fiction* by Ann Charters, St Martin's Press, New York, 1983).

Chapters Four and Five

See James Joyce's letters to his brother Stanislaus (*Selected Letters of James Joyce*, ed. Ellman (Faber, 1975)) for the most interesting comments on his art of the story in *Dubliners*. D.H. Lawrence's letters (*Letters of D.H. Lawrence*, ed. Aldous Huxley, (Heinemann, 1933)) throw light on his attitude to the form. See also *The Short Stories of Thomas Hardy* by Kristin Brady (Macmillan, 1982). Elizabeth Bowen comments on the short story in her introduction to *The Faber Book of Modern Short Stories* (1944) and in the introduction to her own selected short stories (Cape, 1944), both of which are reprinted in *Selected Letters and Essays*, ed. Hermione Lee (Cape, 1986).

INDEX

Absurdity, 141

Accuracy see Exactness

Anecdotal aspect of stories, 27–33, 135, 183

Arnold, Matthew, 117

Association, 108

Art
for art's sake, 1
and mystery, 1–9, 21–2, 48, 150
and real life, 50–7, 65–71
see also Duality

Auden, W.H., 80–1

Austen, Jane, 91–2, 107–8

Authenticity, 70–5, 78–80, 86, 87, 89

Autobiography, 123
see also Writer

Autonomy of discourse, 3–5, 7

Baldwin, Oliver, 86

Baldwin, Stanley, 64

Barrie, J.M., 126–7

Beauty, 151–3

Beckett, Samuel, 158

Bierce, Ambrose, 67

Blixen, Karen, 35, 150

Bodelsen, C.A., 106n

Borges, Jorge Luis, vii

Bowen, Elizabeth, 161–2, 174, 188
The Death of the Heart, 175
'Her Table Spread', 176
'Ivy Gripped the Steps', 161, 176
'Mysterious Kôr', 150, 161, 165–78, 188
'The Storm', 176

Boyle, Kay, vii

Brooke, Rupert, 15

Bunin, Ivan, 115
'The Encounter', 115

Byron, Lord, 5

Camus, Albert
'L'Etranger', 188

Carroll, Lewis, 32

Chekhov, Anton, viii, 110–22
'The Bishop', 119, 186
'The Darling', 185–6
'The Lady with the Little Dog', 54, 111–22, 130,

133-4, 147, 161, 168,
180, 184-5
'The Steppe', 57
Cinema, 103
Class, 16, 18, 21, 150-1
Clodd, Edward, 145
Comedy, 33-4, 46, 80, 111,
127, 159, 174
see also Humour, Irony
Conrad, Joseph, 99
'Amy Foster', 36, 102
'Because of the Dollars', 99
'Falk', 99
'Freya of the Seven Islands',
99
Lord Jim, 36-7, 38, 40, 48
'The Secret Sharer', 38-40,
54, 109
Contextual aspect of stories,
27-31, 37

Darley, George (poet), 7
Death, 185
reactions to, 90-3
and Thomas Hardy, 137-8
de la Mare, Walter, 177
Delusion, 84-95, 97-108, 125,
128
de Maupassant, Guy, 150, 179
'The Necklace', 180-1
Dickens, Charles, 71, 107
Dobree, Bonamy Bernard, 90
Duality, 84-5, 88, 95, 96, 128,
145, 179-82

Eliot, George
Middlemarch, 36
The Mill on the Floss, 175
Eliot, T. S., 101, 134
Endings, 39-40, 57-60
Epiphany, 8, 13, 19, 142, 153,
173, 180, 182, 187
Eroticism, 126, 168
Exactness, 105, 109-17, 142

Fitzgerald, Scott, 150
Flaubert, Gustave, 140, 150
Flecker, James Elroy, 51
Don Juan, 151
Formalist criticism, 2-4, 7,
117
Forster, E. M.
Howard's End, 151
A Passage to India, 67

Gass, William, vii-viii
Ghost stories
'The Phantom Rickshaw',
81-3
'The Turn of the Screw',
48, 50-4, 59, 60
Gogol
'The Overcoat', 36
Gombrich, Professor
Art and Illusion, 71
Gore-Booth, Eva, 24

Haggard, Rider
She, 169, 177
Halpern, David, viii
Hardy, Thomas, 22-3, 24,
123, 134-48
'Barbara of the House of
Grebe', 134
'The Distracted Preacher',
135
'The Fiddler of the Reels',
135
'Green Slates', 24
'A Group of Noble
Dreams', 135
'An Imaginative Woman',
139-41, 146
'A Mere Interlude', 138
'On the Western Circuit',
140-51, 181-2
'The Son's Veto', 135,
136-8, 143

Tess of the D'Urbervilles,
    136–7, 138
'A Tragedy of Two
    Ambitions', 135
'The Withered Arm', 135
his youthfulness, 143–6
Hawthorne, Nathaniel, 158–9
    'My Kinsman Major
        Molineux', 108
Hazlitt, William, 34
Healing, 96
Heaney, Seamus, 20
Hemingway, Ernest, 75–7, 123
    'Big Two-Hearted River',
        80
    'Cat in the Rain', 76–8, 112
    The Garden of Eden, 180
    his idiom, 109–10
    'Indian Camp', 78–80,
        179–80, 187
    In Our Time, 75
    'The Light of the World',
        189
    'The Three-Day Blow', 80
    his will, 77–8
    'Out of Season', 76–7
Hingley, Ronald, 110
Honesty, 21
Howells, William Dean, 61
Humour, 16, 52, 56, 139, 158
    see also Comedy, Irony
Huxley, Aldous
    Point Counter Point, 132
Idiom, 109–10, 152–3
Indeterminacy, 112–13, 118,
    122
    of love, 119
Investigative anecdote, 9–11
    see also Anecdotal aspect of
        stories
Irony, 62, 80, 180
James, Henry, viii, 18, 36, 38,
    90, 105, 123

'The Bench of Desoluation',
    61
The Bostonians, 62
'The Figure in the Carpet',
    49–50
'The Great Good Place', 45
'In the Cage', 50, 59, 60
'A Landscape-Painter',
    40–8, 53–60, 117, 161,
    177–8, 180
'My Friend Bingham',
    59–60, 62
'Paste', 181
'The Story of a
    Masterpiece', 61–2
'The Story of a Year', 56
'What Maisie Knew', 52
Joyce, James, viii, 8, 150–68
    'Counterparts', 154
    'The Dead', 13, 15, 54, 142,
        145, 150–68, 175, 181,
        184–5
    Dubliners, 150–1, 160
    'An Encounter', 162
    'Eveline', 162
    Ulysses, 153, 161

Kafka, Franz, viii, 33, 35
Keats, John
    'The Eve of St Agnes', 13,
        103, 107, 157, 162, 164,
        168, 171
Kipling, John, 69
Kipling, Rudyard, viii, 5, 35,
    41, 64–6, 80–6, 162, 182
    'Baa Baa Black Sheep', 103,
        186–7
    'The Brushwood Boy', 186
    'The Comprehension of
        Private Copper', 68
    'A Conference of the
        Powers', 75
    'The Conversion of St
        Wilfred', 72–3, 76

'Dayspring Mishandled', 70, 84, 97
'At the End of the Passage', 35, 66–7, 81, 83, 88, 91
'The Eye of Allah', 84, 96
'The Finest Story in the World', 74
'A Habitation Enforced', 91
'The Gardener', 94–5, 114
'The Knife and the Naked Chalk', 72
The Light that Failed, 95
'A Madonna of the Trenches', 35, 95–6, 107, 184
'The Man Who Would be King', 67–8
Many Inventions, 74
'Mary Postgate', 84–95, 106, 117, 125, 128, 161, 182, 183–4
'A Matter of Fact', 75
'Mrs Bathhurst', 97–108, 109–10, 117, 120, 125, 128, 161, 182, 183
'My Son's Wife', 91, 108
'On Greenhow Hill', 97
'The Phantom Rickshaw', 81–3
Plain Tales from the Hills, 104
Puck of Pook's Hill, 68–71, 74
'Recessional', 97
Rewards and Fairies, 68
'A Sahib's War', 68, 184
'Soldiers Three', 68
Something of Myself, 68, 81, 98
'The Strange Ride of Morrowbie Jukes', 35, 66–7, 83, 88

'Swept and Garnished', 84–6
'They', 91
Traffics and Discoveries, 120
'Wireless', 103, 107
'The Wish House', 97

Larkin, Philip, 26
'An Arundel Tomb', 20
'Church Going', 16
'Dockery and Son', 12–22, 25, 27, 29, 33
his honesty, 21
'I Remember I Remember', 20
his pessimism, 17
'Symphony in White Major', 18
'The Whitsun Weddings', 12, 20–3, 27
Lavin, Mary, 150
Lawrence, D.H., vii, viii, 20, 40, 113, 123–34
'The Blind Man', 123, 125–7
'The Border-Line', 123, 128–9, 184
'The Captain's Doll', 123, 125, 126, 129, 132–3, 134, 184
'The Fox', 123, 125, 126, 132–3, 134, 184
'The Man Who Loved Islands', 130
The Plumed Serpent, 128
'The Princess', 129–30
'Smile', 131–2
'St Mawr', 123, 125, 129
'The Woman Who Rode Away', 123, 128, 129, 134
Le Fanu
Uncle Silas, 166
Literariness, viii, 2–3, 121

Localization, 117, 121, 136
Love stories, 122

Mansfield, Katherine, 131,
    132, 150
  'Bliss', 124, 180
Markiewicz, Constance, 24
Maugham, Somerset, 179, 181
Melodrama, 97–104, 164–7
Melville, Herman
  'Bartleby the Scrivener', 81,
    83
Middleton Murry, John, 127,
    129, 131–2
Misunderstanding, 152, 180
Mystery, 26, 27, 30–2, 107,
    121–2, 157–8, 175, 183
  and art, 1–9, 21–2, 48,
    150
  of love, 119
  of money, 41

Naturalistic speech in fiction,
    78–9
Neutrality, 160–1
New Yorker type of story, 179
Novel, the, 1, 11, 14, 18–19,
    123, 134, 161, 182
  public preference for, 50

Oates, Joyce Carol, 189
O'Connor, Flannery, 35
Ordinary people, 107–8, 142,
    162

Page, Prof Norman, 87–8, 89
Pater, Walter, 8
Pessimism, 17, 136
Poe, Edgar Allan, 40, 66, 165
Poetry, 2–26, 108, 162, 176–7
Porter, Katherine Anne
  'Pale Horse, Pale Rider',
    110
Powell, Anthony, 70, 78

Precision see Exactness
Priestley, J. B., 74
Propaganda stories, 84–95
Propp, Vladimir, 117
Pushkin
  The Stone Guest, 116
Pym, Barbara, 38

Realism, 161
Real life, 30
  and literature, 50–7, 65–71,
    122–3

Shakespeare, William
  Hamlet, 9
  Measure for Measure, 30
  'The Phoenix and the
    Turtle', 9
Shaw, G. B.
  Pygmalion, 151
Shestov, Leon, 121
Short story
  effect, 8–13, 31, 179, 188
  form of, vii, 23, 83
  ideal, 35–6
  kinds of, 27
  New Yorker type, 179
Significance, 182
Southey, Robert, 4, 6
Stein, Gertrude
  'Melanctha', 150
Stevenson, Robert Louis, 41,
    67
  'The Beach at Falesa', 138
Symbolism, 158–9

Todorov, Tsvetan, 48–50, 56,
    58, 105
Tolstoy, Leo
  Anna Karenina, 112, 117,
    121
Truth, 75, 90
  see also Authenticity,
    Exactness, Real life

Vreker, Hugh, 50

Waugh, Evelyn, 136
Wells, H. G., 107
Welty, Eudora, 150, 166
Wharton, Edith, 150
Wilson, Edmund, 48, 52
Wolfe, Charles
  'The Burial of Sir John
    Moore after Corunna',
    4–13
Woolf, Virginia, 124, 176, 183
Wordsworth, William
  'Advice to Fathers', 11
  'Fidelity', 34

'Lucy' sequence, 11
The Prelude, 8
'Resolution and
    Independence', 11, 21,
    27–35
'Strange Fits of Passion I
    have known', 11
'Tintern Abbey', 2–4, 7–8,
    10, 11, 21
'We are Seven', 11
Writer, reader's sense of,
    38–48, 65, 77, 84

Yeats, W. B., 23, 153, 159
The Winding Stair, 23–6